SWEATING IT OUT

BOB CONDRON

ZIPPER BOOKS

SWEATING IT OUT Bob Condron

First printing July 2000. Printed in Finland by WS Bookwell
Cover photography © 2000 Millivres Prowler

web-site: prowler.co.uk
• ISBN 187374154-5

British Library Cataloguing in Publication Data.
A catalogue record for this book is available from the British Library.

One

A searing blast of steam swirled around the dark, damp sauna. Dense clouds of vapour threatened to encompass all those inside. Diffused light from the shower room filtered through the frosted glass door. And Dirk's stiff cock loomed large in silhouette.

Through sheer size, it refused to be swallowed up. Now bowed before the cock in question, Jens was doing his best to fulfil that particular task. Working his mouth forward and back, the rhythm deliberate and constant. Sweat from his brow dripped from his nose and further moistened the pulsing shaft. A practised technique: slow and steady wins the race. The game plan? Check out the carrot on the stick. Now you see it . . . Now you don't . . .

The Turkish stud drew close. Closer still. Then he stood alongside the pair, with back and buttocks pressed up against the ceramic tiled wall. The whites of his eyes glistened in the darkness. A closer look. Close enough to reach out and touch. And as his eyes grew accustomed to the shadows and light, what could he see? Two muscular, bearded men. Powerfully built men. One seated. One standing. One sucking the other's cock. And it was an awesome cock. Huge. And as he stroked his own erection, the Turk's mouth began to drool.

Even as he felt familiar lips wrap around his girth, consuming him, Dirk had a heightened awareness of this silent observer. He smiled to himself. Everything was going to plan.

*

Sunday afternoon in Berlin was cold and rainy. What better way to spice up an otherwise dreary Sonntag than within the warmth and security of the sauna club - a gay sauna club, that was. A gay Bear sauna, more to the point. Where else? In the past couple of hours Dirk and Jens had done the dry sauna, relaxed in the Jacuzzi and at the bar, made the rounds of the cabins, and all these pleasures leading towards . . .

When the Turk had first entered, both men had looked at each other and grinned: something special. Two men with a single thought, partners in crime. This is what we've been waiting for, they had thought.

They had heard the joke so often. Question: what's the second largest city in Turkey? Answer: Berlin! Sadly, too few Turkish men found their way onto the scene. He had been an exception. And what an exception: a short, stocky powerhouse of muscle, standing no more than 5'6" in bare feet. His shortened muscles bunched up big and chunky. Thick, jet black hair and an equally thick moustache. The white towel wrapped around his narrow waist accentuated the width of his chest and swarthy skin tone. And his face was a beautiful, wholly masculine face: a shadow of stubble on his square chin, white teeth and eyes the colour of Amaretto - and just as warm and potent.

Jens and Dirk had studied him for a good half-hour. Had watched his apparent detachment; how he failed to make eye contact with the potential suitors who circled around him, gently rebuffing the few men who were brave enough to make a pass.

There was no doubt that the Turk had registered their presence - Jens and Dirk were a hard act to miss. At 6'2", Dirk cut an imposing figure, with a full beard and close-cropped, brown hair. The pumped-up curves of his muscular frame were complemented by a lush coating of body hair - a combination that served to further reinforce an inherent animal magnetism. Jens could have been his brother. Little brother, that is - given that at twenty-eight, Jens was almost twelve years younger. Despite his shaven head and goatee, there was more than a passing resemblance. Shorter by a couple of inches, but otherwise more than a match for his companion. Yet even as the Turk's eyes had turned in their direction, they had failed to fully focus, to fully

register, as if he had been holding something back. Maybe, they had thought, maybe he was shy. Maybe he was reserved.
But he was definitely aware.

And the more they had studied him, the more both men had wanted him. Wanted his sex; sensed how to get it and rose to the challenge. They would forget the direct approach, and instead put on a display. Hadn't this tactic worked memorably in the past?

So they had waited patiently until he had headed off towards the hub of all activity, had sneaked in ahead of him, and had taken up their positions.

*

Now inside the welcome confines of the wet sauna, the Turk was hooked and it was, it seemed, simply a case of reeling in the catch. Dirk stretched out a hand and felt his fingertips brush against coarse, black hair coating a solid chest. Yet no sooner had he made contact than his hand was removed, put aside. For a moment, Dirk was perplexed. But the Turk didn't move. Seconds passed, and he still continued to watch their sex play intently. His signalled his interest by his closeness, his eyes devouring the junction of cock and mouth only inches away. Gotcha, thought Dirk. Gotcha now!

Standing there with one hand covering his crotch, the Turk remained silent and unmoving, watching and waiting. Or so it seemed. Dirk, fresh from one rebuff, was determined to try again. His hand reached out once more, this time in the direction of the Turk's groin. Their fingers touched tentatively, and the Turk moved his hand to the side, exposing his arousal, indicating his acquiescence. Dirk took hold of the hardening phallus, feeling its length, the throbbing mass of twitching muscle. And in the instant, he felt his own dick swell to bursting point in Jens' mouth.

The Turk remained passive as Dirk toyed with his shaft, then reached down to play with his balls. First one and then the other, rolling them around between his thick fingers. Other than this, though, there was still no response. Fuck it, Dirk thought. It was time to up the ante a little and to see if the guy was really worth the effort. Easing his way out of Jens' mouth, Dirk ducked down and lapped at the head of the Turk's throbbing gristle. The response was instantaneous. The other man became animated, arching his body upwards, inching his dick slowly into Dirk's throat. Inch by inch, Dirk swallowed the pork sword until the entire Kebap was buried deep in his aching gullet. Hitting base, nose pressed up against a dense thatch of pubic hair, the Turk reached down and held Dirk by the back of his neck, stabbing into him with rising desire.

Dirk concentrated on breathing through his crushed nose. Keeping his throat open, he suckled as long as he was able. Relax and breathe. Long, wet draining breaths - like he was sucking the air from the Turk's bollocks. He could feel the Turk's body responding, straining upwards, angling his body to try to keep his rigid penis inside that warm, wet hole, until Dirk reluctantly withdrew his wet mouth.

Finally, upright again, Dirk spread his hand once more against the Turk's chest, but this time he wasn't being brushed away. Instead, the Turk stretched upwards and kissed Dirk hungrily on the lips, opening his mouth and extending his tongue. Fierce, passionate kisses. Full and fiery. Hot and lustful. Dirk could feel the tension simmering. Almost smell it. The Turk broke away, but only for an instant, long enough to whisper in Dirk's ear. His voice was hoarse, husky, hungry.

'I want to be together with you. You have cabin?'

'Yeah, we've got a cabin . . . ' And now for the clincher. 'But my friend will be coming along too. Okay?'

Dirk endured many anxious milliseconds before the Turk replied.

'Yes. We meet us in shower outside.'

And then Dirk watched him weave through the cluster of heaving, sweaty bodies and disappear in the steamy twilight.

Jens. Must get Jens, he remembered, almost as an afterthought. Then: Where the fuck is he?! Turning towards his last-known position, Dirk was somewhat surprised to find Jens otherwise occupied - sucking hungrily on one more anonymous dick. Some fit young guy was thrusting his sizeable erection in and out of Jens' hungry mouth. Dirk bent down to whisper in Jens' ear about developments concerning the Turk, but Jens carried on regardless.

'At least give me the key to the cabin!' Dirk said dryly - amused that his partner seemed too preoccupied to even acknowledge his presence.

Without missing a stroke, Jens held up his wrist to allow Dirk to take the key band off for himself.

'Meet you back there?' Dirk enquired.

Breaking off at last, Jens gasped. 'I thought he wasn't interested?'

'He suggested going back to the cabin!'

Still, Jens wasn't convinced. 'I don't know . . . '

Dirk began to panic; he had visions of the Turk losing interest and that would be an end to it. What was Jens playing at? Hadn't they agreed? Now Jens seemed to have lost the plot.

In a flash, an idea sprang to Dirk's mind, 'Bring your friend back with you. Let's make it a foursome.'

'Hmm . . . I don't know.'

Enough! Enough time wasted. 'Look, I'll see you back at the cabin?'

Out of the darkness and into the light, where the Turk was waiting patiently at the side of the shower room. Each man eyed the other and neither was in any way disappointed. Dirk shot the Turk a grin whilst leisurely soaping up, showing off his buff, hairy body while still keeping an eye on the door to see if Jens was going to appear.

No show.

Leading the way through the maze of corridors, Dirk finally stopped before number 318 and unlocked the door to the double cabin. The Turk entered first, Dirk following at his heels. The door closed behind them, and Dirk left it off the latch. Then, he turned to face the Turk, as he reached out to untie the knotted towel round the other man's waist and let it fall to the floor.

'What's your name?' Dirk asked.

'Ömer,' the Turk replied, his voice tapering off into a low moan as Dirk swiftly dropped to his knees before him, enveloping the crown of his beautifully circumcised cockhead between practised lips.

First licking and lapping from tip to base and back again, he eased the Turk's rod once more down his open throat. Dirk was so preoccupied with the task at hand that he barely clocked the opening door. When eventually he opened his eyes and looked up, Jens was standing behind the Turk, tweaking his little bullet nipples whilst exchanging wet, sloppy kisses.

For his part, Jens was equally surprised. In the wet sauna he had only seen the Turk brush Dirk's hand away before he himself was distracted. He had genuinely thought that the guy was not in the least bit interested. Not really. But even as he opened the door to the cabin, the Turk had reached out and offered up his mouth in a kiss. Now, pressed up behind him, toying with the man's tits, he felt the passion unleashed. All defences dropped; all barriers down. This guy didn't just kiss, he feasted on face. Jens was swept up by the Turk's blatant enthusiasm. His prick swelled in seconds and pressed into the cleft between the Turk's ample buttocks. And then Jens' eyes finally met Dirk's.

'Jens, meet Ömer.'

'Hello, Ömer!'

'Hello.'

'And I'm Dirk.'

Ömer nodded politely as both men introduced themselves, parting his lips to reveal a toothpaste smile.

Formalities over with, it was time to get down to serious business. Ömer sprawled back on the double mattress. Jens and Dirk lay either side, making him the filling to their sandwich. Then the kissing began. Three mouths, one kiss. Tongues fighting for space. Ömer writhed uncontrollably beneath them, drowning happily in kisses. Then he angled from one to the other, spoilt for choice.

Dirk was the first to break free, shifting position, letting his mouth fall onto Ömer's blistering erection and sucking like a vacuum pump. Jens brushed his hand over Ömer's taut, straining belly. Finding the navel, he dipped his finger in, played with it and, all the time, continued eating face.

Gasping for air, Ömer pulled back. He clasped the back of Jens' head and pushed him down to suck on Dirk. Then his own mouth consumed Jens. Not a daisy chain, but rather a triangle of lust. First this direction, then that. It appeared as if Ömer wanted to do everything and all at the same time. Then it was time for all to change places. Ömer pounced onto Dirk's meat, cramming as much as he could down his eager throat. Out of the corner of his eye, Jens could not help but watch Ömer gag willingly on Dirk's mammoth shaft as Jens himself, in turn, took the weight of both Turkish bollocks into his mouth. He gently chewed on the two heavy orbs, teasing their potency with his versatile tongue; urging them to manufacture a copious load. Then he released them, glistening wet, and worked his wriggling tongue downward. Ömer already was eagerly parting his own buttocks, ready for Jens' favours.

Jens could see nothing now but the sole focus of his attention - one tight little bud of a hairless arsehole. As his fingers prised Ömer's buttocks wide, his tongue darted against the quivering sphincter. The Turk's reaction was electric. If only, Jens thought, he could see Ömer's expression: eyes closed tight, as wave upon wave of sheer pleasure swept over his handsome face. Sucking violently on Dirk muffled the Turk's moans of pleasure, but hardly disguised them. And suddenly, Ömer yanked his head back, again gasping for air.

'This so horny! So horny! I think I come soon.'

Dirk found his voice. 'Hold on. Hold on a while longer.'

Jens eased back. 'Just relax.'

The heap of bodies collapsed down. Once more they lay alongside each other but this time simply cuddled close. All three breathing hard, slowly coming down from the high of a few moments before. Dirk ran his fingers through Ömer's chest hair, now drenched with sweat. Jens slid his palm over the moist skin surface, sliding down over the contour of Ömer's waist to firm thighs and back up again. Massaging the Turk's body, enjoying the feel of muscle and skin, body hair and sweat, and the thud of a racing heartbeat, pumping just below the surface of his ribcage.

Relaxing fully into the mattress, Ömer slipped an arm around the shoulders of both of his playmates and gave them one of his huge grins. Fuck, thought Dirk, this guy is soooo fucking handsome. But Dirk managed to smile back and, without breaking their gaze, he put out his tongue and took a long, slow lick of Ömer's armpit. It was sweaty - like the rest of his body - and heavy with musk. Intoxicated by the masculine odour, Dirk's head swam as he licked again, even more slowly, nibbling and sucking at the tender skin. Ömer let out a low moan. Dirk went in for the kill: licking and sucking, nibbling, kissing and moving his hot, wet mouth up and down Ömer's pit. Jens, having pinned the Turk's wrists above his head, had joined forces on the other side, thus forcing Ömer to writhe in tender agony. No mercy. None.

Dirk reached down his hand and began to play with his own cock, rubbing it against Ömer's, taking both of them in his fist and slowly jacking them off together. At the same time he leaned over and kissed the Turk. Ömer groaned in pleasure and opened his mouth wide, eager to accept Dirk's probing tongue, pushing back with his own tongue, wrestling it furiously. The pace was picking up again.

Jens released Ömer's wrists and shuffled down to groin level. He examined the twin fleshy poles intently. Dirk's was the bigger of the two, but not by much. And Ömer's cock certainly was beautiful. Perfectly formed. Nothing much to choose between the two. Maybe taste? And so he began sucking both cocks alternately. First a long, slow, glide down Dirk's swelling prick. Licking the shaft, leaving it slick with spittle. Then, while gently massaging the head of Dirk's erection with one hand, Jens moved to run the tip of his tongue over Ömer's cockhead, dipping it into the piss-slit, circling the ridge below the purple helmet, then gulping the entire length in one swift movement. He felt an exquisite fullness in his throat as he hit home, the ballsac pulsating beneath his chin. No, he couldn't choose. He wanted them both. The choice would have to be made for him.

There was to be no contest. Ömer flipped Jens over and brought him to his knees. His fingers roughly explored Jens' lubricated hole whilst the Turk muttered - half in German, half in Turkish. From over his shoulder came Dirk's translation.

'He wants to fuck you while I fuck him.'

'How do you know?'

'Trust me. Sign language speaks volumes.'

'So? Hand out the rubbers!'

Moments later, Ömer was positioned squarely behind Jens. Then he stabbed the full length of his thick, long cock into Jens with a single thrust of the hips. Jens took it effortlessly, begging for it. Slamming back on to it.

Swiftly, Dirk positioned himself at Ömer's rear; the bulbous head of his weapon pressed up tight against the Turk's throbbing ring. For the briefest moment, Dirk wondered if the Turk could accommodate him; or would he simply split in half? He chuckled, then slowly entered the other man. Ömer gasped as the tubular fullness slipped ever deeper inside. It was obvious that he was holding his breath, unable to take it more than halfway. Establishing a rhythm was tricky to achieve, but achieve it they did. Dirk reached down and gripped Ömer's balls, pulling them tightly towards him, feeling them strain and tug as

Ömer's stiff cock was pulled in another direction, plugged into another socket, pumping in and out. Jens was slamming back into the Turk like a sparring partner - absorbing each lunge, giving as good as he got. He ground his arse back on the Turk's pole, forcing every millimetre of cock up inside. Meanwhile, Dirk continued to ease his own prong up inside Ömer's willing and widening hole. With a moan of pleasure, the Turk pressed back, violently wriggling his hips, barely accommodating the width until, at last, it seemed he could savour the feeling of fullness. Every inch of Dirk's fat cock was now deep, deep inside him.

Dirk buried in Ömer; Ömer buried in Jens. Both active cocks were encircled by a desperate, gobbling hole. Three bodies were fused tight. Two cocks were gliding now in perfect unison, each thrusting as deeply as possible. Hips arching and bucking to push respective knobs deeper inside. Jens began to withdraw ever so slightly each time before plunging back, spearing himself on Ömer's power pylon. Then he ground his hips in a circular motion, willing the power tool to drill deeper, to spill its seed, to fuck him to Kingdom Cum.

This was so hot. Hotter than any fucking sauna. Sweat sprang out of every pore, free-flowing man-sweat mingling and lubricating their intimate body contact. All three of them were intent now on the one shared aim. Ömer's hands were busy on Jens' tits, kneading, pinching, tweaking. Dirk was cupping his hands under and around Ömer 's bubble-butt while Jens himself, with a glazed look in his eyes, worked his right hand furiously over his oozing hunk of a dick, pumping the foreskin back and forth.

Then Ömer began to lose it, whipping his head from side to side. Through gritted teeth, he cried out: 'I come. I come . . . ' Then he was yelping, pumping hot, Turkish sperm deep into the centre of Europe. Blasting up and out of his balls, spraying his primal energy like a geyser, flooding the rubber to bursting point.

Dirk's orgasm was triggered by this display. It was all just too fucking horny. He pulled out, ripped off his condom and jerked furiously. 'Double load,' he groaned, 'Double load!' And with this, he shot wad upon wad of milky white seed over Ömer's taut, tan buttocks. As for Jens, his body was fucked; his balls were blown. Easing free of Ömer's tool, he leapt to his feet and let fly over his two tormentors. He cascaded come over their heads, splattering their shoulders, their bellies, their softening dicks. Letting it fall on fertile ground. Then Jens leaned back against the cabin wall and lovingly stroked his tender man-meat, eyes closed tight, savouring the moment. All three were savouring the moment.

Ömer finally broke the silence, delighted with himself. 'This was my first time with three!' he announced, proudly.

'And how was it?' asked Jens, with a satisfied sigh.

Ömer paused, thought it over briefly, grinned and replied, 'I have no words enough.'

'We'll teach you a few new words,' Dirk offered, dropping to his knees to face the Turk and tugging gently on Ömer's softening tool.

'Yeah.' Jens chuckled. 'Along with a few other things!'

'I want you teach me. I learn quick!' Ömer was beaming.

Dirk pressed his mouth hard against Ömer's yielding lips. 'Come here,' he said, lustily. 'Time for lesson number two . . . '

Two

Jens drifted back into consciousness and, for a couple of moments, had no idea where he was. Reaching out a hand, he felt the damp patch on the sheet beside him and realisation began to dawn. He opened his eyes slowly, allowing the dim amber light from the lamp above the single bedside shelf to steal its way into his vision and illuminate the tacky, laminated walls of the cabin. He was alone. Ganz allein.

Wie spät ist es? What time was it? How long had he been asleep? Time seemed to lose all meaning within the boundaries of the sauna. It was always midnight in here; there were no windows to the outside world. Reality was not allowed to intrude, for this was never-never land.

He heard the lock on the cabin door click open and turned his head to catch sight of Dirk entering. He had a satisfied smile on his face, two bottles of beer in hand.

'You're awake!'

'Where have you been?'

'Saying good-bye to our little friend.' Dirk sat on the bed, took a swig from his bottle of Beck's and handed the second to Jens.

'Why didn't you wake me?' Jens rubbed his eyes.

'You were dead to the world.'

It was Jens' turn to smile. He ground his tender arse against the mattress. 'Fucked?'

'On more than one occasion!' Dirk punctuated his observation with a throaty chuckle - a catch in his throat that was both distinctly masculine and uniquely Dirk at one and the same time. And a characteristic that never failed to charm Jens.

'Still, you should have woken me.'

Dirk reached out a hand and rubbed Jens' hairy, muscled calf from ankle to knee and back again. 'Naw. You looked so peaceful. It would have been a shame.'

'But I didn't get a chance to say good-bye.'

'Au revoir.'

'Au revoir?'

'Until the next time.'

'There might never be a next time,'

Dirk placed his bottle on the shelf and reached out to the breast pocket of his plaid workshirt, which hung on the wall alongside them. He fumbled around and retrieved a big, thick cigar. 'Don't be so sure.'

Jens' eyes narrowed. 'Do you know something I don't know?'

Dirk grinned sheepishly as he peeled off the cellophane wrapper. 'He was keen to have our phone number, so I gave it to him.'

Jens sat up. 'But Dirk, we agreed. That kind of decision - return matches - we make together. You should have asked me.'

'You were asleep. I thought you'd be happy.' With a flick of his lighter, Dirk lit his cigar. 'If it makes you feel any better, I gave him my Handy number.

No. It didn't reassure Jens to know Ömer had been given the private number to Dirk's mobile phone. Why would it? He had no control over it. Dirk realised he had dropped a bollock and attempted to smooth Jens' ruffled fur. 'Anyway . . . he was big into you . . . '

'Even so.' Jens took a gulp of beer. His jaw relaxed. His eyes began to twinkle. 'He was into me, wasn't he?'

Dirk puffed out a cloud of aromatic smoke, clamped his teeth on his cigar and grinned. 'In a big way.'

Now it was Dirk's turn to take a nap. Jens was just toying with the idea of another beer when the announcement came over the tannoy - the announcement signalling an Aufguß. Jens knew that he would only have a few minutes to grab a seat in the dry sauna before the Aufguß began. Then, with all the other guys piled in together, he would be able to enjoy the benefits of water mixed with aromatic essential oils being poured onto the hot stones. The temperature inside the sauna would rise rapidly and the blistering heat would open every pore. The sauna had its benefits, not least the feeling of being squeaky clean. And Jens loved being clean.

He grabbed his towel and headed off, padding down the corridor. On the way to his dry sauna, he passed by the gallery of paintings and posters illustrating a gay Kama Sutra of sexual activities. There was no mistaking what this place was about. He glanced up at the clock face suspended overhead. Nine p.m. The night was still young. Doubtless, Dirk would still be keen to hit the bars. As he passed by the glass wall fronting the Jacuzzi, he glanced in. Blue tiles, a potted palm, and subdued lighting. Four towels on four hangers. And a scrum of hairy Bears splashing about in a group grope amidst the foaming waters.

Jens remembered the time he had been followed into the very same Jacuzzi by another swarthy hunk. A visitor attending a conference. Big and beefy. Tanned and toned. Dark and handsome. Closing the sliding door behind him, the guy had said 'Hello' as he removed his towel and placed it on a hook. Which had been unusual enough. In a Jacuzzi, most guys didn't acknowledge each other with words, rather with actions - with looks, with smiles. And then there was the more direct approach, under the cover of the bubbles. As the newcomer had climbed the metal steps, Jens had sneaked a peek at the guy's tackle. Soft but substantial. A thick length of pipe and low slung balls surrounded by a thick bush of pubic hair.

As he had slipped beneath the waves, the newcomer had spoken again. His first question was to ask if Jens spoke English. The second was to enquire where all the women were - it turned out that this guy had stumbled upon the place accidentally. He had seen the sign for Sauna and simply came in off the street. Jens could not even begin to guess how the newcomer had managed to ignore the million and one signs that made this particular sauna's function abundantly clear. How could someone miss the array of sex toys prominently displayed in the glass case beside the cash desk - gargantuan dildoes, butt-plugs, rubbers and lube; or the posters, the paintings, not to mention the guys blatantly advertising their wares through their open cabin doors? Some stroking their erections, others face down with their bubble-butts in the air.

Either the guy had been totally naive, blind, or in denial. And Jens had decided to put him out of his misery. He had shuffled along the seating, for there had been just the two of them in a pool to seat nine. Side by side, Jens had then thrown an arm casually around the edge of the pool behind the guy's back and allowed his hand to inch forward, to subtly brush his fingers against the visitor's smooth, broad back whilst he had told him, in no uncertain terms, that this sauna was gay - for men who wanted sex with men.

Having dropped the bombshell, Jens had awaited the fallout. There had been none. One would have expected any red-blooded heterosexual man to have been shocked, at the very least. Would have expected his jaw to drop, even if he didn't go so far as to run screaming for safety. But this revelation had had no discernible impact on the guy, for neither his facial expression nor his body language had altered in anyway.

Did the visitor have a name? Yes, Frank. Did Frank have a girlfriend? Yes, back home, but - Frank had added with a grin - he had no idea what she was up to. So . . . had he ever kissed a man? And finally, a reaction: an embarrassed laugh, as if the question could not be serious. No, Frank had said incredulously, his hands raised in protest before him. Still, he hadn't moved away from Jens' fingers as they increased their pressure: stroking his shoulder, kneading his warm, pliant flesh.

Put it down to beer or bravado, but Jens had decided it was time to push the boundaries. He had lifted his arm from around the visitor's shoulders and lowered it to rest below the waterline. Then tentatively, Jens had slipped his hand around Frank's inner thigh. And Frank had let it lie. No resistance. His big brown eyes had grown wide, wider still as Jens had let his fingers do the walking. Still no resistance, even as Jens had gripped Frank's thickening phallus in his fist. A first time for everything? Frank had been in good hands. Firm hands. And Jens? He had caught himself one big fish.

An hour after Dirk's well-deserved nap and Jens' reflective soak in the Jacuzzi, the pair were exiting Nollendorfplatz subway station - just a stone's throw from their favourite gay haunts, and a second stone's throw to their apartment right in the heart of this gay enclave. They stopped to cross at the traffic lights opposite The Metropol, just as a big, fuck-off, red Lamborghini pulled up in front of them: music blaring, top down. The soft top down in the midst of winter? What was this driver trying to prove? Behind the wheel sat a guy with Ray-Bans perched on his forehead. His thick grey hair was parted down the centre and pulled back in a pony-tail. And with gaudy gold jewellery glittering in the amber street light, he looked every inch the oldest swinger in town. He looked them up and down, making his interest clear. In your dreams, thought Jens. But he didn't need to say anything. Dirk knew exactly what Jens was thinking and raised his eyebrows in agreement. They quickened their pace.

Gay men of every description were on the streets, wrapped up warm, collars turned up against the biting winds, for they were not going to be deterred from a night on the hunt. Gay men heading this way and that, towards bars and cafés to suit every colour of the Rainbow Flag - not to mention a few shades in between. Jens and Dirk glanced through the glass frontage of Zwilling, the disco bunny bar. It was packed to overflowing. Wall to wall with designer yuppies, gossiping and flirting, dressed up to the nines, swapping fashion tips. Jens and Dirk exchanged a look, shook their heads and carried on towards their destination, their local Kniepe, F-FABrik.

Heavy, black, felt curtains were pushed aside as they stepped into the cigarette smog. The bar was to the left; tables and chairs were to the right and the pinball machine was situated in the far corner. Directly ahead was an archway leading into the inner sanctum. Here there was a second bar, a pool table, toilets and the extensive back-room beyond. Disco music throbbed from big, bass speakers and a blue haze of cigarette smoke hung in the air. The pungent smell of fresh piss was almost overpowering.

Rüdiger, the barman, waved to the pair over the heads of the customers sitting at the bar. Jens and Dirk crossed the room.

'Hi, guys. The usual?'

Dirk nodded. 'What's with the smell?'

'Rubber party this afternoon.' Rüdiger popped the caps off two bottles of beer with practised ease and slapped them on the bar before them. 'The last of the punters just left.'

Jens paid. 'Piss party, you mean?'

'Any chance of investing in air conditioning in the near future?' Dirk added.

Rüdiger laughed. 'You've been coming here long enough. What do you think?!'

Silly question. F-FABrik was a dump of the first magnitude - this was considered part of its charm. The lights were kept low with good reason. For in the cold light of day, it would doubtless look like a bomb site. Fortunately for all concerned, the lighting system was on par with a forty-watt bulb throughout. And no big deal, because the clientele didn't come to F-FABrik for the decor. They came to come.

Suddenly, Jens and Dirk felt themselves swept up from behind in a giant Bear hug. It was Bodo - one of their best friends and an occasional fuck buddy of Dirk's. He greeted them by rubbing his whiskers against their cheeks, roughly. Built like a brick outhouse, Bodo had the look of a wild Scottish Highlander: an unruly head of copper-coloured hair with full beard to match and sparkling, green eyes. He claimed he could trace his ancestors back to Scottish settlers to Berlin in the fifteenth century; supporters of Bonnie Prince Charlie who were, at that time, on the run from the Brits. And it would have taken a brave man to argue the point. He was, first and foremost, an intimidating figure. A characteristic that made him perfect for his chosen profession - that of security. Mostly at organised events, but sometimes even as a bodyguard.

Dirk and Bodo went back a long way. Many, many years in fact. When Bodo had first arrived in Berlin, Dirk had been his first pick-up. They had gone out together a few times, but it was something that wasn't meant to be. Still, the sex had been fabulous, and Bodo was a lot of fun to hang out with. And that was about the sum total: no romantic chemistry, but the potential to be big buddies. So after a couple of months, when it had become clear that they were not destined to be life-long lovers, their relationship had changed into a comfortable, almost effortless friendship. Though a friendship where, from time to time, either of them could end up an evening in the other's bed.

When Jens had come on the scene, Bodo had retreated for a while. It had turned out that he had the hots for Jens himself. Sad but true. But up to press, the potentialities had never been seriously pursued. Bodo was - first, last and always - Dirk's friend. Sure, he would flirt with Jens. Unmercifully at times. But the emphasis was squarely on the buddy aspect. Bodo was, perhaps, the Bear that Dirk most liked and trusted in Berlin. After Jens, that was. For Bodo was a big lug, but his height and muscular bulk belied a surprisingly tender soul. Dirk found him to be perceptive, warm and loving. And now committed, however questionably, to his own little home-Bear.

Bodo smiled from one to the other. His gruff voice came like a sonic boom out of his hairy, barrel chest. 'I thought there was a funny smell in here! I should have guessed.'

Jens was delighted to see their pal. 'Bodo, you old grizzly. Long time no see. How the fuck are you?'

'Glad to be back speaking German.'

Dirk rubbed Bodo's beefy shoulder. 'Oh, yeah. You've been away. Florida, wasn't it?'

'That's right. Bear convention.'

'Did Volker go with you?' Dirk asked. Volker was Bodo's cute, little Bear cub of a boyfriend.

'No. Couldn't get the time off work.'

'Shame,' said Dirk, with more than a touch of irony.

Jens grinned. 'I bet those American Bears didn't know what hit them!'

Bodo let out a roar of laughter. 'Not just American. Canadian, Mexican, Brazilian . . . ' He counted them off on his sausage-like fingers.

Dirk cocked an eyebrow at Jens. 'You name them - he had them!' He raised the neck of his beer bottle to his lips.

Another roar. Bodo slapped Dirk on the back with such a force that he almost sent Dirk's beer bottle rocketing skyward.

'This guy doesn't know his own strength,' Dirk spluttered, mopping down the front of his plaid workshirt.

'Surprising he's got any left!' Jens quipped. 'You don't seem to have got much of a tan to say that you were in Florida.'

Bodo threw his arms around their shoulders once more as if he was sweeping them up into his confidence. 'Too busy exploring the great indoors, my friends!'

'How did you get on with speaking English?'

'It was no problem to make myself understood.'

'We don't doubt that for a minute - do we, Jens?'

Jens grabbed his crotch and made a thrusting action. 'No. Not one minute.'

Bodo rolled his eyes. 'Less of the comedy double-act.' He released his grip on the pair and rubbed his huge hands together. 'So. Are we going to make a night of it?'

'No. I'm just having the one beer, then off to bed.' Jens grimaced. 'Work in the morning. But Dirk's out for the evening, aren't you, Dirk?' Jens smiled at Dirk knowingly. 'Maybe you can keep him company, Bodo. Keep him out of trouble . . . '

'Get me into it, you mean!' Dirk retorted.

'Get him out of here at least.' Bodo sniffed the air. 'Man, it stinks!'

Dirk smiled. 'Some people like the smell.'

'Yeah? Must be an acquired taste. And not one I'd be pushed to acquire, that's for sure.'

'You're not into piss play, Bodo? You surprise me!'

'Piss is okay in its place -'

Jens leaned in towards Dirk's ear. 'Yeah. Gushing into his mouth, splashing over his beard, spraying all over his fur . . . '

Bodo gave Jens a look that said 'you better shut up if you know what's good for you, pal,' and finished off his sentence. '- but I don't want to wade in it.'

Dirk put his empty bottle on the counter. 'C'mon, then. Let's make waves.'

Another hour, another bar. Dirk was upstairs by the pool table, waiting for Bodo to come back with the beer he had promised. But there was no sign of it happening any time soon. The bar was pretty crowded that evening and Bodo had a habit of making new friends - or fuck buddies - wherever he went. Or at least, whenever there was enough people that he could find someone to interest him. Dirk allowed his eyes to wander over the crowd. The usual faces - skinny skinheads with would-be tough guy expressions sipping their Beck's beer to make it last the best part of the evening; the leather queens with their 1000 DM butch drag that didn't fool anyone and the SM gang, with their coloured hankie codes. Each looking about as intimidating (or submissive, depending on your particular preference) as a cage full of gerbils. In other words, just a typical leather/cruise bar crowd. Dirk's eyes, however, were drawn to a Bear couple - one early thirties and the other in his fifties. A Daddy/Son couple for sure, out on the prowl for either another Daddy or Son to make up the family numbers for the evening. Dirk was certainly in the mood to let a Daddy play around with him - and a three-way was always appealing.

Both men were in identical gear - check-shirts, jeans and work-boots. Their hair was cropped short, and both were bearded - though Daddy Bear had a longer, fuller beard. A bit like Walt Whitman's, thought Dirk. He continued staring at the couple, who by now had met his gaze across the crowded bar and were staring back. Then the Son whispered something to Daddy and, with one last look over at Dirk, they both disappeared down the stairs into the cruising cellar. Dirk looked around again, wondering where the hell Bodo had got to; there still wasn't any sight of him. And now there was the added complication of the growing boner in his pants. Figuring that his absence wouldn't cause Bodo too much distress, Dirk made his way through the crowd and walked downstairs.

At the bottom of the stairs, Dirk waited a couple of moments to allow his eyes to adjust to the gloom. If he had thought that upstairs was crowded, here it was heaving. Men everywhere, and most of them Dirk hadn't seen before - and he had been in the bar for over an hour, so these guys must have been shagging down here all of that time. Get it while you can, Dirk thought to himself, allowing himself a wry smile. Now the question was, which way? The darkroom branched off in two directions, one leading to a series of cabins and a totally dark area, while the other went to a pair of so-called theme rooms, one 'wet' and another with a sling. Dirk figured that his Bear couple probably weren't heading toward those rooms but, then again, you could never be sure. Dirk decided to sit and wait this one out. If they were really interested, they would come looking for him.

Dirk sat back on the wooden bench, his back against the dry stone wall, both feet resting on the lip of the cropped oak barrel before him that otherwise acted as a table and settled down to wait. One hand was clutching his bottle of beer. Now and then, he raised the bottle to his lips, taking a long, slow gulp, and then returned it to his lap. It was an effortless gesture, a relaxed gesture. The monitor fixed to the opposite wall played standard gay SM porno. Mind numbing. Different costumes, a different backdrop, but the acting was as uninspired and uninspiring as ever. The screen cast the only light in an otherwise dark and steamy cellar. A cellar where nothing was stored, save for the aromatic memories of countless copulations.

Out of the darkness, a shadow emerged, easing into Dirk's field of vision, and Dirk flicked his eyes towards this distraction with deliberate disinterest. Mustn't seem too keen. Though the Son who now stood with his back against the wall directly opposite him was making no bones about his interest. His eyes were boring a hole in Dirk's crotch. A hand was stuffed inside his checked workshirt, fingers pinching and tugging the pierced nipple on one seriously hairy chest. Then, with a little nod, he gestured over his shoulder, turned and walked towards the darkroom.

Dirk sprang to his feet, and followed the leader down the dark corridor. Turning a corner, he thought he spied the Son up ahead, standing in the entry to the darkest area. Dirk moved through the crush of bodies and, as he stepped through the doorway, he pressed his body against the Son. Sure enough the pressure was returned and the Son followed him a couple of steps inside. Once there in the darkness, Dirk was spun around. His shirt was ripped open, his stiff nipples were tweaked mercilessly and his head was drawn down for a kiss. Passion exploded. Tongues clashed as Dirk fought to open the buttons of the Son's shirt, exposing a leather harness hidden underneath. He let his hands roam over a solid chest, cupping the chiselled pecs, pinching the pierced nipples, and ruffling the rug of chest hair. They continued to kiss and Dirk felt someone come up behind him. He could feel the long beard being rubbed against the back of his neck, as Daddy Bear reached around to play with his nipples and then moved his hand downwards to pop open the buttons of Dirk's jeans. And Dirk was enjoying this. Son, meanwhile, had slipped down to suck on his tits - first taking one swollen nipple and then the other between tongue and teeth, nibbling and licking - making them hard.

At the same time, Daddy Bear was rubbing his not-insubstantial crotch against Dirk's arse, grinding it in while both of his hands gripped Dirk's shoulders and slid down his upper arms as he chewed on Dirk's neck. Dirk's cock was out and getting harder by the minute. He was loving this. Every fucking moment of it. Just what he enjoyed most - being the centre of attention, allowing others to do the work. This way he could concentrate on pure physical pleasure. But then, almost as suddenly as it had begun, the two guys disentangled themselves and moved away into the darkness, leaving Dirk standing alone, his pants around his knees, his engorged cock straining to burst. What's this all about? he thought. Maybe these guys just liked to play a little? But it wasn't at all clear. He wasn't pissed off, exactly, but he still had a stonking hard-on.

Dirk went back upstairs to see if he could find Bodo, but there still was no sign of him anywhere. He's probably gone off home, Dirk thought, maybe I should do the same myself. Moving slowly towards the front of the bar and the exit, however, he noticed a little Bear in a baseball cap sitting all alone in the corner nearest the door. He looks cute, thought Dirk, conscious of his still-throbbing cock. What the hell, he could have one more beer and see how the final part of the evening developed. As if on cue, the little Bear looked up, caught Dirk's eye and gave a welcoming smile. That's settled then, thought Dirk, one more beer and then . . . if I'm lucky?

He made his way back to the bar and ordered. The whole time he gave little glances over his shoulder to show his continuing interest. Beer in hand, he walked up to the empty stool just a couple of metres from Bear Cub, and sat down. Resting his back against the wall, Dirk pulled a second stool over beside him and, looking over in the direction of Bear Cub, he indicated the new stool with a glance and a questioning look. Bear Cub smiled. He got up from his place and came over to sit with Dirk.

Dirk spoke first. 'So, what's your name?'

'Lutz. And yours?'

Dirk leaned over and kissed him on the lips. 'Dirk,' he replied softly, and kissed him again.

Lutz moaned and opened his mouth wider. Dirk ran his tongue around Lutz's lips, nibbling on the lower lip, sucking on his top lip. Slipping his tongue in between both. Lutz captured Dirk's tongue instantly, sucking on it rapturously. Deep soul kisses, drawing them ever closer to the point of no return. Lutz's fingers found the buttons of Dirk's shirt and opened it. Fingers moved to nipples and squeezed them. As his nipples were already tender from the workout they had had downstairs, Dirk did not simply feel his body catch light, but imagined he could actually hear the 'whoof!' as he burst into flames.

Shamelessly, Lutz's hands travelled downwards, down to massage Dirk's bulging crotch. He ran his thumb over the prominent outline of Dirk's cock, whilst at the same time cupping his balls. He felt Dirk's rock-solid prick strain to burst free of its enclosure. Lutz got up from his stool and positioned himself between Dirk's thighs, bulging crotch now rubbing against bulging crotch. Their passionate, slobbering kisses increased in their intensity, as their tongues wrestled for supremacy. At last Lutz sighed into Dirk's mouth, capitulating. His lips yielding, wanting gentleness. And he got it. Sweet and tender kisses.

'Funny. I thought you would be different,' said Lutz, during a break for air.

'How do you mean?' Dirk asked, though he already knew the answer.

'Well, it's how you look. You know. Big, tall, cropped hair and all.

You look like a really tough guy, and then this . . . ' Lutz kissed Dirk again. It was something Dirk had heard at various times - how his aggressive looks belied his tender sexual preferences. But then, it wasn't something that had ever troubled him. He figured it a strength, not a weakness.

They kissed again, passionately, and Lutz began to undo the buttons of Dirk's jeans. Dirk didn't do anything to stop him. In this sort of bar it wouldn't matter anyway. Sure - wasn't this the place where he and Jens had seen two guys get fist-fucked by a third - the receiving pair lying back on the pool table while the third guy - bollock-naked - stuck an arm up each of their rear ends. The funny thing was, then as now, people around were acting as if it was a completely normal and everyday occurrence. Berlin was a funny place sometimes.

Dirk's cock was now fully free and Lutz was slowly working it with his fist. Then, dropping to his hunkers, he licked the tip and then took the entire length in his mouth. Dirk moaned, enjoying the feeling of his cock in the warm hole. A slobbering, desperate hole, thought Dirk. Hungry for man-meat. Desperate to have the aching emptiness filled. And Dirk's dick was enough to plug the deepest orifice. Lutz relaxed his throat muscles and swallowed Dirk whole. He seemed to be luxuriating in the fullness, for it was a perfect fit. He was unwilling to let Dirk go. He was holding on for dear life.

Dirk struggled to release himself. 'Let's go somewhere more comfortable,' he said, stroking Lutz's head tenderly. Lutz gasped, his jaws still open, his tongue lolling out hopefully. He was still hungry - and he wanted to be fed. Finally, he nodded his agreement.

Downstairs offered a measure of privacy in the form of small cubicles. Though only a measure - and little more than cosmetic. Tissue-thin walls closed in on three sides, with a door at the fourth. The floor was strewn with paper towels from the dispenser on the side wall and used condoms, knotted and discarded. Dirk rested his back up against the back wall - the only one that would support his weight - whilst

Lutz fell to his knees once again and resumed his suck-fest.

Reaching up, Lutz's fingers played with Dirk's scorched nipples. Dirk's length responded by vibrating deep, deep within the other man's throat. Then Dirk pulled Lutz up onto his feet, forced Bear Cub's mouth down on his tits, forcing him to suck on each bullet in turn. Forcing him to devour them. Lutz stripped off Dirk's shirt fully, exposing his forested armpits, ripe and lickable. He hooked the shirt over the towel dispenser as quickly as he could, and then buried his mouth in one hairy pit. Buried it right on in there.

Then like a man possessed, Lutz spun round, unbuttoning his shirt and hoisting it up his back, dropping his jeans and jock strap to his ankles. He pushed Dirk's cock between his crack and ground his arse back into Dirk's groin. 'We need to be safe,' he gasped.

'Naturally.'

'You have condoms.'

'Of course.'

'You mind if I talk dirty?'

'Not at all.'

'I mean, do you mind if I talk unsafe?'

'Whatever turns you on, baby. I don't have a problem with words.'

Lutz needed no more encouragement. He pressed ahead, full throttle. 'Oh man, I want you to fuck me. I want you to fuck me so bad. I want to feel you come inside me. To feel your come dribble out of me.'

Dirk felt his cock stiffen, sandwiched between Lutz's hairy cleft. Felt a smile play across his lips. This guy was some actor. 'You want my big dick pumping deep in that tight arsehole of yours, baby? Want me to baste your insides with my juices?'

'Oh, yeah, bigman. I want that. Man, do I want that!' Lutz increased his backward motion even as he started yanking on his own cock, beating his meat to a pulp. 'You can do whatever you want to me, bigman. Anything at all. What do you want? Tell me, bigman. Anything you want, I'll do.'

'Get on your knees, where you belong. Worship my cock. Worship it!'

Within the instant, Lutz was on his knees, gazing reverently at Dirk's awesome prong. Trembling. 'Please, bigman. Please, can I stick your beautiful dick in my mouth?'

Dirk smiled down upon him. 'C'mon, baby. You can do better than that!'

Lutz reached out a hand but Dirk brushed it aside.

'Please, bigman!' Lutz eyes were pleading. 'Please! I want it in my mouth. Fuck my throat. I want you to come in my mouth. I want to taste your come. To roll your come around my tongue.'

Dirk smiled once again. 'Oh, baby!" He leaned down and clasped the back of Lutz's neck. 'You've got such a dirty little mouth. All that dirty talk coming out of your dirty little mouth. I think I'm going to have to wash it out for you. I'm going to have to flood your mouth, flood it with all the love in my big, big balls. Do you a big favour. Wash it clean.'

Lutz whimpered. Visibly shaken, he was turned on to the point of overload. And then he launched himself onto Dirk's knob, sucking it with a vengeance. His tongue worked furiously up and down the length of Dirk's mammoth organ, traced the line of the engorged veins and, in doing so, sensed the need, the deep abiding need within Dirk's ballsac to empty its wealth of contents.

'I'd love to be naked in bed with you.' Lutz gasped and sucked. 'I'd love to watch you fuck my boyfriend.' He gasped and sucked. 'To watch you shove your big, fat cock inside his tight, little arse.' He gasped and sucked. 'To watch you fucking him.' He gasped and sucked. 'I'd like to fuck your boyfriend. To watch you fuck mine while I fuck yours.' He gasped and -

Suddenly, Dirk grabbed Lutz by the collar and manhandled him up on to his feet once more. Pinching his mouth between his fingers, Dirk hissed, 'Shut that dirty mouth and make me come, baby.' He fell forward, chewing on Lutz's chin, his moist tongue flicking around his jawline. Then lips found each other once again and passionate kissing threatened to overwhelm them both.

Pressing solid, hairy chests together. Rubbing pecs against each other. Delighting in the friction of flesh on flesh. Dirk was working his cock, about to come.

'Oh, baby. That's a good baby. You wanted my bigman come. You're going to get it. All over your belly, gallons of bigman come. Going to shoot it now. You ready? You ready, baby?!'

'I'm ready. I've never been more ready.'

Lutz's lips held Dirk's tongue in a vicelike grip as Dirk shot his load, stifling his groans as he jerked his creamy wad over Lutz's hairy crotch. Lutz reached down and felt the wet sticky discharge on his fingers. He rubbed it in, massaged Dirk's load into his groin and along the length of his stiff dick. Jerking furiously now, jerking like a crazy man, he shot his own load. Nuzzling into Dirk's neck, he too smothered his guttural outpouring. Groans pulsating, vibrating against Dirk's burning flesh. Drenching Dirk's crotch. Spurting his copious load up over Dirk's bollocks, over his hairy thighs.

At last, all was still save for heaving chests. For the first time, Dirk became conscious of the unnatural silence; became aware of the distinct possibility of ears outside straining to hear. Pressed up against the walls? Sharing vicariously in their pleasure. But inside the cubicle, sweet little lip kisses were what were being shared: a final intimacy in the aftermath of orgasm. Then Lutz and Dirk mopped up. Buttoned up. Zipped up. Hugged. Opened the door to the strange world outside. Nothing much had changed. The corridor was still packed, with the hungry still on the prowl.

'Got to go . . . ' said Lutz regretfully. 'My boyfriend will wonder where I got to.' And with that, he led the way upstairs.

Dirk leaned on the bar, finishing off his beer. Daddy and Son passed by on their way out of the curtained door. Daddy squeezed

Dirk's arm; gave him a knowing smile. Dirk smiled in return, a genuine smile. A charming smile. His white, white teeth thrown into contrast by his chocolate-brown beard. Daddy nearly melted under its influence.

Maybe another time.

Three

With his coat collar turned up against the bitter chill, Jens stood shivering before the double doors. Before he was buzzed into the steel and concrete building, he paused briefly to shake the snow from his baseball cap. The logo of the Miami Bears had almost been obliterated on the short walk from the subway station. Berlin was under a blanket of snow.

As he stepped into the welcome warmth of the elevator and slowly began to thaw, Jens wondered if he would ever be used to the winters in Berlin. Either the length or the severity. In winter, chill winds cut through the body like a knife and his own breath frosted his goatee. Already on his third winter, he somehow doubted it.

At times like this, it was all too easy to forget the wonderful summer months and he found himself muttering, as so often before: 'So just what is keeping me here?!' If he had been in a more reflective move, then the answer would have undoubtedly been 'Dirk'. But he wasn't feeling reflective. He was feeling playful. So the reason that sprang to the forefront of his mind was 'Cock.' It was that simple. It had to be. Big, thick, links of German sausage. A seemingly endless supply. Fresh meat on every incoming plane and train. The fact was, what had brought him here brought here to Berlin had brought them all - the promise of a life lived to the full. Free from the constraints of tiny minds and small-town mentalities. The old, old story. And in his case, Palm Vista, Florida now seemed a world away and he wasn't about to swap planets.

Earlier that day, he had been cruised on the platform of the subway. Hardly the first time, but somehow it still came as something of a shock to be so brazenly pursued by hungry eyes. The guy had asked Jens for the time; had recognised his American accent and been delighted to have the opportunity to practise his limited English vocabulary on a native speaker. That was if 'Do you want me to fuck you?' counted as English practice.

And later, as he had slipped inch by thick, long inch of his gloved penis ever deeper into Jens, the stranger had uttered all the stock clichés of an American porno actor.

'Ooh, yeah! You love phat big dick inside you, don't you? Yeah! Take phat big cock!'

It was all Jens could do not to laugh being confronted with the Catalina method of language learning, an audio-visual technique he wouldn't normally exploit in the classroom. He didn't have the heart to point out that the stranger needed some serious work on his 'th's.

Even as Jens entered the office, Sabine, the receptionist and secretary was reaching for her coat.

'Would you mind locking up tonight? I'm leaving early, if that's okay?'

'Hot date?'

She raised her eyebrows in mock reprimand. 'I have an appointment with my landlord. Definitely not a date! '

Her command of English never failed to impress Jens. Perfect diction with only the merest hint of an accent. Invariably, she took the initiative and forced Jens into speaking English. She would always argue that she needed the practice more.

'Yeah, I'll lock up. No problem,' Jens assured her.

'Only, you're the last one in the school tonight . . . ' She pulled a woolly cap down over her ears and tucked any stray hair away neatly. 'Oh, and only one of your students has arrived so far. Jürgen.' She paused, raised her eyebrows, and lowered her voice. ' He is such a flirt!' she hissed. 'He told me I have beautiful eyes!'

'But you do have beautiful eyes, Sabine!' Jens laughed.

She pursed her lips in mock reprimand. 'I sent him through to the coffee room . . . ' She grabbed her bag and sped past him.

Jens checked his watch. 'Still five minutes. I've time for a coffee myself.'

'Make the most of it!' She threw a look over her shoulder as she disappeared out of the door. 'Rather you alone with him than me!'

The door slammed behind her and then - silence.

He poured himself a coffee in the teacher's room and, perching on the edge of a cluttered table, watched the snowfall outside the window and allowed his mind to drift. Berlin had been under a blanket of snow the night he had arrived, too. The taxi had eased through the slush-filled streets. The city had been alive with lights. Late-night shoppers had skidded down the Kurfurstendamm, carrier bags in hand, collars turned up against the bitter winds. His companion had sat alongside him on the back seat; like tonight, she had been chattering away ten to the dozen, glad to escape the cold outside. But he had been deaf to her words. He had finally arrived. Berlin. Finally, Berlin.

Sabine had been waiting for him at the arrival gate in Tegel Airport. A hand-made sign bore his name - Jens Müller. Sabine had been the welcoming committee, in its entirety.

'Sabine Koch?'

She had smiled in greeting. 'Jens Müller?'

Sabine had a charming smile, and a warm and open face. Small and slim, with brown, shoulder-length hair, she had a childlike quality that Jens had warmed to straight away. Even then he could tell that they were going to become the best of friends. 'That's right, but please call me Jens.'

'Did you have a good flight?'

'Let's just say, I feel more comfortable with my feet on the ground!'

'So, do you want to keep them there? There's a taxi waiting outside.'

'Please -' he gestured '- lead the way.'

Once they were finally in the vehicle, Jens had looked out through the passenger window, through the frosting of snow, and been mesmerised by the glittering city that seemed almost to reach out and embrace him.

'Jens? Jens!' Sabine's voice had finally registered and brought him back to the reality of the taxi-cab..

'Sorry. Did you say something?'

'Yes. Where was it you said you came from?'

'Palm Vista.'

Sabine had raised a quizzical eyebrow.

'It's a couple of hours from Miami . . . You know, Miami . . . as in Florida.'

Sabine had shrugged. 'Never heard of it.'

'You've never heard of Miami?!'

She had laughed. 'No! What you said - Palm Vista.'

He had laughed, too. 'Can't say I'm surprised you've never heard of it. It might sound exotic, but don't be fooled. It's the kind of place that, even if you did know it ,you would be glad to forget it.'

'I love America. Really love it. I hope to live there one day.'

'But not in Palm Vista. Not unless you want to die a virgin.'

'Too late for that, I'm afraid.'

Jens had laughed at her candour, and Sabine had followed suit.

There had been a pause, one that allowed Jens to flip into German. 'Konnen Wir ein bißchen Deutsch sprechen? Can we speak German? I need to get into the habit.'

Sabine looked a little disappointed. 'Your German is good.'

'I should hope so. My parents are German-American. They've never really learnt to speak English properly. I spent most of my childhood translating.'

'That must have been a big responsibility.'

Jens shrugged. 'Good training for a language teacher.'

'So here you are . . . '

'So here I am . . . Free at last!'

'Palm Vista can't be that bad. Surely?'

'Can't it? Why do you think I've flown the coop?'

'Berlin has its attractions.'

And he had looked out the taxi window and smiled. Never a truer word. In that moment, he had felt like he had been swept up in a whirlwind and now found himself in the fabled land of Oz, a magic land. And that feeling had never faded - not once in all the years he had lived in Berlin.

Palm Vista. To the uninitiated, the name might conjure up visions of a paradise idyll but, for Jens, the mere thought of it was enough to make him shudder. He would never go back, of this he was certain. He had not simply left - he had run the hell away. Far away from the stifling confines of a small-town mentality and traditional values. Away from a family who would see his spirit crushed by conformity rather than acknowledge his difference.

Graduating from university without a job, he had been forced, reluctantly, to return home, though he had never intended this to be any thing other than a short-term strategy. He was determined he would not be forced back into the closet. He had tasted gay life in Miami, and he liked the taste.

First day back, he had even told his mother, just as she busied herself with the washing-up. 'I'm gay, Mom.' Just like that. What had he expected? The worst? He had not been disappointed. Her primary concern had been that his father should never know. 'It would kill him!' she had cried theatrically, like the kitchen-sink drama queen she was. All the while rattling her pots and pans to drown out his protests. In any event, she had got her wish - the last wish he would ever grant her. No need for his father ever to know. Jens was now a world apart.

Jürgen was looking out of the window into the blackened night as Jens entered the coffee room. Momentarily unaware of his presence, Jürgen puffed manfully on the cigar held fast between thick fingers whilst his other hand clutched a cup of coffee in its powerful grasp. A white T-shirt stretched across his powerful back, criss-crossed with the braces from his blue overalls; the seat snugly fitting one magnificent Knack-Arsch. Jens' reflection came into view as Jürgen exhaled a stream of smoke.

'Ah! Hello, Jens!' Jürgen said, placing his cup on the sill, and turning to extend one meaty paw in greeting.

'Jürgen!' Jens took his hand and felt Jürgen's thick fingers grip like a vice and squeeze tightly. 'Only you here tonight?' Jens enquired, hopefully.

'I think it.' Jürgen shrugged. 'Work is very busy in the moment.'

'In the moment or "At" the moment?'

'At the moment!' he corrected himself, his eyes sparkling.

'But this is the last lesson. I won't get to say good-bye to the other guys.'

'Then I get full attention?'

'Guess so.'

Jens had learned a lot about Jürgen over the past several weeks: that Jürgen was thirty-two years old; that he came from the former East - the island of Rügen on the Baltic Sea coast - and had moved to West Berlin shortly after the Wall came down; that he was recently divorced with two small children; that he was currently employed as an in-house fireman at one of the large American manufacturing subsidiaries that peppered the city and that his main passion (against all blue-collar appearances) was that of stamp collecting. A hobby he had been introduced to by his father. When he had first told Jens of this, his hobby, he had grinned and lowered his eyes like a bashful boy. Jens had been forced to conclude that Jürgen was possibly the most unlikely stamp collector the world had ever seen.

Jürgen was learning English as part of his job, as it was the company language of the multinational concern for whom he now worked.

And he'd been a joy to teach. Partly because his enthusiasm and commitment meant that he learned quickly, but mostly because he was fun to be around and a pleasure to look at. At around 5'10", he was stocky, muscular and hirsute - just the way Jens liked his wank fantasies to be. With dark-blond hair, cut super short around his ears, longer on top, a moustache and four-day beard framing an almost-permanent grin.

Jens decided to abandon the lesson plan, even before Jürgen stubbed out his cigar. There was no point going through to the classroom.

'Take a seat, Jürgen. We'll be more comfortable in here.'

Jürgen sat down on the leather couch. Resting back, he crossed his feet at the ankle and splayed his solid thighs. 'We are alone in the school?'

'Yes. Tonight it's just the two of us. So let's talk. Practise your fluency.' Jens sat alongside him on the other end of the couch. 'How was your day?'

Jürgen thought a moment. 'A long day. I started work at . . . half past six and finished at seventeen o'clock.'

'Seventeen o'clock or "five p.m."?'

He grinned, familiar now with Jens' techniques for correction. 'Five p.m. And had a little time to shower -'

'You have showers at work?'

'It's filthy work sometimes.'

'Dirty work.'

'Yes, dirty work. Oil and . . . sweat?'

Jens nodded.

'Yes, much sweat. And we shower . . . '

'We or I?'

'We. My colleagues and me.'

'You're not shy?'

'Shy?' His face took on a puzzled expression.

'Shy would be what you would feel if you were uncomfortable being naked in front of your work mates.

'Ah . . . schuctern! No! I'm not shy! Why to be shy?'

Good question, if he looked as good out of his overalls as he did in them. Still, the possibility of seeing him in all his naked glory certainly struck Jens as a big deal. Standing alongside Jürgen in the shower. Soaping his back. Dropping the soap. Bending down to retrieve it . . .

'Hell - lo!' Jürgen was waving a hand in front of Jens' face. 'Where go you?'

Reluctantly, Jens snapped out of it. 'Sorry, Jürgen. I was lost in thought for a moment.'

Jürgen leaned back, stretching his arms to the ceiling, and then laced his hands behind his head. Rearranging himself on the leather upholstery, he threw an arm over the back of the sofa and brought one knee up to rest on the seat between them, spreading his thighs even wider in the process. The bulge at his groin stood out dramatically, straining at the fly. Separated on either side of the stitched gusset, lay the sumptuous curves of each loose-slung ball. Reluctantly, Jens averted his gaze.

'So, after you showered?'

'Went for a beer, maybe two . . . '

'You're not driving tonight, I hope?'

'No.' He looked Jens straight in the eye. 'I come home with you . . . You drive!' And he laughed.

'In this weather? I was lucky to get here. I don't even want to think about going home.'

Jürgen chuckled. 'Then we stay the night?'

Did Jens blush? Certainly, he was flustered. 'Let's see . . . ' he began, swiftly changing the subject, 'I know a lot about you, but you know very little about me. So, ask any questions you like. Okay?'

'Okay,' Jürgen replied. 'How old are you?'

'I'm twenty-eight years old.'

'Where you live in Berlin?'

'Nollendorfplatz. I have a really nice apartment. Three rooms. Seventy-five square meters.'

Jürgen paused, concentrating. 'You are married or not?'

'No. Next question.'

'You have a friend?'

Jens laughed. 'I have many friends, Jürgen.'

'I mean a girlfriend?'

'No. Next question.'

'No girlfriend?' The look that crossed Jürgen's handsome face was almost audible. 'You like much more men?'

Word order was Jürgen's biggest problem, but in this instance it seemed almost churlish to correct him. 'Yes. You could say that. But better, I like men much more.'

'You like men much more . . . ' Jürgen savoured the sentence in his mouth, then grinned shamelessly, revealing a perfect set of milk-white teeth between moist lips. 'Then I can say . . . I also?'

'You mean, "Me too" . . . ' Now it was Jens' turn to grin. 'We have an expression in English, Jürgen: actions speak louder than words.' Now if he had said that line to a native speaker, Jens thought, it would have sounded like the cheesiest line of the century! Fortunately, Jürgen was oblivious.

'What means this?'

Jens laughed. 'It means that I think you are a very handsome man . . . ' Jens abandoned this form of explanation. 'It means this . . . ' He reached across the short distance between them and placed his hand squarely in Jürgen's lap, cupping the big, bulging basket.

Jürgen gazed intently into Jens' face. 'You have beautiful eyes. '

Laughter bubbled up out of Jens' lips. He shook his head. 'Our secretary had you pegged, Jürgen. She said you're a flirt, and you are. You are such a flirt!'

'I enjoy to flirt, it's true.' Jürgen held Jens in his meaningful gaze. 'But a flirt is only playing. I don't just play.' The cushioned leather seat creaked as Jürgen leaned closer - close enough for Jens to feel the warmth of Jürgen's breath on his face. 'No. I don't just talk, I do it.'

Any reservations Jens might have had were quickly smothered by the ferocity of Jürgen's kiss. Powerful arms enfolded him, ruling out any attempt at resistance. And Jens was not about to resist: he responded fully. His mouth worked furiously, feasting on face now. Jürgen's hands clutched at Jens' body through the confinement of clothing. Hungry mouths clamped together, tongues dancing around each other like some ancient fertility rite. Jürgen's tongue proved to be the more energetic, now forcing Jens' to dance backwards as he ploughed his long, wet tongue deep into Jens' cavernous need.

Jens' eyes were closed tight. Behind closed lids, it was as if a thousand stars were exploding in a night sky. His whole body was electrified. Jürgen's hands were all over him. Gripping and groping. Squeezing and tweaking and twisting. Jens yanked his mouth free, gasping for air. Jürgen wasn't about to let him off so easily, and he lunged once more towards him, tongue outstretched. Jens raised his hands, clasped Jürgen's head in his palms, holding him at bay before covering his face in kisses.

'Do you want me to fuck you?' Jürgen blurted out the question, direct and urgent, and, as if to drive the question home, he buried his warm, wriggling tongue in Jens' ear. Jürgen's need, and his desire, were both overpowering. It was an aphrodisiac all by itself. The temperature was rising and at breakneck speed. From a spark to a flame to a forest fire.

Jens reached for his own belt buckle in turn and worked it open. Why play hard to get? What was to be gained? He wanted this guy, big style. Now was the time to make his feelings known. No holding back. No holds barred. Jürgen had Jens' trousers and pants around his ankles with a single swift tug. For a split second he gazed reverently at Jens' stiff, throbbing cock and then he leaned forward, his dripping tongue poking out of his mouth and flicking the tip of Jens' swollen cock-head. Jens grabbed his own balls, gripped them tight, sure for one terrible moment that he was about to shoot his bolt in that instant. But, thankfully, he managed to keep his climax at bay - if only just.

Cradling Jürgen's chin in the palm of his hand, Jens watched him swallow his fat dick whole. Wide-eyed, Jürgen looked up, directly meeting Jens' gaze.

'And I thought you wanted to talk?'

Jürgen pulled back. 'Later. Talk later.' And once again his open mouth swallowed the length of Jens' tool.

Clamping his lips tight shut, Jürgen held on with the determination of a dog who is not about to surrender his bone, whilst still managing to unlace Jens boots and yank them off. Jens peeled his jumper and shirt over his head, throwing them to one side and, kicking his feet free of his trousers, he finally lay naked before Jürgen.

Jürgen's coarse, workman-like hands now traversed the entire surface of Jens' body. His lust was palpable. Jürgen flipped him over, manhandled Jens around so that he lay face down, on his belly. Jens' nose met the heady stench of leather from the cushioned upholstery and his arse was in the air, exposed to Jürgen's thorough examination. For Jürgen was prising open Jens' buttocks and spitting into the gash. Jens shivered, reflexively, as a coarse finger traced around his tight and tender hole. And then Jürgen pressed that same thick finger up against the entrance. Gently but firmly, he forced his way in. More spit, then a second finger. Finally, a third. Spreading his fingers wide, Jürgen opened up Jens' ring-piece like a flower in bloom. Jens was lost in a sea of sensation. He ground his arse backwards, rotating his hips, cramming as much of Jürgen's hand inside himself as was humanly possible. Up to the knuckles now, Jürgen flexed and contracted his fingers, swivelled his hand around, first clockwise then anticlockwise. Pressing down now, his talented fingers massaged Jens' prostate. It was all too much to bear. Just too fucking wonderful to endure. To have a big man's fingers buried deep up another's hairy hole - could there be an act more intimate? Open, exposed, penetrated. And willingly. Alive in the moment. Connecting. Connected . . .

When the phone rang, Dirk was fresh from the shower. Wearing only a sweatshirt top and jogging bottoms, he flopped down on the sofa and lifted the receiver.

'Hello.'

'Hello. Here is Ömer.

Dirk allowed himself a triumphant smile, and snuggled back against the cushions. 'Hello, Ömer. I have been thinking of you.'

'Really?'

'Yeah, really. Thinking about you.' Dirk let his mind drift to their last assignation. The one Jens didn't know about. The one that occurred whilst he had been in the cabin, dead to the world. 'Remembering your fierce and tender kisses in the dark, damp sauna. Remembering your beautiful face looking at me as you stood outside the shower cubicles. Your beautiful face giving me no choice but to invite you to join me for one last quickie. And so I have the pleasure of remembering the stiffness of your dick as you quickly jerked out all the come from your big balls into the palm of my open hand.

A pause. 'Can a man call another man beautiful?'

'Yes, if he's brave enough. I'm brave enough, Ömer. And you are beautiful.' Dirk felt his groin stir into action. 'So many memories of our meeting. Sitting and talking. My hand slipping down your broad back and cupping your arse. My toes touching your toes on the cool, tiled floor under the hot shower. Listening to the sounds from your throat as you moaned and groaned out your pleasure. This was music to my ears. And later as you made to leave, over by the lockers. Opening your towel again and again just for another glimpse of your naked body, another glimpse of your delicious cock. Pressing my cock up against your cock. And all the time I wanted you. Would have licked you up and down - from your toes to your nose. Could have eaten you up. You turned me on in a big, bad way. I remember this.'

There was a catch, a quiver in Ömer's voice as he replied. 'When we see us again?'

'Soon, Ömer. The sooner the better.'

'Are you alone?'

'Yep, Jens is at work. It's his late night. And you?'

'Me?'

'I was going to ask if you're alone too. But it occurs to me that I don't know very much about you. Do you live alone?'

'I live with my brother and his family.'

'So I guess that rules out us coming over to your place some time as a possibility.'

Ömer continued quickly on. 'But my brother's wife and children fly to Turkey in the winter. They are there now. And my brother, he works the late shift tonight.'

'I wish you'd given us more notice. Like I said, Jens is working.'

'I look for a place of my own at the moment. Maybe in between time I can come to you?'

Dirk sighed, regretfully. 'Also not possible, I'm afraid. Jens and I, we agreed we don't invite people home. Hey, but we'll sort something out. There's always the sauna to fall back on.'

'I think on you both. I want make sex with you, bad.'

Without fully realising what he was doing, Dirk slipped his hand under the waistband of his jogging bottoms and began to toy with his stiffening penis. 'You say you're alone at the moment?'

'Alone, yes.'

'What are you wearing?'

'Please?'

Dirk released a throaty chuckle. 'I said, what are you wearing?'

'A blue T-shirt and jeans. Why you want to know?'

'I want you to do something for me, Ömer. I want you to take them off. I want you to take them off very slowly. And I want you to tell me exactly what you're doing.'

Jens lay back on the sofa and looked up at Jürgen, towering over him. Naked. All muscle and hair. Yanking on his mammoth dick. Grunting. 'Want a dose fresh from the tap?

'Less talk, more action . . . '

'Okay, then. But you are not to touch me?'

'Whatever you say, Jürgen. Whatever . . . '

Jürgen puffed up his chest, naked and proud before Jens. 'Am I not handsome?' he asked.

'Beautiful . . . ' Jens replied, in awe of Jürgen's massive, circumcised dong. Dripping wet. Pre-come glistening on his gaping slit.

'Lie back and take it . . . ' he instructed Jens, now resting his knees on the edge of the sofa astride him whilst he positioned his heavy basket over Jens' thick mat of chest fur.

Jürgen's erection overwhelmed Jens. Up close, he could see heavy veins pulsing with life blood; a sprinkling of hair along the thick under shaft. And Jürgen's balls . . . big, big, balls resting in a slack, hairy sac. And a mammoth helmet. Lowering his chin to his chest, Jürgen spit a glob directly onto the bulbous, purple head and began to caress it.

Reflexively, Jens reached out a hand to cradle and scrunch Jürgen's bollocks, but Jürgen's hoarse whisper put a swift end to that idea. 'I said don't touch me!'

Jens did as he was told. He didn't mind sharing in Jürgen's power game. It was fun. If Jürgen wanted to play top, it was okay by Jens. So Jens rested back and let Jürgen do his thing. Clasping his own stiff prick, Jens began to tug and await the inevitable. His eyes were closed, intent and focused on one aim.

Jürgen began to mutter. 'Look at my big cock. Look at it, Jens!'

Jens eyes snapped open.

'You like my big cock?' Jürgen looked down upon Jens' with mock sympathy. 'You want to taste my big cock? Poor baby. You look so hungry.' Jürgen's shaft was glistening now, glistening with spit and pre-come as he slid his fist backwards and forwards. 'Poor baby wants Jürgen's big cock? Wants to see it come? Needs to see it come? Jürgen's hot Sperma squirting onto his hairy belly. Wants me to make him finished? Jürgen wants it too, Jens. But you have to beg me for it.'

Jens pummelled his own stiff meat and groaned. 'I want it, Jürgen. Give it to me, you big, horny fucker. Make me finished.'

'You must do better than that . . . ' Jürgen tormented him.

'Give me your load, Jürgen. Don't hold back. Let it pour. Spray me full! Come on, do it. Do it! Fucking do it!'

Jürgen scoffed and sneered. 'I love it when you beg me. Makes me want to take pity. You look so hungry!' Jürgen's cock shimmered above his target. His tight grip grew more sustained. 'You see this big dick, Jens? This big dick was made for pussy. For filling up some soft, wet pussy. It's for making babies, Jens. I got two babies already. These eggs are full of life. But you want that life too, don't you?'

'Yeah, ' Jens gulped. 'I want it. Oh, man really, I really want it . . . '

Jürgen's face contorted with exertion. The veins on his tube were engorged to bursting point as he jerked with full force.

'Now, Jens, now I'm ready. Oh, Jens, you are going to get it now. You are going to get all you deserve. Big dick and big balls just aching to come. I come soon. I come now. I come . . . '

Jürgen's mouth fell open, his eyebrows knitting together, as a tortured groan escaped his lips. The first bolt of jism was propelled onto Jens' heaving chest. Jürgen's eyes opened wide and looked directly into Jens' as he poured forth, quaking and trembling, gushing and squirting load upon load upon load. Each one a direct hit. And, in that same split-second, Jens came too. Erupting wildly, come flying high and wide, belly and bollocks drenched in the sudden downpour.

Almost empty, Jürgen directed one last spurt onto Jens' goatee. Then dropped to his knees and fell forward. Much to Jens' surprise and delight, Jürgen stuck out his soft, pink tongue and slathered up his own come from Jens' bearded chin. He swallowed it down with loud, noisy smacks.

The expression, 'waste not, want not' came to mind. But Jens decided to keep that particular English expression to himself. It would have sounded as cheesy as 'actions speak louder than words'!

Sweatshirt top and jogging bottoms now discarded over the arm of the sofa, Dirk lay back, his sturdy thighs spread wide as he caressed his erection. His cock stood upright, the crimson knobhead pointing straight up at ninety degrees as he manhandled his pliable meat. Spit lubricated his palm, and lubricated his poker-stiff penis, as well, as he slid his hand from top to tail.

'Tell me again, Ömer.'

'My cock is drooling. Pre-come on the tip. I'm so hard. Let me come, Dirk. Please.'

'Not just yet, Brother Bear.' A pause. Dirk maintained control, walking a fine line. He would keep Ömer on the brink of orgasm for as long as he could, knowing that when he did finally come it would blow him away. 'Now. I want you to sweep up that juice on your index finger.'

'Okay, I do it.'

'Now, very carefully, without spilling a drop, I want you to bring that finger to your lips. Now, part your lips. Now, slip that finger between your lips. Stick it in your mouth. Suck it clean for me, baby.'

He could hear Ömer whimper even as he suckled on himself.

'Now, baby. Imagine it's my cock you're sucking. My big, stiff prick filling your mouth.'

More whimpering.

'Now you can come. Come now, my sweet little Bear Cub. Come

for Dirk. Dirk is going to come for you.' Dirk was now beating his meat with a toe-curling vengeance. Matched, he could only conclude, by the tremulous whimpering at the other end of the line by Ömer himself. His nuts ached as they bounced in the wake of his pummelling fist, so eager was he to spill his seed. But he held back. Held back just long enough to hear Ömer reach his peak and let fly. It happened not a moment too soon.

'I come, Dirk. I come now. I come - just - for - you!' Then came the squeal, the long protracted squeal.

And as Dirk imagined Ömer's milk-white jism spraying high and wide, he let himself blow like Moby. Moby Dick, that was.

Jürgen leapt to his feet, surprisingly still brimful of energy. He pulled on his T-shirt and stared down at Jen, who was still lying naked on the leather couch, splattered with come. He winked. 'Maybe we can do this again sometime?'

'Maybe . . . ' But Jens had no intention of seeing Jürgen again. A man like that? It would be too easy to grow attached and Jens didn't need that complication in his life. Better just to consign this man to the stuff of memory. Albeit a beautiful memory.

'Now, Ömer, take your underwear, your white underwear, the underwear you described so well, and mop up all your thick, milky sperm.'

'I do it.'

'That's right, soak it all up.'

'It is everywhere.'

'Don't miss a drop.'

'I do it.'

'Now, when you put the phone down, Ömer, I want you to slip your briefs into a plastic bag. Put the bag in a big brown envelope and send it to me. Would you do that for me, Ömer?'

'I go do it now.'

'That's a good boy.'

'I need your address.'

'No problem. You got a pen.'

'Somewhere here . . . Ugh! My fingers are sticky!'

Four

Sabine was on the move, single once again. At the weekend she would leave this large apartment, one she had shared with her former long-time lover, Achim, and move to a smaller, more affordable one. One free of ghosts. Jens and Dirk were recruited to help her decorate before she left. It had to be done - it was stipulated in her tenancy agreement. And, with less than a week to go, there was plenty still to do.

Jens was in the kitchen, dressed in paint-splattered overalls, running a roller over the ceiling, coating it in white emulsion. The difference was startling. Having sanded down the first coat, Sabine was painting the kitchen door. Dirk was preparing to leave - he had an early start in the morning and it was already ten in the evening with no sign of finishing up soon.

'Sorry to have to run out on you guys.' Dirk slipped on his jacket.

'No need to apologise,' Sabine replied cheerily. 'You've done more than enough already.' She brushed the hair out of her eyes with the back of her hand. 'Is the same time tomorrow, okay?'

Dirk leaned down and kissed her cheek. 'You're a chancer, Sabine!'

'Don't ask, don't get - that's my motto!'

'See you tomorrow.' He turned his attention to Jens. 'See you later, sweetheart?'

'Much later, by the look of things. I'll try not to wake you.'

'Ciao.'

'Ciao.'

They waited until they both heard the front door slam before returning to the tasks at hand.

Sabine loved Dirk. In a way, she felt as close to him as Jens, despite the fact that she did not see him half as often. She took pride in the fact that she had been a witness on the day that they met. Had, in fact, introduced them. Jens, the teacher, to Dirk, the student - or, rather, a department head from a big engineering concern that was expanding into Eastern Europe. Therefore, Dirk needed to improve his English. One-to-one lessons had delivered much more than they had promised.

A shared love of opera had led to her own relationship with Dirk developing. Jens refused point blank to accompany Dirk anymore - he claimed he could not stand to watch people screeching in pain as they ran around the stage searching hopelessly for a tune. Sabine had stepped into his shoes and become Dirk's 'Opera Buddy'. And she really appreciated the time she got to spend alone with him. He was warm, witty and entertaining. His opera knowledge was impressive. And, most importantly, she loved the way he talked about Jens. He adored Jens. Of this, she had no doubts.

But something was wrong. Put it down to female intuition, she thought to herself, but something is definitely out of kilter. Jens had been unusually silent all evening. Now that Dirk had gone, she was determined to find out if her suspicions were founded.

'Something on your mind?'

'Eh?'

'I said, is there something on your mind?'

'Oh . . . Nothing really.'

Sabine raised an eyebrow. 'Nothing?'

'Relationships.'

'Oh, those. Tell me about it!'

'You've got enough on your plate at the moment.'

'If you are referring to my ex, then please feel free to talk away. It would only take my mind off the bastard.'

'It still hurts?'

'Not really.' She grinned. 'Good riddance. He did me a favour.'

'Running off with your best friend?'

Taking hold of a screwdriver, she prised the lid from yet another tin of gloss paint. 'Clearly, she was not my best friend. In fact, she was no

friend. Believe me, she's welcome to him. They deserve each other.'
Kneeling down, she began to paint the skirting board. 'Anyway, you're
my best friend. Now, if he had run off with you, then I would have
had something to complain about.'

'Whatever happened to commitment?'

'You are in philosophical mood, aren't you?!'

'I don't know . . . Things seemed so much simpler when I was
younger. Things were more black and white.'

'Ah, yes. "The Good Old Days". They were simpler, weren't they,
Granddad?'

'Fuck you!' Jens could not resist smiling. But almost as quickly as
the smile appeared, it disappeared. He frowned. 'It's like, years ago I
remember reading this advice column in some gay rag. And there was
this letter from "Heartbroken of Philadelphia" or something like that.
And he was broken-hearted because his partner was screwing around
left, right and centre whilst this guy wanted a "monogamous" relationship. Now, it was obvious that the guy was being eaten up by jealousy. He was really hurting.'

'Keep painting!'

'Oh, yeah!' Jens smiled again. He ran his roller across the paint tray.
'So the advisor told him to stop being such a tight-arse. Told him to
lighten up. Told him monogamy was a heterosexual concept and not
applicable. Told him essentially: "If you can't beat 'em - join 'em".' And
it made me fucking furious. I thought, what kind of advisor is this?!

'One pushing his own agenda?'

'Exactly, and trampling all over "Heartbroken of Philadelphia" in
the process.'

'What would you have advised then?'

'Dump the boyfriend and find someone who wants the same as
you.'

'Sounds reasonable.'

'Except that now I've "joined 'em". My boyfriend screws around and so do I.'

Sabine thought about that for a moment. 'But you enjoy it, don't you? You're always saying it's just recreation. I do Step class. You do horizontal aerobics.'

'Sure, I enjoy it on one level . . . '

'But . . . '

'I'm really scared that it's doing damage to the relationship on some deeper level. You know, we started out with the intention of being monogamous. I don't know, somehow we just seemed to drift into this situation.'

'So drift out of it.'

'If only it was that simple.'

'Like trying to put the lid back on Pandora's Box?'

'You got it in one.' He laid his roller up against the step ladder. 'I need a break.' He crossed to the fridge and pulled out a beer. 'Look, Sabine. I didn't mean to dump this on you.'

'Make me a Hagebuttentee while you're over by the kettle, will you? And, anyway, you're not dumping - you're sharing.'

Jens checked that the kettle was full, flicked the switch, and reached into the wall cupboard taking down a mug. 'You see, I feel that if I asked Dirk to go back to the way it was, he would agree.'

'Sorry? So where's the problem.'

'He would agree and then, after a while, he'd fall into the old pattern. Except this time he'd have assignations behind my back. And that would be worse than being up front. At the moment, at least, we're up front about what we get up to. At least I think we are . . . ' Jens toyed with his goatee. A nervous habit, a quirk.

'But then, it's clear. Trust is the issue, isn't it? You don't trust him.'

'Oh, it's worse than that.' He lowered his eyes. 'I don't trust myself.'

'You mean, you can't trust yourself to be faithful, either?'

'I don't know. I really don't know. All I do know is that I love Dirk and if I want to be in a relationship with him, then I have to accept that he likes to play around.'

'Is it that clear cut?'

'Yes. Yes, I think so.' The kettle clicked off. He poured the boiling contents over the Teebeutal now resting in the mug. 'You must think I'm crazy!'

'Not at all.'

'But like with you and Achim? How did you feel when you found out about . . . '

She lay her paintbrush down and got to her feet. 'About him "screwing around"?'

'If you want to put it that way.' He handed her her tea.

Sabine leaned up against a work surface. 'Oh, you know. What was it the man said? Monogamy is just a heterosexual concept?' She blew on the steaming contents in her mug. 'To be honest, I wanted to chop his balls off!'

'You see? We must sound crazy!'

'Not at all. My first thought was, I want to chop his balls off. But afterwards, when I thought about, I realised I was actually relieved.'

'Relieved?'

'Yes, relieved. It was a bad relationship. It had been for the longest time. I was just too dumb or too lazy to end it sooner. Like I said, he did me a favour. But you and Dirk? You have a great relationship, at least from where I stand. It just needs regular maintenance, that's all. You love each other. You can work it out.'

'We do love each other.'

'I know you do. If you didn't, we wouldn't be having this conversation.' She smiled. 'Now pick up that roller ,and get on with it!'

Five

The doorman was no doorman, but a glamorous transsexual. A beautiful, statuesque, exotic transsexual. Her long, glossy, black hair was pulled tightly back into a pony tail. Her make-up was impeccable and her cleavage was equally impressive. Jens watched her interact with Dirk, watched them flirt. Transsexuals and transvestites inevitably flirted with Dirk. Drawn as much by his height - he always towered above them, stilettos and all - as by his masculinity. For his part, Dirk was charmed by the attention. He admired courage in all its many and varied manifestations.

Having paid the entrance fee, been stamped and processed, Ömer led the way into the main venue. The hall had undergone a significant transformation. Dirk had long been familiar with this place - in its present incarnation it was called Elektrik Barbarella - but the venue itself had long been renowned for hosting alternative events of every description. It had once been the premier punk venue in Berlin, though with the way it was currently decorated it was hard for Dirk to picture himself back there and seventeen again.

Linen curtains with pastel, ethnic patterns hung from the ceiling and adorned the walls, creating another ambience entirely. The pungent smell of incense filled the air. To one side, a raised platform was strewn with oriental carpets and cushions. At the far end of the room, the main stage was colourfully set for a theatrical performance of some sort. On the edge of the stage sat a small band of musicians playing traditional Turkish folk music before a small but appreciative Publikum. The audience were seated on rows of wooden benches.

It was still early, Ömer informed them. The show proper wasn't due to start until ten p.m. Twenty minutes to go. They each grabbed a beer, found a seat and began to soak up the atmosphere. The exotic and unmistakable smell of Patchouli oil perfumed the air. The audience was a mixed bunch - gay, lesbian and straight. Mostly Turks, but with more than a fair sprinkling of their admirers. Some listening to the music, others chatting or welcoming friends as they arrived. Glamorous drag queens made their theatrical entrances, positioned themselves where they could be seen and admired. The room quickly filled to capacity and the sense of expectation grew in direct proportion.

Manic, stressed and hyper, Ömer sat stiffly upright on the bench, sandwiched in between Dirk and Jens. His excitement was palpable and it was most definitely not because of the show to come. He would lean first this way and then that, sharing a joke, an intimacy and then suddenly bolt upright once again. Dirk would tease him but he did not always 'geddit', the joke getting lost somewhere in translation. When he finally began to relax, Dirk reached across and rubbed his belly, took his hand, held it. Ömer's little finger rubbed Dirk's little finger. His eyes darted around the room. Unfocused. Refusing to settle. He was jabbering away, talking too much. Nervous, shy and overcompensating.

'I can not believe that guys like you would be interested in someone like me,' Ömer said at last. The words tumbled from his mouth, all in a rush.

'Are you joking?!' Dirk replied. 'You're a fucking hunk!'

Ömer dropped his gaze, examined Dirk's hand still clasped in his own. Then he squeezed it. 'Do not get me wrong, I appreciate the compliment . . . But I do not feel like a hunk.'

'But Ömer,' Jens smiled. 'That is part of your charm.'

'He is charming, isn't he,' Dirk seconded.

'A born charmer, I'd say.'

Ömer held on to Dirk's hand and took hold of Jens'. 'Thank you, guys.'

Just then, the musicians took their bows and left the stage to warm applause. Their timing could not have been more perfect.

The show that followed after was ablaze with colour. It took the form of a revue. Comedy sketches, live and on video, were liberally interspersed with the drag performers' specialities - lip-syncing to Turkish pop songs or doing the obligatory belly dance. It was a hoot, as many of the jokes were aimed specifically at German 'correctness'. Dirk and Jens had no problem seeing the funny side, and they laughed along with the best of them. The show alone was well worth the entrance fee. And despite lasting for at least ninety minutes, it seemed to be over much too fast.

Time out. Whilst the attendants cleared the room and made space for the disco to follow, Ömer went to the bar. Dirk and Jens took a seat in the carpeted, cushioned and curtained area at the side and waited. And waited . . . The disco began. The dance floor began to fill. Where had he got to?

Dirk nudged Jens and indicated that he should look over his shoulder. 'What's going on there?'

Ömer had been on his way back, but had been stopped. Now he was standing over by the coat check, in conversation with another Turk. His body language seemed to speak volumes. His head bowed, listening as the other guy spoke into his ear. Three beer bottles clutched close to his chest as if in a gesture of defence. Finally the transaction was over and Ömer turned towards Jens and Dirk. He walked towards them with his eyes lowered. Preoccupied in thought.

Even as Ömer had turned towards them, the stranger had cast an eye in the direction of Dirk and Jens and had locked eyes with the latter. A smile had split the stranger's face but it wasn't a warm smile - more a curl of the lip, a smirk. Whatever the motivation, it made the little hairs on the back of Jens' neck stand up. The guy looked like a real bruiser. Taller and broader than Ömer and blue-collar brawny. His jet-black hair was clipped short, a thick, full moustache covered his top lip, and between bottom lip and the deep cleft in his chin was a perfectly sculpted triangle of facial hair. He wore blue jeans held up by a thick leather belt, trainers and a white V-neck T-shirt. A black leather jacket was hooked on the index finger of his left hand and was casually slung over his shoulder. A surfeit of chest hair burst out of the low-cut neckline and above it, around his muscular neck. He wore a pale, beaded choker that offset his natural tan to perfection. And he wore a smirk. The mystery man cocked an eyebrow, and then he turned his attention to the neck of his beer bottle and disappeared off in the opposite direction, losing himself in the bustling crowd.

Ömer arrived back alongside them and handed over Jens and Dirk's beers without comment.

'Who's the hunk?' Dirk asked pointedly, elbowing Ömer in the ribs.

Ömer looked over his shoulder at nothing in particular. 'Oh, him?' He rolled his own beer bottle between his palms. 'That is my brother, Ahmet. My older brother.'

'You kept that one quiet!' Dirk said, punctuating the sentence with another jab to Ömer's ribs.

'Your brother's gay too?' Jens asked quietly, exhibiting a little more sensitivity in his delivery, since he was aware that Ömer was experiencing some discomfort.

'If you asked him, he would say no.'

'What does that mean?'

Ömer shrugged.

'Why is he here, then?' Dirk still hadn't got it.

'He says he is curious to see the kind of places I hang out.' Ömer didn't seem convinced. Nor did he seem comfortable with this line of questioning. Dirk opened his mouth to ask a follow-up, but Jens handed him his bottle and, plucking Ömer's from his grip, handed it over, too.

'Look after those. Me and Ömer are going for a dance.' And without further ado, he manoeuvred Ömer by the shoulders onto the heaving dance floor.

Dirk edged closer to the bar and found a high table to lean on over by the side. People were still piling into the club in a seemingly endless stream. The line for the coat check stretched from the far side of the bar way, way back out of the double doors and down the corridor leading towards the entrance. Someone was making big money. And it didn't seem there was any limit to the numbers that were going to be allowed in. The air was now thick with the smell of bodies and cigarette smoke. As more people entered, the level of chatter rose up and clashed with the pounding music in a losing battle to be heard.

Heads were bobbing, bodies were swaying in anticipation. Everyone was eager to dump their jackets and the like and get into the fray. Necks were straining to see what awaited them on the dance floor. Singles, couples, and groups stood in line: men, women, drag queens; the young and the more mature; the good, the bad and the ugly. All human life in a midnight circus, standing in the wings waiting to climb into the ring. Into the spotlight.

Suddenly, a friendly face appeared, head and shoulders above the crowd. A hand was raised in greeting, and Bodo made his way towards Dirk. He was dragging with him Volker, his little Bear Cub. Within moments, Dirk found himself engulfed in a double Bear hug.
Having almost back-slapped the life out of him, Bodo held Dirk at arms length. 'We really must stop meeting like this!'

'Well, Bodo, if you rang ahead of time once in a while to make an arrangement . . . '

'I know. I know . . . '

Dirk turned his attention to Volker, who looked up at him with shining eyes. 'Good to see you too, handsome. Did he finally manage to persuade you to leave your snug little Bear cave and venture out into the wilds?'

Bodo answered for him, pleased with himself. 'I sure did!'

'I was talking to the organ grinder, not the monkey, Bodo.'

'You should be so lucky to have him grind your organ, my friend,' Bodo quipped. 'It is no problem for me to admit that he is my little organ grinder.' He threw an arm around Volker's shoulders and pulled him to his side. 'You are, aren't you, sweetheart?' Volker blushed. Bodo guffawed. 'Ahhh! Isn't he cute when he blushes?!'

'Just as well. He must get plenty of opportunity to practise around you. You're enough to make a navvy blush.'

Volker just smiled, his eyes twinkling. There was a sweetness about Volker that was undeniable. And he loved Bodo, that was obvious. A meeting of opposites turned into a perfect combination. Volker who preferred to stay home and make a home. Volker who gave Bodo a long, long leash, secure in the knowledge that his big Bear would always find his way back there.

And it was probably best for all concerned that Volker stayed at home out of harm's way because the guy was some dish. Short and chunky, gym trained. A thick, blonde beard and a crew cut. An agricultural student, with a fresh-faced complexion that seemed to come naturally from a life spent mostly outdoors. Wearing a leather waistcoat, checked shirt and faded Levi's, he was a tempting little morsel. Still in his early twenties, there was a vitality about him that seemed to shine out of every pore. His desirability had certainly not been lost on Dirk. But Bodo and all? Dirk did not need that kind of grief!

'You want a beer?' Dirk asked.

'Naw. We aren't staying. Just dropped in for one. Checking the place out.'

'And what do you think of it, Volker?'

'He . . . '

'Shut it, Bodo! Volker?'

'Interesting.' Volker didn't sound convinced.

'Some nice arse,' Bodo chipped in. 'We just saw Jens out on the dance floor. That guy he's with? He's a fine thing!' Bodo licked his lips like a cartoon lecher.

'Yeah. And you can keep your big, hairy paws off him! He's all ours.'

'Like that, is it?'

'Yeah. Like that.' Dirk grinned. 'But if you're very good, we might fill you in on all the grizzly details.'

'Now that, I look forward to.'

It didn't take long for Dirk to muscle in. The three of them gyrated their bodies together in the middle of a packed and heaving dance floor. But, for Jens, it had swiftly grown untenable, sandwiched as they were on all sides by a heaving mass of people. And then again, there was the strange but unnerving feeling that somehow he and Dirk were now both competing for Ömer's attentions. Dirk was making his interest patently obvious - with looks, with smiles, with body contact. Jens could not quite put his finger on the reason why, but he felt like he was being pushed aside.

He was feeling ignored; was feeling like there was something going on between the two of them - and only the two of them. Dirk had not simply joined them, he had barged in and was taking over, taking command of the situation. It was typical of Dirk, and one of his least attractive characteristics. Jens had never been into competitive sports and that was exactly what this felt like - a game. A game that he quickly decided he did not want to play. He capitulated without argument and pushed his way through the crowd towards the sidelines.

Dirk and Ömer remained on the dance floor doing their own variation of Dirty Dancing. Dirty Belly Dancing? Hardly. They were certainly using more than their stomachs. They couldn't seem to keep their hands off each other, not to mention all the other body parts. And as Jens looked on, he was beginning to feel more than just a little jealous.

In an attempt to distract himself, he cast an eye up onto the brightly lit stage. Earlier in the evening, this is where the cabaret had taken place but now, two Turkish Go-Go-Boys were shaking their considerable booty in little more than a silver codpiece and a transparent veil, each. Surrounded by a crush of bodies, Jens could barely move. It was hard enough to take a slug from his bottle. Then he felt the hand on his arse.

At first, he thought this intimate contact must have been accidental. A consequence of too many bodies sharing too little space. But now the hand was clearly and deliberately cupping his buttock and kneading the taut flesh that lay beneath his faded jeans. Jens froze, not knowing quite what do. He was outraged and yet somewhat flattered by the attention. Thick fingers found the fringed tear in the seat of his pants and slipped inside, manoeuvring their way slowly and inextricably towards his hairy crack. That tipped the scales, Jens swivelled his head and looked around over his shoulder, prepared for the worst - to be confronted with a gargoyle - and prepared to tell that gargoyle in no uncertain terms to climb back on his perch. Instead, he found himself looking into the glittering eyes of Ömer 's big brother, Ahmet.

Ahmet was smirking, again. Up close, he was even more intimidating than at a distance. The first shock was his eyes - not brown, but pale-blue. The pupils were dilated and as black as coal but the iris that bordered them were of the palest hue imaginable. They had a hypnotic quality and they were fixed firmly on Jens' own. Ahmet sighed and his breath was like sweet perfume, wafting over Jens' face, flooding his senses as he, in turn, inhaled. He quivered, a big man suddenly made weak at the knees.

'Come.' Ahmet gestured with his head in the direction of the bar, more a demand than a request. He then turned to forge a path through the crowd. Jens followed without argument, followed in his wake. Ahmet had the difficult job, cutting through the drunken throng, finally emerging on the far side of the dance floor where the crush thinned to an acceptable level. On towards the bar and then, much to Jens' surprise, Ahmet swung a left and entered the long dark corridor leading to the entrance. He slipped his jacket on as he walked.

The corridor was as trashed as the rest of the club. Tatty posters, advertising numerous alternative events, were peeling off the scuffed, black walls. To one side, the long, wooden benches were strewn with party revellers, who were all glistening with sweat and taking much-needed time out. Animated chatter bubbled above the smothered bass boom from inside the packed dance hall, but Ahmet strode purpose-fully on. Past the toilets, past the cigarette machine, past the box office and on past the security. Jens hung back as Ahmet stood in the doorway and slipped his jacket on before turning around to hold up and display the front of his fist. 'You have your stamp?'

Jens nodded, bemused.

'Then they let you back in. Come.'

Dirk took Ömer by the hand and led him to the side of the dance floor.

'Where do you get your energy from?'

'I younger than you!'

Dirk held up his fist. 'Watch it, Buster!'

Ömer slipped his arms around Dirk's waist. 'We have fun, yes?'

'We sure do.' Dirk cast his eyes around the room. 'I wonder where Jens has got to.'

'You think he is gone? Maybe we make him angry? He think we ignore him?'

Dirk ruffled his hair. 'Not, Jens. He's a big Teddy Bear. He's proba-bly over at the bar, getting chatted up by countless admirers.'

'And you do not have a problem with this.'

'Why should I?' Dirk reached around and grabbed Ömer's firm, round buttocks. 'I've got my hands full just taking care of you!'

Outside the club, the streets were frosted with frozen rain. Jens took a deep breath, filled his lungs with the cool, damp, night air, and the city smells were momentarily neutralised. Ahmet marched on ahead, disappearing around the street corner. After a pause, Jens followed him.

Ahmet had been waiting just out of sight, waiting for Jens to catch up. Now he turned and crossed the street and made directly for the building site opposite. Berlin sometimes seemed like one big building site, especially over in the East where they now were. Construction areas proliferated, making up for all the years of architectural neglect. There were still gaps to be found between buildings where bombs had dropped, and fifty years later the scars remained vivid. Like the exterior of buildings still pockmarked with bullet holes, awaiting the inevitable facelift.

The building site was quiet, deserted, unsupervised. The skeleton of some modern monstrosity springing up in the empty space between two traditional, ornate apartment buildings - like a thorn between two roses. The perimeter was ringed with chain-link fencing, and just inside were two, prefabricated huts - workmen's huts - canary yellow and stacked one on top of the other. Ahmet strode purposefully towards the padlocked gate.

Jens turned the corner with some trepidation. He could never mount that fence! And what if they were caught trespassing? But, much to his relief, Ahmet dispelled his fears by producing a heavy bunch of keys from his pocket. He proceeded to unlock the gateway to the inner sanctum.

'What?' Jens asked, somewhat surprised.

'I work here.' Ahmet pushed open the gate. 'Come. Inside.'

Jens did as he was bid, walking ahead, picking his way through the rubble. Ahmet locked the gate behind them then, stuffing the keys deep in his pocket. Then he led the way behind the prefabs. It was dark back there. There was only the glint of the moon on Ahmet's belt buckle as he stood with his back against the wall of the hut and reached a hand down to unzip his fly.

'You like it here? You glad I brought you?' Ömer was asking Dirk.

'Yeah. It's . . . different . . . interesting.' Dirk laughed and wiped the sweat from his brow with the back of his hand. 'Didn't expect there would be so many straights, here though.'

'The organisers do their best to keep straight men out.'

'They have to keep them out? Why would straight men want to come here anyway?' This was no oblique reference to Ahmet. Dirk had forgotten about him already.

'Straight women. They come for the straight women.'

'And straight women are here in their hundreds.'

'Oh, sure. Straight Turkish women like it here. Here is safe. They can let their hair down, can drink and dance and have fun without hassle.'

'You mean free from the hassle of constantly having to fight off straight Turkish men? I should be so hard done by!"

'You know what I mean.'

'Not personally, but I get what you mean. Dirk smiled. 'Nah, it's all these straight couples I have a problem with. Thinking it's cool and trendy to hang out with gays is one thing but all this kind of thing -' Dirk pointed in the direction of a couple nearby who appeared to be holding a wrestling match with their tongues '- where do they get off on flaunting their heterosexuality in our faces?!'

Ömer slipped a hand around Dirk's neck and, gripping it firmly, pulled Dirk's head down towards him. 'We show them how it is done . . . '

Jens was on his knees. Faced with Ahmet's throbbing member, his reserve began to crack. His heart leapt into his throat and he almost choked. 'What if somebody sees us?!'

'So what if they do, my friend? Ahmet waved his stiff prick just inches from Jens' drooling mouth, like he was laying down a challenge. 'We let them watch if they want. We let them share in our pleasure.'

Jens closed his eyes and took a deep breath, trying to regain his equilibrium. No use. When he opened them again, Ahmet's cock was still there and just as tempting. Jens licked his lips. 'Oh, to hell with it!' Caution thrown aside, he was silenced by the stiff, circumcised cock that now filled his throat to capacity.

Ahmet began to slide his length in and out of Jens' willing orifice. 'That's it,' he moaned. 'Take it all. Just take it.'

Jens struggled to accommodate him, consciously relaxing his throat muscles. He felt the fullness, luxuriating in it.

Ahmet began to buck his hips, fucking Jens' throat with increasing vigour. Pumping his hips forcefully now, clutching the back of Jens' head. Refusing to lighten up even when Jens began to gag, began to struggle. He fucked the other man's mouth with the dick of a donkey, as he gripped the base of his balls in a fist and slapped his low-slung ballsac against Jens' chin.

He laughed as Jens' mouth gagged reflexively, uncontrollably, willingly.

'Chew on it, use your teeth. Ooh, yeah! Just like that. Don't stop.'
Jens was not about to.
'Suck my beauty. It's a beauty, isn't it?!'
All Jens could do was nod.
'You want to see me come later?'
Another nod.
'My wife likes to watch too. It gets her pussy all wet.' Ahmet pulled free. He slapped his cosh against Jens' lips, against his cheek. Then his fingers clasped the proud, crimson helmet, buffing and polishing it till it shimmered and shone.

Looking down, he caught sight of Jens, his eyes glazed over, his tongue hanging out, dripping wet. Cock-worshipping. Ahmet chuckled as he worked himself up into a lather.

Jens bent forward, flicking his tongue over the juddering cockhead, his face, his lips, his nose now buried in Ahmet's hairy crotch.

A curious expression crossed Ahmet's face. A mixture of mock disgust and sincere delight. 'Enjoying this, are you?' And so saying, he returned his focus to the task in hand. Working his sturdy fist up and down the solid shaft. Unhurried. Slow and easy, from fruit to root. Reflexively, he spread his thighs wider, bending both knees for comfort and support, and relaxed into it. The crack of his arse parted ever so slightly to reveal a crop of blue-black curls. Jens traced the line with his finger.

Ahmet's breathing came more heavily, his expression more intense. He stopped the slow jerk and squeezed tight. Pre-come oozed from the piss-slit and balanced like a glistening jewel on the crown of his knob. Sweeping it up on his index finger, Ahmet examined it, then held it out at arm's length towards Jens. When he spoke, his throat was thick with lust.

'Want it?'

Jens' mouth dropped open. He wanted it. He was terrified of how much he wanted it. But Ahmet wanted it, too. Five, maybe ten seconds passed until Ahmet stuffed the finger in his own mouth.

'Now go, suck.'

No resistance. Jens pounced willingly on the cock presented to his hungry lips. Tension filled the space between them, crackling like electricity, and there was not even a feeble attempt by Jens to defy Ahmet. Ultimately, he felt compelled to obey the Turkish man's firm and masterful instruction. He was a sucker - literally - for a little domination. And the situation left little room for negotiation. Ahmet had set the terms. One false move on Jens' part and Ahmet could easily withdraw from the game and Jens was not about to give him an excuse.

Jens stared up with glazed eyes, then re-focused his gaze on Ahmet's intent, cruel expression. His lips were curled; his eyes shut tightly. Jens was forced to accommodate Ahmet's prong, every thick, long inch of it. Ahmet gripped the back of Jens' head and held it in place so that Jens worked his mouth like a piston, aggressively pounding up against Ahmet's pubic bone, consume the whole glorious length of his pride and joy. Forward and back, forward and back. Plunging his pork sword down into the moist depths. Withdrawing. Plunging again.

Jens' eyes blinked back tears, but continued to stare up. Eyes - now accustomed to the light - drank in the whole of Ahmet. He was so indescribably handsome. At that very moment in time, everything Jens had ever considered attractive in a man seemed to be all wrapped up in this one package. No. More than a man. A bull. A big stud bull.

Ahmet's big, booted feet trembled involuntarily. The intensity of expression around his mouth and eyes reflected the vehemence with which Jens' mouth now gripped his cock as it pumped out a rhythm to beat the band.

'You love it, don't you?' Ahmet's voice quivered, his breathing laboured.

Jens gulped, his response inaudible. Ahmet felt the vibration along the length of his shaft.

'Love servicing my big, fat dick.'

Jens gagged.

'Take it all.'

Another gulp.

'Can't get enough, can you?'

Jens reached up, grabbed Ahmet's big, shaved balls and tugged them hard. Sign language. 'Come!' Meanwhile, his eager mouth never missed a stroke.

Abruptly, Ahmet yanked his cock free. Let his hands fall to his sides. His colossal dong slapped against his rigid stomach and strained upwards past his navel. Eyes closed now, his chest heaved from his exertions.

'What?' Jens asked, perturbed.

"What? What?!' Ahmet mimicked him irritably.

'Why did you stop?'

'We make a break.' Ahmet fell silent, leaned back against the workman's hut.

They both fell silent.

Moments passed. Ahmet's breathing grew more regular. His lids remained drawn over his eyes, affording Jens the opportunity to look closely at the other man. Nipples, small, taut and erect, poked out from the thick flush of chest chair. Like a carpet, Jens thought. His eyes traced the fine line that led down to the deep cleft of Ahmet's navel, and then blossomed out into the luxuriant pubic hair that surrounded his still-pulsing tool. Engorged with blood, it twitched in one direction whilst his big bollocks rested low in the opposite.

Jens' eyes continued their downward glide over athletic thighs, chiselled knees, and substantial calves. Turkish footballers legs. Then, past the jeans resting around his ankles, to his booted feet.

Finally, Jens took his chance. Couldn't resist. Holding his breath, he hesitantly wrapped his hand around the back of Ahmet's calf. It felt hot and solid. Slowly, he slid his hand back and forth, kneading the curve, feeling the friction of hair against his palm. Tension ebbed away and the muscle grew more malleable as Ahmet let out a deep, extended sigh. Finally, he spoke - but quietly, this time.

'What are you doing'?'

'What does it feel like I'm doing?' Jens held his breath.

'Don't know. Feels good,' Ahmet grudgingly admitted.

'Does it?'

'Yeah.'

Jens let both hands mould around Ahmet's upper thighs. 'And this?'

'Maybe.'

'What do you mean, 'Maybe?!"

'Yeah . . . '

'Yeah, what?'

'Yeah . . . it feels good.'

Jens' fingers massaged Ahmet's warm and pliant flesh in ever-increasing circles. Inevitably, his thumbs brushed against Ahmet's knob-sac. His nuts responded involuntarily to Jens' touch, first rising and then lowering. Ahmet shuddered and groaned. Ahmet groaned again as Jens cradled his tender bollocks in the palm of his hand. And again, when Jens dipped the tip of his tongue into Ahmet's navel, before sliding down slowly to bathe his bulbous cockhead.

'Let me love it,' Jens pleaded, his mouth watering. 'It's so big and fat and juicy. Let me love it, Ahmet. Let me . . . '

Jens kissed the gaping piss-slit and pressed his moist lips downwards to part and slide over Ahmet's polished helmet. Then Jens paused, circling his tongue around and around the circumference, and then, clasping the head in a vicelike grip, he sucked long and hard.

Ahmet's response seemed to lurch up and out from the very pit of his stomach. He grabbed the back of Jens' head once more and thrust his cock deep down Jens' throat. 'I don't need you to love it,' Ahmet hissed in a whisper. 'Just fucking eat it! Don't play with it. Eat the fuck-er!!'

The ferocity with which Ahmet's hand clasped the back of Jens' neck and forced him to swallow barely registered, so desperate was Jens' need to taste cock. His throat yielding as Ahmet's thick dick bashed against the sides and disappeared into the depths. Ahmet was pumping now, pumping with a fury, stretching Jens' jaw wide. Ploughing a trough. Drilling a path to his stomach.

'Take it! Swallow that fucker!!'

Jens began to gag.

'What's the matter? I too big for you? My cock too big for you, is it? More than a mouthful?' Ahmet held fast.

Jens' mouth and mind were blown. He began to thrash about. Desperate to accommodate all of Ahmet's mammoth dick, but struggling to contain his length and struggling to breathe, as well. It was a losing battle. Once Ahmet relaxed his grip, Jens yanked his head back reflexively. His fist curled around the shaft of Ahmet's glistening prick and began to pump it. Jens' face was only inches away

'I'm going to come. I'm going to shoot for Turkey. And you? You are going to watch. You are going to watch me shoot.' Roughly, Ahmet pushed Jens back to sitting position. 'Play with my balls. Go on. Tug them. Tug them hard.'

Jens reached out a hand and did as he was bid whilst Ahmet looked down directly into his face. Once again, that cruel smirk twisted his full, wet lips. Ahmet was grinding his hips, thrusting them up to meet his pummelling fist.

'My cock is beautiful, or?' Ahmet cooed.

'Oh, yes.' Jens swallowed hard. 'It sure is beautiful. Make it come. Come soon. I want to watch it shoot.'

'And it is going to blow. Any second now it is going to blow. Here it comes, boy. Here it comes. Coming now. Coming . . . '

And, with a last flick of the wrist, Ahmet spewed an arc of come over Jens' head. He turned to the side and Jens watched him spurt in profile. Thick ropes of creamy, white jism pulsed out of Ahmet's yawning piss-slit. Hand over fist, he was firing on both steaming cylinders. Splattering the dust. His head thrown back, his teeth clamped together in a vain attempt to smother the groans of his powerful orgasm.

Jens' cock erupted too, then. Trapped within the confines of his jeans, he sprayed the inside of his briefs, soaking his underwear. The warm wetness of his spunk pulsing against his skin.

Ahmet squeezed the last pearl of come free from his slowly softening penis, and Jens watched transfixed as it balanced on the very tip.

'You sure come a lot, man!' Jens was profoundly impressed.

And again that smirk. 'Normally, I charge for such a show. Fifty Deutschmarks. But I give it you free.'

Jens was about to laugh, and then thought better of it. There was no humour in the way Ahmet told it. He stood up with difficulty, rubbing the cramp from the back of his knees and reached out a hand, steadying himself with the aid of Ahmet's shoulder. Solid as steel.

When Jens returned to the club, his first port of call was the toilet. Locked inside a cubicle, he peeled off his sodden pants and mopped up, discarding both briefs and tissues in the flip top bin by the door as he made his exit. Fortunately, the coast had been clear. He found Dirk and Ömer in a clinch over by one of the loudspeakers. Dirk had Ömer pinned to the wall, and their mouths were locked together in a bout of passionate kissing. Jens did think of tapping Dirk on the shoulder to get his attention, but decided to bide his time. Let them enjoy their fun. He simply stood and waited for time out.

Eventually, Ömer opened his eyes and caught sight of Jens watching them intently with a long-suffering expression on his face, followed quickly by a grin. Ömer grinned back. Dirk turned his head to see what the unwanted distraction was.

'Where the fuck have you been? We've been looking all over for you?' Dirk wore a look of some concern.

'Really? Worried, were you?' Jens looked them both up and down. Cocked an eyebrow. 'Good that you had Ömer here to console you, then!'

'Cut it out. Where did you get to?' Dirk leered. 'Off whoring were you?'

'Popped out for a Kebap.'

'Oh, yeah?' Dirk was not convinced. 'From that nice little Imbiss in Hamburg, was it?'

'Come off it, I wasn't gone that long.'

'Well, you certainly took your time.'

'It was roasting in here. It was lovely and cool outside. I went for a walk . . . '

Ömer had been silent throughout this exchange. Suddenly, he put up his hand like a schoolboy who wants to leave the classroom. 'I go piss.'

He and Dirk exchanged a look. Dirk nodded. It was a subtle exchange, but it still registered as odd with Jens. Ömer disappeared off.

'He has to ask for your permission to go to the toilet now? You've got him well trained.'

'I wanted to ask you something?'

'Why am I not surprised?'

'Would you mind if we brought him home with us tonight?'

Jens narrowed his eyes, turned his head away. 'Dirk, we have an agreement. We don't bring tricks home.'

'These are special circumstances.'

'Yeah? Really!'

'Yeah, really. We can't go back to his place - you've seen the brother. And, anyway, Ömer's not a trick.'

'What is he then?'

Dirk was shifting his weight from foot to foot nervously. 'A fuck buddy? A friend. I like him. He likes you. You like me. What's the problem?'

'The problem is, we made an agreement. We're always making agreements. I think they're fixed; you think they're flexible. We negotiate ground rules, you move the goal posts.'

Jens was pouting.

Dirk saw Ömer making his way back through the crowd. 'Have I pissed you off?'

'No. Not really.'

'If you say no, it's okay.'

'What? And deny you your bit of fun?'

'Yours too.'

'Okay. But can we go like this minute?'

Dirk turned to Ömer as he arrived alongside. 'Get your coat, you've been pulled!'

Six

On the high street outside the club, Dirk flagged down a passing cab and the three of them tumbled in. The journey took only fifteen minutes or so, but throughout the duration Dirk sat impatiently in the back alongside Jens, drumming his fingers on his knees. Jens cast a sideways glance. Dirk was definitely on for it tonight. Ömer sat up front, chatting amiably with the taxi driver who, in turn, seemed to be showing more than the usual interest in his passengers, for he spent more time looking in the rear view mirror than watching the road in front.

As the taxi pulled up outside their apartment, it was Jens who had the job of dissuading the driver from following them upstairs. He was keen. Boy, was he keen. A gay taxi driver, and not at all unattractive. But, tonight at least, four was definitely going to be a crowd.

Dirk fell out of the taxi and led the way. Like a lamb to the slaughter, Ömer followed willingly. Dirk led him by the hand through the wrought iron gates, across the patio, to the porch. This achieved, it took Dirk an age to wrestle with the lock on the front door. Finally, it swung open and, flicking the light switch by the entrance they headed up the stairs to the first floor, Jens followed quickly behind. Dirk handed Jens the keys to the apartment. Jens fumbled with the lock momentarily, then opened the door wide and stepped back to let them through. Inside, all was pitch black. Dirk launched himself on Ömer from behind, manhandling him through the door and into the hallway. Slobbering and grunting, Dirk ground his groin into Ömer's arse whilst cursing endearments. 'In here?' he gasped, throwing the door to the bedroom open.

They tumbled forward and fell to the floor. Lost in the moment, Dirk wrestled Ömer on to his back. Within minutes, Ömer's jeans and underwear were yanked over his ankles, and his hard, dripping dick

- 72 -

was released. Dirk raised Ömer's thighs to his chest and buried his face in the crack of the other man's arse.

All of a sudden, the bedside lamp was switched on. Quite how long it took Dirk to register the imposing figure of Jens as he stood by the bed fully dressed, Dirk could not be sure. But there he was: arms folded across his chest, leaning up against the door frame.

'Mind if I join in?' he asked dryly. 'Or should I just leave the two of you to get on with it?'

When Jens arrived late home from work late the following Friday, he found Dirk on the sofa, reading, listening to Monteverdi. The kiss he gave Dirk on the forehead was little more than perfunctory before he disappeared into the kitchen to rustle up some food.

Jens was rattling pots and pans as Dirk joined him, standing in the doorway.

'Are you going to tell me what this is all about or do I have to suffer your silence indefinitely?' Dirk asked, as light-heartedly as he could muster.

Jens busied himself. 'What are you on about?'

'What am I on about? Dirk crossed the kitchen and hugged Jens from behind, holding his arms, preventing him from further activity.

'I'm hungry!' Jens whined.

'Well, you won't starve if you wait ten minutes. C'mon, what's the problem?'

'Problem?'

Dirk spun Jens around to face him. 'What the fuck is wrong with you? You've been walking around like a Bear with a sore head for the best part of a week! Are we going to talk about it, or what?'

Jens shrugged.

'C'mon, out with it.'

Jens sighed. 'Saturday night, Sunday morning . . . '

'Yes?'

'I just felt like a spare part, that's all.'

Dirk shook his head, smiled, 'What do you mean?'

Jens turned his head away. 'Ömer. He was all over you like a rash.'

'You're jealous?'

Jens was close to losing it. 'No! I'm pissed off, that's all.'

'But he likes you.'

'He likes you more.' Jens broke free from Dirk's grip. Walking through to the lounge, he plonked himself down on the sofa and folded his arms across his chest in a defensive posture.

Dirk followed. 'What is your problem?'

'My problem is: I didn't want to bring him home in the first place. I didn't want to share our bed. I didn't want to sleep with him sandwiched in the middle. What else? He focused all his energy on you. Did he rim me? No. Did he suck my toes? No. I was like a spare prick on a honeymoon!'

Dirk adopted an expression of quiet resignation. 'Don't you think you contributed to this?'

'Me?' Jens was indignant. 'How?'

'Well, I don't think it helped that you took yourself out of the action and sat drinking beer on the floor beside the bed, time after time.'

'I enjoy watching, you know that.'

'Yeah, but does he know that? I think you're blowing this out of proportion. The guy really likes you.'

'Yeah!'

'Yeah. He told me so. What he actually said was, you're his "ideal".'

Jens was not convinced. Sarcasm tinged his response. 'Really?'

'Yeah, really. He said, you're a man. A real, honest-to-goodness man. And he loves that about you. Now, why would he say that if he didn't mean it?'

'You tell me?'

'Because it's true!' Dirk crossed to the sofa, sat down beside Jens, put his arm around him. 'Lighten up, baby. He likes you. He really does. You just need to open up a little bit.'

'And when exactly did he say this?'

Dirk crooked an eyebrow, grinned. 'While you were out of the room, getting yet another beer.'

Jens looked suddenly thoughtful. 'You want this?'

'Want what?'

'Him as a fuck buddy?'

'To be totally honest? Yes. Damn right! He's fucking gorgeous.' He nudged Jens in the ribs. 'C'mon, admit it!'

Jens shrugged, unwilling to commit himself.

'But if you have a problem with him being a fuck buddy . . . ' Dirk frowned, brushed an imaginary fleck of lint from the front of his flannel shirt. 'I just wish you'd told me the way you feel earlier. I mean, we've arranged to see him this Sunday for the Naked Sex Party.'

'You really think he likes me?'

'I don't think, I know.'

'Then I'll give it another shot.'

'Okay. That's good, baby. Now, you want to go out and eat?'

'Depends.'

'On?'

Jens smiled wanly. 'If you're paying then, yes.'

Dirk leaned forward and kissed him. 'My treat.'

Five bare butts sat on bar stools. Ömer would never forget the sight that met his eyes as he, Dirk and Jens stood at the cashier's window. It was all he could do not to laugh. Over the cashier's shoulder, five bare arses were on display, warmly welcoming them in. Each arse seated at the main bar, each punter drinking his brew of choice. Nonchalantly nude. Boots and socks were the only attire. A shiver of excitement ran through Ömer's whole body. So, this was to be the introduction to his first Naked Sex Party. Since these events had been introduced onto the

Berlin gay itinerary by a couple of bars some years earlier, they had really taken off. To the extent that you could now go to one any night of the week - and on some nights you'd be spoiled for choice. Jens and Dirk, however, tended to go to the same place - a centrally located leather/cruise bar where the parties took place every Sunday in the late afternoon. The timing was perfect for attracting lots of guys who were 'just out for a Sunday stroll', or were 'off having a beer with the lads'. If only their wives and girlfriends knew! The event also attracted a good mix of men, young and old, hairy and smooth, and from out-and-out sex pigs to guys who were, if not exactly shrinking violets, weren't going to lie down on the pool table and let themselves be fucked by rote. It was this variety that appealed to Dirk and Jens, that and the fact that there was something almost sacrilegious about going to an orgy on a Sunday afternoon. Whatever, it certainly beat the afternoon tradition of coffee with cheesecake and cream, hands down!

Having handed over their five Deutschmarks admission money, the trio were each doled out a blue bin bag and a numbered wrist tag, before being buzzed in through the main door. Inside, disco music bounced off the dry stone walls while all monitors were screening a variety of porno videos. There was something for every taste, and this helped to set the tone for the event. Heading towards the cloakroom they could see that it was still only about one third full - hardly surprising, since it was still early. While admission was restricted to one hour only, most guys tended to hang on until the last ten minutes or so before the doors were shut, hoping to arrive when the orgy was in full swing. Wouldn't want to disappoint them, thought Dirk, as he eased his jeans over his muscular thighs. Jens was already packing his clothes into the bag. 'Come on then, hurry up you guys,' he remonstrated. Ömer was being the slowest of all. It seemed as if it was all a bit too much for him. Which, in a way, it was. It wasn't every day that you could walk into a room of maybe thirty buck-naked men, all geared up to fuck and suck for the next couple of hours. The prospect was almost too overwhelming.

At last Ömer was ready, his clothes neatly folded and packed away into the bag. He handed his bag over to the collector and made his way over to the bar where Jens and Dirk were already standing waiting for him.

'You certainly took your time,' was Jens' only comment.

'I guess you were getting a little distracted, eh Ömer -' Dirk looked down at Ömer's semi-erect cock '- and it shows.'

Ömer just shrugged. 'Move over, guys.'

The lights were low, flattering naked flesh. Their three bare asses joined the five at the bar and Dirk ordered. Ömer didn't know where to look. Feeling mildly embarrassed, he turned his eyes heavenward. Overhead, combat netting was slung across the high ceilings, billowing in waves. Lamps hung from the rafters. Dirk handed him his beer and just then, Ömer caught sight of the video screen above the bar. A welcome and legitimate distraction. He was transfixed. Some porno star was sucking himself off. Ömer was mesmerised - a fact that was not lost on Jens.

Jens leaned in close to Ömer's ear and asked. 'Don't they have porno in Turkey?'

Ömer replied, never once taking his eyes from the screen. 'You think we are the Flintstones? You think Turkey is in the stone age? Of course we have porno!'

'What? Gay porno?' Jens was incredulous.

'No! Straight porno. We have porno cinemas, you know? In Istanbul at least. And, of course, gay men go there too.'

'To blow the straight men?' Dirk asked with a grin.

'Or the married ones who like to think they're straight,' Jens added pointedly.

Whether Ömer missed the point or simply chose to ignore it, was anybody's guess. Either way, he didn't reply. His eyes remained glued to the video action, watching the guy gobble his own donkey dick. He shook his head. 'I thought that was not possible for a body!' he muttered in awe.

'Really?' Jens chuckled. 'Didn't you know that Dirk can do it? It's his party piece!'

'Fortunately, we don't go to parties very often,' Dirk added with a wry smile.

'I tried it but I can't do it,' Ömer admitted with some consternation.

Jens rubbed Ömer's shoulder in a conciliatory fashion. 'Have a word with Dirk. I'm sure he'd only be too happy to show you some stretching exercises!'

Ömer remained engrossed in the video for the next fifteen minutes. Precisely the amount of time it took for the porno star to suck himself off. 'Wow!' said Ömer, genuinely impressed. 'I never see this before. Never. Can you really do this, Dirk? Maybe I could look sometime?'

Dirk grinned. 'One thing, Ömer. Don't believe everything that Jens tells you. I wish I could suck my own dick, though. It would have saved me a lot of hassle when I was younger. You know those years when you're horny as fuck, but you've no idea what to do, where to go, or any of that? That's the time I would have loved to just lay back and suck away to my heart's content. Sadly, buddy, it was just a dream. And now it's even more of one.'

'And I was beginning to look forward to seeing it live . . . '

'Well, maybe I can make it up to you in other ways.' Dirk reached out to stroke Ömer's tempting man-meat. 'How about it?'

Jens watched the exchange and felt a sudden surge of jealousy threaten to overwhelm him, much the same as it did in the club. Anything to change the subject. 'Which reminds me. Ömer, I saw your brother in the park earlier. At least I think it was your brother. Ahmet, isn't it?'

Ömer's smile dropped. He looked down at his hands. 'Uh-huh.'

Jens continued, turning to Dirk. 'Yeah, over by the table-tennis tables. There were a group of Turkish guys, hanging out together. Taking turns, playing against each other. Anyway, I saw him out of the corner of my eye. Saw that he saw me. I turned, smiled, waved. I said, "Hi" . . . And guess what?'

Ömer bit his thumb nail. 'He ignored you?'

Jens looked suddenly surprised at being guessed right, and nodded. Then continued, 'Absolutely. He looked straight through me. I thought, maybe he didn't recognise me -'

Dirk interrupted. 'What? With all your clothes on?!'

'Very funny! Shut your mouth!' Jens turned to Ömer. 'So I waved again. Nothing. He turned to his friends, shrugged, and carried on playing. And I'm just standing there -'

'As opposed to kneeling?' Dirk again.

'I said, shut it! So I'm just standing there . . . '

'Like a big prick?'

'You are asking for it, lover boy!' Jens raised his fist.

Dirk grinned. 'And the other one!'

Ömer sighed heavily. 'I apologise for my brother. He can be a real arsehole at times.'

'Yeah, but why? I only wanted to say hello.'

'Ah, but then he would have had to explain you away to his friends. How does he do that? "Oh, this is the American guy I met in the gay club?".'

'And just what exactly were these men doing playing table tennis right next to the cruising area?' Dirk interjected. He didn't get the benefit of an answer.

'I would have played it straight. I wouldn't have embarrassed him in front of his mates.'

'But he doesn't know that. Appearances are everything to my brother. And you have to remember that the culture we Turks come from, the close community we live in . . . ' Ömer's voice trailed off. 'He's a family man.'

'Even so . . . ' Jens was not mollified.

Ömer reached out a hand and rubbed Jens' hairy belly. 'If it helps to know, this is nothing to do with you. It is my brother's stuff. Don't worry about him; he wouldn't worry about you. He is much too busy always thinking about himself.'

The flashing of the lights signalled that the doors were now finally closed. From this point on, there would be no more guys coming in to disturb the scene, only ones who had shot their load, leaving to rejoin their life outside. Just as well, the place was now packed. From this moment on, for the men in this room, there was only the party. Sex. Naked bodies. Hard to avoid, if not impossible. Fucking. Sucking. Rimming. That was about it. Until the next party, that was.

Dirk led the way downstairs. Here the light was even dimmer than in the bar, and there wasn't much air. Most of it had been consumed by the heaving mass of naked flesh that moved along the narrow darkened corridors. Hands reached out to touch nipples, rub bellies, arses, cocks, whatever. It was a free-for-all. Ömer was mesmerised. He had never seen anything like this before; had never experienced this amount of hot action in one room. It was intoxicating. The smell of sweat; the feel of bodies sliding past each other in the passageways as Dirk led them further into the depths. After a couple of minutes, their destination was reached. A small semi-private area, enclosed on three sides with partitions. Inside hung a sling. And as luck would have it, it wasn't in use. Standing together in the semi-darkness, their bodies locked together in a group kiss.

Ömer had never seen a sling before, so Dirk suggested he try it out. He helped Ömer into a prone position, and Ömer lay back. It was surprisingly comfortable. His body was suspended effortlessly, his head resting back on the leather pillow while his feet were up in the stirrups.

'Ready for action?' Dirk enquired, dropping down onto his calves. Without waiting for a reply, Dirk held Ömer's buttocks wide and buried his bearded face between them. Long strokes of his tongue ran the full length from arsehole to balls. Reflexively, Ömer reached up to tweak and play with his own nipples. Jens watched for a minute or so, watched from the sidelines, until he too bit the bullet and joined in, lowering his head to suck lazily on Ömer's stiff, juicy pole.

How long was it before Jens realised they were being observed? He cast an eye in the direction of the entrance. Someone had indeed come by to watch. A younger guy, mid-twenties at the most. Clean shaven, but with cropped hair and a hairy chest and back. He looks a bit like a navvy, thought Dirk. The guy stepped forward, hesitantly at first but then seemingly encouraged by Jens' fixed stare. He positioned himself with his crotch close to Jens' arse and, leaning over, he began to play with Jens' tits. Still bent over and still sucking on Ömer's achingly erect dick, Jens reached behind him and took hold of the guy's cock, positioning it between his legs and out of harm's way. Jens gripped the navvy's stiff prick between his thighs and began to pump backwards. The pace was quickly starting to heat up. Jens was holding his own - and both of theirs. Working his body. Working their bodies. Working up a sweat.

Dirk looked on at the whole thing, enjoying the voyeuristic aspect of it all. Enjoying the sight of Jens and the navvy getting it on whilst Dirk kept Ömer's arse well lubricated with his spit. The hairy-chested navvy whetted Dirk's appetite all the more and Jens' too, apparently. His mouth released Ömer's rock-hard prong and he eased up straight. The navvy held him from behind, buried his teeth in Jens' neck as he thrust his cock between his thighs ever more purposefully.

Dressed for the occasion, Dirk retrieved the condom and lube from out of his sock. It was time to take centre stage once again. Standing tall, Dirk positioned his cockhead against Ömer's moist ring-piece and he pressed gently forward. Ömer wriggled his arse to facilitate entry. Dirk's cock slid effortlessly into the warm, welcoming embrace of his brother Bear's bolt-hole, and he started to fuck him, easing his cock in and out of Ömer's willing and needful arsehole. He was gentle at first, but quickly got into the rhythm. Suspended from the roof, the chains of the sling starting to rattle, the leather straps creaking, Ömer swung back and forth, back and forth.

Dirk heard footsteps behind him. Someone else had come to watch, or even to join in? Dirk recognised the guy almost as soon as he appeared around his shoulder and came into full view. He had seen him in the bars many times before. Older, maybe in his late forties. Stocky, with a goatee and balding. Handsome - distinguished, even. Jens and he had commented on how they had never ever seen this guy with anyone. So Dirk was surprised to see him here of all places, at an event like this. Life was full of surprises. Still, it didn't put Dirk off his stroke. He continued to fuck Ömer. As he drove his dick home, Ömer's buttocks slapped against his thighs as the sling continued to swing and creak. Back and forth, back and forth.

Mr Goatee simply watched for a while, licking his lips and stroking his engorged cock. Dirk began to wank Ömer's dick, and catching the older man's eye, he indicated down to it, holding it up to the light like a precious jewel. Mr Goatee didn't need a second invitation. In seconds, his mouth was around Ömer 's purple helmet, sucking.

Dirk pulled out and went up behind Mr Goatee. Flinging his own used condom to one side, he took a fresh one out of his sock and rolled it over Mr Goatee's cock. It was a tight fit. But tighter still when the older man slipped it inside Ömer's aching gash and began to plunge into the heart of him. Ömer began to rock back in his cradle, whimpering in agony, in ecstasy. Dirk shut him up with a well-placed thrust between the lips. Soon enough, Ömer was happily sucking on his comforter.

Then the navvy came with an ear-splitting yelp, splashing his come over Jens' thighs. Grunting and groaning and spurting, he collapsed forward onto Jens' back as he in turn sprayed the floor. Each spasm profoundly felt as his juice was expelled. He was acutely aware of his spunk being squeezed out of the tube, shot for shot, glob for glob, onto the filthy concrete floor.

It was all too much for Mr Goatee. He pulled out of Ömer, tore off his condom and jerked his cock wildly. Dirk's eyes were fixed on the juddering fist as it brought that hunk of a dick to a ball-shattering climax. Mr Goatee shot his load over Ömer's belly, as Ömer beat his own meat into second place. Juice spurted high in the air, before crash-landing on his own heaving belly. Dirk came last of all, but didn't give a shit. It wasn't winning the game that counted, only the pleasure of taking part. He pulled free of Ömer's mouth and let fly over Ömer's hairy, heaving pecs. His come splattered on top of spunk on top of spunk. His belly awash, Ömer reached around and spread the puddle of sperm across his chest. Rubbed it in. Exhausted, but happy. And the sling swung to standstill.

Dirk and Jens said their good-byes to Ömer outside the club. Cuddles and kisses and promises to meet again. No worries. This was gay turf. They watched him unchain his bike from the lamp post, throw a muscular leg over the frame, position his pert buttocks on the saddle and sit with some difficulty. No wonder. Fucked twice over, his arse was a little more than sensitive. They watched and waved after him as he disappeared into the distance. Finally, they turned for the short walk home.

Dirk was a happy man. 'So, how was that? Feel better now?'

Jens face clouded over, he stuffed his hands in the pockets of his leather jacket. 'Feel better? Are you joking?!'

Dirk frowned. 'What is the matter now?'

'The matter?!' Jens threw up his hands. He was close to blowing his top. His voice rasping, little more than a hiss. Seething with anger. 'I was completely superfluous. If it hadn't have been for the other guy . . . '

'What? What are you on about now?'

Jens was not to be deterred. 'Completely superfluous! You and him? You two had the time of your lives. What did you expect me to do, just referee the fucking match?!'

Dirk's rage erupted. 'I can't believe you! You were just as nice as fucking pie to the guy.' He imitated Jens, exaggerated his manner. 'See you, Ömer. It was swell, Ömer. Take good care of yourself, Ömer...You're wasted on teaching, you are. You should be a frigging actor. You'd win a fucking Oscar hands down.'

'I did that for you. Not for him. For you. I know you fucking want him. It's fucking obvious. You practically wet your pants every time he walks in the room.' Jens swallowed hard. 'Far be it from me to spoil your fun.'

Dirk was livid. Sarcasm dripped from his response. 'Well, thank you so much. Thank you for sacrificing yourself for me, for my sake. You are so hard done by, aren't you? A fucking saint, aren't you?'

Silence. Jens lowered his head purposefully, and carried on walking.

Dirk was not about to let the matter drop. 'If you felt that way, why didn't you just say so! Am I a mind reader?'

Silence.

Dirk was exasperated. 'You think I wouldn't say, "Enough. No more," if I knew you were so uncomfortable?'

'That's the problem. That is exactly the problem. I don't know.'

'Well, fuck you!' Dirk made to turn in the opposite direction and walk away.

Jens came to his senses suddenly. 'Don't walk away. That doesn't solve anything. Let's talk about it.'

Too late. 'Fuck you!' And Dirk was long gone.

Seven

It had been an exhausting day at work and Dirk was tired to the bone. A situation that was not helped by the thought of what awaited him back home. Since the argument he had had with Jens a few days before, the atmosphere in the apartment had been nothing short of unbearable. He hated it when they argued. Hated the silences that inevitably followed. It didn't help that it was a rare occurrence. It also didn't help that Jens was usually the one who made up first when a fall-out did occur. Because this time, things were different. This time Jens seemed determined to drag the argument out. Sleeping on the opposite side of the bed, back to back, as far away as physically possible. Dirk knew he should have made overtures, but instead had sought solace by working late and then heading off to the bars. He knew it didn't help and yet he could not seem to help himself. Even so, he was aware that he couldn't keep avoiding the issue forever. And tonight he was dog tired. Tonight he was definitely staying home.

Turning the key in the lock, he was surprised to hear music gently playing in the background. He hadn't expected Jens to be home, and had secretly hoped he would not be. Wasn't tonight one of his nights to work late? Dirk came into the living room to find Jens stretched out on the sofa reading.

'Hi, Dirk. You're late this evening.'

'Am I?'

'Yeah.'

'It's been a particularly rough day, at the end of a pretty rough week, and I've just about had it.' Dirk threw his jacket on the sofa. 'I thought you were supposed to be working?'

'Well, I guess that you've struck lucky this evening. The class cancelled. So, your bath is ready, if you want to slip into it, and by the time you get out your dinner will be ready,' said Jens, while moving into the kitchen. 'There's beer cooling in the fridge. Want one?'

'I'd prefer whisky, ice, maybe a slice of lemon.'

'Whatever you want.'

'Eh, yeah. What's this all about, Jens?' Dirk looked bemused but he kept his voice even. 'Why are you being so . . . nice?'

'I'm your partner. I'm allowed to be nice.'

Dirk arched his eyebrows. The message was, 'You know what I mean?'

'Nothing really,' Jens continued after a pause. 'Well, not "nothing" as such, but more, well, I've been thinking for a while of how I seem to be out all of the time, and then when I'm here, you're out. And then there's the situation with Ömer and stuff. And it's just like we never have time for us. Just the two of us. Know what I mean?'

Dirk knew exactly what he meant. His own head had been filled with the same thoughts for the past couple of weeks. Trying to work out this complicated love triangle stuff in his head. What did it mean, where was it going, and what did Jens really think of the situation? But these thoughts were soon far from his mind, as he settled into the steaming waters of the bath that Jens had drawn for him.

Sipping on his whisky, watching the candles flicker and listening to the relaxing sound of an Eric Satie CD playing in the background, Dirk felt his whole body just slide into that state of deep peace that only such physical indulgence overload can induce. He needed this. He really needed it. In the background he could hear Jens bustling about in the kitchen. But that was somewhere else. All Dirk had to concentrate on was the warmth of the whisky as it slid past the back of his throat and the warmth of the water that caressed his body. He could feel his muscles heat up, relax, begin to soften.

After what seemed like minutes, though it had involved his glass being refilled, Jens announced that dinner was ready. Dirk climbed out of the bath and after a brisk towelling-down, wrapped himself in the thick white cotton sauna gown - the one that Jens had bought him and that made him look like a boxer coming out into the ring. At least, Jens said so. Whatever.

In the kitchen, there were more candles on the table. Red wine in the glasses, and the food on the table.

They ate in comfortable silence.

'To us,' said Jens, raising his glass for a toast.

'Yeah. To us,' Dirk replied, looking Jens directly in the eye. 'I do love you, you know. Really.'

'I know. I know you do. And I love you too. But somehow I get the feeling that we just don't say it often enough. Or can you say something like that often enough?'

'Don't know really. I know that I don't ever get tired hearing it.'

'Me neither. Me neither.'

'And I never get tired of you, Baby Bear.'

'Glad to hear it, Daddy Bear.'

'Should we take the wine into the bedroom?'

'What about dessert?'

'That's exactly what I had in mind!'

Jens was lying on his belly on the bed, his legs spread. Starting at the top of his head, Dirk traced a line with his tongue down over the back of Jens' shaved head, pausing to gently bite the neck, and then on down the length of the spine until he reached the crack of his arse. Parting Jens' buttocks, he allowed his tongue to flick from one side of the crack to the other, inching towards the arsehole, but stopping millimetres away from it. He returned to Jens' head, but this time he concentrated on kissing, licking and nibbling every part of it. Then he moved from neck to ear and back again, caressing with his tongue, bathing Jens in his love and devotion. His own body arched over that of Jens and he could feel his erection rubbing against Jens' buttocks, allowing it to slide into the cleft and rest there.

Moving down to the shoulders, Dirk lavished his attention on first one side and then the other. He reached around to Jens' chest to play lazily with his nipple, while Jens, in turn, reached back to grab hold of Dirk's cock, gently retracting the foreskin and massaging the cockhead with his fingertips. Dirk continued to lick, suck and chew on Jens' willing flesh, enjoying the sensation of tongue on skin, the wetness, the sheer pleasure in such a simple act of devotion.

Now Dirk had worked his way down the entire length of Jens' back and was poised, once more, at the top of his arsecrack. Allowing his tongue one more glide along the slit, he gently parted the buttocks to reveal . . .

'You've shaved, Jens!'

'Yeah. That was the little surprise I mentioned to you. I was wondering when you would finally get to it!'

It was beautiful. Jens' rosebud was framed by smooth, pinkish, hairless flesh. A little world all to itself. And the key to the heart of Jens' passions. Dirk ran his tongue up and down the crack a couple of times, before settling in to devote his attention to Jens' ring-piece. He licked and sucked and then, gently, he inserted the tip of his tongue into the hole. Pressing gently, waiting for the rosebud to open up, and all due to Dirk's tender care and attention.

'More . . . ' Jens growled, raising his arse off the bed. Offering it up for worship.

Dirk's fingers came into play as his mouth continued to gorge itself. Slowly, carefully, he worked both of his index fingers into the hole, one on each side, pulling it open to allow increased access for his probing tongue. Jens was writhing in ecstasy now. His whole body was quivering with sensation.

'More!' Jens growled again, thumping the pillow with his fist.

Dirk chuckled into Jens' crack. 'What's your hurry? I plan to take my time. I plan to enjoy this. He shuffled up the bed, manoeuvred himself to lie behind Jens. Their bodies cupped together like two spoons in a kitchen drawer. It had been a while since they had been this close. This together.

Dirk placed his cock between Jens' slick arsecheeks. Rubbing backward and forward, building up friction...and tension. Jens arched his body, pushing his arse back, pressing his cheeks together to constrain Dirk's throbbing member.

'Oh fuck . . . More!' Jens' breathing had become heavy, his throat thick with lust.

Reaching back, Jens took hold of Dirk's cock and began to stroke it. Thrilled by its size, its stiffness. He wanted it badly. Needed it. Needed to feel his entire insides get pummelled by this cock. Dirk's cock.

'I want to be inside you,' Dirk whispered in his ear as he nibbled the lobe.

'Oh, yes!'

'You want it too, don't you, baby?'

'Oh, yes!!'

Dirk rolled onto his back. 'Then you know what you have to do?'

Jens rolled over, reached down under the side of the bed and retrieved the condoms and lube. And it was with intense pleasure that he filled his palm with a dose of the thick, sticky come-like substance, before spreading it over Dirk's rock hard prong with one practised hand. Dirk's toes curled, his hips rising up involuntarily from the mattress. 'Oh . . . '

Hand over hand now, Jens manipulated Dirk's glistening manmeat. Squeezing, tugging, stroking it to ball-bursting erection. He bit the lip of the foil enclosing the flesh-coloured condom and tore it open. With thumb and forefinger squeezing air from the teat he rolled the circle of latex over Dirk's crimson cockhead, down over the ridge, down over the full, aching length until it was fully encased in a second skin. Dirk nipped the base where balls met shaft and held proud whilst Jens squeezed another dose of lube from the tube onto the tips of his fingers. Dirk's fingers found their way effortlessly to Jens own tender, aching ring-piece, spreading a generous dose of lube around the rim, teasing his orifice, lingering at the entrance before Dirk's middle finger slipped effortlessly through the porthole. Jens' whole body convulsed. Shuddered with pleasure as a second finger joined the first, and the promise of fullness that might come.

Dirk looked up in to Jens' face. Eyes closed, an expression of rapture, of intense sensations, flickering across his handsome face. Pleasuring himself, pleasuring Dirk as a consequence. Only a matter of time. Jens opened his eyes, looked directly into Dirk's. They both burst out laughing.

'What are you looking at?'

'You.'

'Why?'

'I'm your partner. I'm allowed.'

'Well, partner, you just lie back. Let me do all the work.' Jens straddled Dirk's thighs, reached back and took hold of his swollen dick, placed the fat head up against his puckered anus.

'Whatever you say.'

And without another word, Jens eased back, mounting Dirk's cock. Wriggling his butt to facilitate entry, he gasped as the bulbous helmet entered in. Jens could feel his ring tightening around the rim of Dirk's cockhead before he slid effortlessly down the full length of the greased-up pole. Buttocks touched base and Jens released a satisfied groan.

Dirk's hands cupped and cradled Jens' firm, hairy buttocks as the they began to rock slowly backwards and forwards. Luxuriating in the tight fit. Jens loosening himself up for the inevitable upsurge in activity. Dirk could feel Jens' sphincter tighten and relax, drawing him ever deeper into him. Dirk felt reassured, deeply reassured, to not only have his cock accepted but actively welcomed home. No man had ever wanted him more. No man had ever made him feel so desired. Only Jens. Jens turned fucking into an act of love.

Jens raised himself upwards controlling the depth of penetration.

One, two, three, four inches of slick dick were exposed, then consumed again with one single downward thrust. And again and again. Building up speed until Jens was bouncing up and down, slamming down to meet Dirk's upward thrusts. Then he suddenly held still, his buttocks pressing down against Dirk's thighs, as Dirk continued to thrust up into him. Dirk looked up and saw the intensity of feeling mapped on Jens' sweet, familiar face. Eyes closed, his thick eyebrows knitted together, his lips parted. With every thrust another grunt escaped his throat. Jens now began to grind his arse around and around. Now raising himself up, Dirk's cock fully released. Jens' arsehole yawned hungrily then swallowed Dirk's dick in one single gulp.

'Oh, I love you. Love you. Love you!' Dirk's voice trembled with his exertions, with the weight of Jens' solid, chunky butt crushing down on him. 'I'm going to come. Come inside you. All my love inside you.'

Jens increased the pounding he was giving Dirk's rod. 'So, come. Just do it. Fucking do it. Give it all to me. Give all of yourself to me. Now!'

'Yeah . . . '

'Now!'

'Oh, yeah . . . '

'Now!'

'Oh, fuck! YEAH!! YEAH!! YEAH!! YEAH!!'

Mopped up now, tissues and condom discarded on the floor beside the bed, they held each other close. They lay that way for a good long while, their bodies spent, their powerful, hairy limbs wrapped around each other. Basking in the afterglow. Their sexual appetites might have been sated, but not their need for love and affection. Cuddled up close, Dirk yawned. Jens followed suit, then snuggled his cheek up against Dirk's chest. Sleep was about to come quickly, but not before Jens had the chance to realise he wasn't thinking at all. No troubled thoughts. No worries. If only for this night - this moment even -

Ahmet and Ömer did not exist. It was just him and Dirk. The world held at bay outside these four walls. He felt his whole body sigh with relief. And then he joined Dirk in dreamland.

Eight

It was the first day back after Christmas and New Year break, another one of those all too familiar early mornings when Jens really was not feeling up to working. Dirk was the early bird, whereas it took Jens all his time to crawl out of the bed. But early mornings came with the territory. Naja - that's life! Things could have been a lot worse.

In the event, the sun was shining. It was one of those crisp winter mornings when you actually get a sense of spring just over the horizon. And Jens could feel his spirits rise in anticipation. Well, maybe he was not entirely happy, but then he wasn't exactly unhappy either. It was just that this morning he was off to teach 'in-company', one of those jobs where he had to travel halfway across the city to the outer suburbs in order to teach a group of clients in their workplace. He didn't really mind this - apart from the early start and the long journey and the lousy salary, of course! But, hell, at the same time, it had its advantages. It gave him time to read, to think, to reflect. All three were exactly what he had been doing for the whole trip out to Wannsee, and was what he was intending to continue to do as the connecting S-Bahn pulled in to the platform.

Dirk had been a sweetheart over the holidays; had been a sweetheart ever since they made had up after that awful row. With presents galore on Christmas morning and champagne flowing on New Years Eve, Jens felt that Dirk had really made an effort to put things right. But then again, hadn't he still suggested that they should remain friends with Ömer. Insisted even that they could be friends and fuck buddies. Why not? Wasn't it the grown-up thing to do? Dirk loved Jens after all, didn't he? Nothing was going to change that, was it? Shouldn't Jens just lighten up and not worry?

But worry he did. Worried about the impact Ömer would have on their partnership. For hadn't they agreed long ago that their 'open' relationship was limited to fucking around with the understanding that there would be no emotional involvement? Ömer was something different, he was a fully-rounded individual. A sweetheart and a hunk. The other guys were no competition. But Ömer?

The incoming train slowed to a halt and, as the automatic doors opened, Jens stepped inside. He looked around to find a seat, only to see Ahmet, Ömer's drop-dead handsome elder brother Bear, already seated and staring at him. Jens didn't know what to do, and was about to turn and go elsewhere, when Ahmet gave him a broad welcoming smile and, with a slight nod of his head indicated the empty seat opposite him. Jens wasn't sure what was going on. His mind was racing - full of conflicting thoughts. This guy had some nerve. Hadn't he ignored him just a while back? And now here he was boldly suggesting that Jens should come over and sit with him. It took Jens a little time to make up his mind. And he berated himself silently: Why do I always feel I have to be so fucking agreeable?!

He walked slowly over and sat down directly opposite Ahmet as the train pulled out of the station. Ahmet's face was a picture, lit up with a big smile that showed off his white teeth. It was, however, the eyes that betrayed his inner thoughts. Lustful, I-want-to-fuck-you, thoughts. Ahmet's eyes looked at Jens and slowly but deliberately undressed him. Jens could feel every stroke.

'Hi,' said Jens blandly. 'Nice day, or?'

'Better now that I meet you again. I have been so wanting to see you ever since that day in the park. I saw you looking at me. Saw you waving. But I couldn't do anything. My friends . . . ' His words trailed off. He shook his head regretfully. Was this guy for real?! 'I was with all of these Turkish guys, and they would have wanted to know how I knew you. It would have been complicated. You know how it is in our culture . . . '

This last sentence was said in that pleading, you've-got-to-understand-me voice that appealed to the caregiver in Jens. Without thinking of the fact that Ömer never used his cultural background as an excuse for anything he did or did not do, Jens waded in, 'Yeah, don't worry about it. I understand. It's a difficult situation for you.'

'It's not that I don't like you,' Ahmet continued, allowing the wet tip of his tongue to rest momentarily on his lower lip whilst looking Jens directly in the eyes, 'but . . . I guess that it's just that I want to say that, in public . . . Well, when I'm with a group of Turkish friends . . . It's hard to be myself. If you know what I mean?'

'Sure. Sure I do.'

There followed an awkward pause. Neither of them quite knowing what to do or say next. However, it should have been clear that Ahmet was attempting to take control of the situation, when he dropped his voice a couple of octaves and continued in a honeyed, husky, sexy tone, 'I have a longing for you . . . ' His provocative words were accompanied by another one of those sleepy-eyed looks, and another smile. Jens could feel his resolve wilting. He lowered his eyes but, perhaps unfortunately, they fell onto the significant bulge in Ahmet's jeans. As if on cue, Ahmet let his thumb brush against the outline of his stiffening member. At that moment, Jens could almost taste Ahmet's fat circumcised cock once again on his tongue. The sense memory sent a shiver down his spine, made the tiny hairs on the back of his neck stand up, made him salivate.

Again. As if to hammer the point home. 'I have a longing for you . . . '

Jens gulped. Mouth wet, throat dry. 'Me too.

Ahmet smirked seductively. 'I would like to see you again. Maybe we could arrange to meet up sometime. Somewhere private? Just the two of us?'

'You have a telephone number where I could reach you?'

'You have pen and paper?'

Jens felt in his coat pocket and produced both.

Ahmet took them and began to scribble down his name and number. 'I will give you the one for my mobile. If I am not there, I have voice mail. I get back to you. Okay?'

Jens nodded.

'I promise. Okay?'

Jens nodded.

The rest of the journey passed by like the scenery - like a blur. It was only afterwards that Jens wondered about the speed of this ten-minute seduction scene. That was how long it had taken the S-Bahn to make the trip from Wannsee to Potsdam Hauptbahnhof. Ten minutes for his supposedly steely resolve to crumble. And for what? The chance of a rematch with Ahmet? Jens had surprised himself. And why? He could still see the bulge in Ahmet's pants; could feel his own dick start to throb. So much for setting boundaries, he thought. Why not behave just like the rest of them, just like his darling Dirk? Why not let his cock do all the thinking for a change? Why not go with the flow? Just this one time, it would be worth it. Wouldn't it?

Nine

Dirk hit forty. Or maybe it would be better to say that forty hit him. It felt like a knockout blow. He felt down, but he was not out for the count. Not for a long time yet. Fortunately, he still had Jens as his encourager. On that memorable birthday, Jens had made him a special Bagel Frühstück. Breakfast in bed. He felt suitably pampered. But, even so, this gesture could in no way dissipate the cloud of doom and gloom that hung over his head.

Having eaten, Dirk pushed the tray aside and pulled himself out of bed. Naked and bleary-eyed, he stumbled to stand in front of the full-length mirror that hung on their bedroom wall. True, he was in excellent shape. True, he still had the look. The thick head of hair, but wasn't his full, dark beard now tainted with just a hint of silver even as it framed his square jaw? Of course, there was no denying his big cock and balls hung just as proudly as ever, but it did feel like he had crossed a bridge, the end of an era.

Under that stocky, hairy physique, under that muscle monster exterior, he was sure the could hear his body clock ticking away ever more rapidly. A body he had worked so hard to achieve. He struck a pose, ran a palm over his flat, tightly muscled belly and turned his head towards Jens who now stood in the doorway. 'Enjoy it while you've got it. It's all downhill from here.'

Jens let out a gust of laughter. 'There you go again - always looking on the bright side!' It was typical of the half-empty-glass syndrome that Dirk was prone to indulge in. Jens' laughter could always puncture Dirk's bubble of negativity. Jens was used to Dirk's moods, but he wasn't about to give into them.

Dirk shrugged. 'It's okay for you. You're still a young man . . . '

Jens was having none of it. 'Get real. Firstly, forty is not old. Secondly, you're a Bear and Bears improve with age. And thirdly -' Jens produced a present from behind his back '- I got you that book you wanted: Muscle for Life. Just keep up the good work, Grandpa.'

The book had proven an inspiration and Dirk had set to work with a vengeance. A twelve-week programme designed to give him his best body - ever! And twelve weeks to the day his body was in kick-arse shape. Better than it had ever been. The exercise programme in the book had been invaluable. But, hell, Dirk had to take some credit. The finger that pulled the trigger was his. He didn't flag, not once. Six days a week, he had remained totally focused. On the seventh, like God, he rested. Jens watched his progress with a compassionate eye, and still he kept asking how you can improve on perfection. To his mind, Dirk's body had already been in kick-arse shape, but he knew better than to argue.

By the eleventh week, Dirk was strutting around the gym, proud of his efforts, showing off, feeling once again in control - not only of his body but of his destiny. It seemed like he couldn't get through his routine without some young guy asking what he was taking, what he ate, how old he was. It was such a buzz to hear that sharp intake of breath and the inevitable, 'Man, you've made some excellent progress'.

Now Dirk was sitting in the Jacuzzi with yet another admirer, hearing the compliment again. Dirk had never talked to this particular guy before, but he was a hard act to ignore. He had seen him around at the fitness studio often, but other than exchanging a friendly smile and a wave they had never spoken a word. The gym was a place of work; Dirk's programme was intense. It wasn't a place to chat or cruise or make new friends but a simply place a place to workout. Now, resting back in the Jacuzzi, muscles battered by bubbles, Dirk allowed his focus to shift.

'Thanks,' Dirk replied. 'Good of you to notice.'

'Are you kidding? All your hard work? You've been a real inspiration to me.' A firm, meaty paw appeared out of the water and was held out towards Dirk as he leaned forward. 'My name's Hagen. My friends call me Hagen.'

Dirk took hold and felt his iron grip. 'Pleased to meet you, Hagen. Mine's Dirk.'

It was early morning, a time Dirk loved to train. Lunch time and evenings could be unbearably busy. Thank God for flexible working hours, he thought to himself, only me and the handsome stranger in the Jacuzzi. Plenty of room to stretch out and relax. Hagen's hand disappeared once more under the foam and brushed Dirk's foot as it rested on the shelf beside Hagen's butt. It lingered just a moment too long, then moved away.

Hagen grinned. 'Sorry.'

Dirk smiled. 'No problem.'

The Jacuzzi stopped, the bubbles disappearing. Hagen stood up and stretched his pumped, bull-like muscularity, then reached over to press the restart button. As the pump kicked in, he returned to a seated position, but this time slid alongside Dirk. Closing his eyes, he rested his neck back against the rim of the pool. Seconds later, he spread his knees wide so that his thick, muscular thigh rested against Dirk's.

Hagen let out a tortured sigh. 'I think that maybe I overdid it today. My muscles are so stiff.' He opened his eyes, raised his head, and turned it towards Dirk. 'You wouldn't believe how stiff I am.' And then came the almost imperceptible increase in pressure of his leg against Dirk's.

Dirk turned his head to face Hagen, saw the unmistakable twinkle in his clear-blue eyes. So much for this being a straight gym, one Dirk and Jens had chosen for its potential lack of distractions. He let his eyes linger on Hagen's face - a chiselled, almost sculpted face. Golden, cropped hair, a peppering of stubble on his top lip and cleft chin. Slowly, Dirk reached out a hand under the foaming waves. His finger tips brushed the erect column between Hagen's spread thighs. Hagen's dick was colossal. Dirk could feel its immense girth and its pulsing length vibrate at his touch. Hagen trembled, and so did Dirk. His fingers strained to wrap around the circumference as Hagen again closed his eyes and leaned his head back. Dirk turned to check the glass panel in the door that looked directly out onto the passageway. One man wandered back from the gym, casually wiping a towel over his brow, a second passed the first on his way towards the sauna. Both were oblivious, neither looked their way. What would they have seen? Only two heads bobbing above the water. The real action was hidden beneath the foam.

Hagen reached out a hand to stroke Dirk's inner thigh, brushing against Dirk's own erect member. His touch was surprisingly tender, kneading the muscle like a masseur. Dirk's fist tightened around Hagen's rock-hard penis, felt it swell to bursting.

'Take me home,' Hagen groaned. 'Let's go for the full workout.'

Dirk clambered out of the Jacuzzi and reached, dripping wet, for his towel.

Hagen was awe-struck. 'Man, you are one Big Daddy!'

Towelled dry, dressed in a pair of light-grey briefs, Hagen looked like a professional wrestler. No tattoos, no piercings, shaved smooth. Unadorned. His body was a statement on its own: 'Don't fuck with me!' A statement Dirk had every intention of ignoring. Finally dressed in jeans and workboots, a white T-shirt stretched tightly across his V-shaped chest, Hagen led the way downstairs, and out through the lobby, onto the crowded street.

It was Dirk's turn to lead. 'I only live a few minutes away. Follow me.' He slung his sports bag over his shoulder, thankful that Jens was away teaching on a residential seminar until the weekend. 'How long have you lived around here? I presume from your accent that you're not a local?'

'Been up from Bayern a couple of months, living with a buddy and his girlfriend. Now she has decided that three's a crowd.'

'Really?' A silence fell. 'Got a trade?'

'Electrician. And you?'

'Engineer.' Another pause. 'How old are you?'

'Me? I'm twenty-two.'

'You look older.'

'And you?'

Dirk flinched. Shrugged. 'Forty.'

'Man! I hope I look that good at forty! You look much younger.'

'You're full of compliments.'

'Hey, it's all the same to me. I prefer older guys. I really do. Anyway, the way I look at it, if you're hot, you're hot.'

'Yeah?'

'Used to be a time when older guys allowed themselves to fall apart. Got themselves a bad name.'

'That's not about to happen to me.'

'Clearly.' Hagen skipped a step. 'Yeah. To my mind, older guys have that little something extra.'

'Oh, yeah? And what might that be?'

Hagen bumped playfully into Dirk's side, almost knocking him off balance. 'If I'm lucky . . . the experience to know how to use that big cock of yours!'

They reached Dirk's apartment building and entered through the security door. Upstairs, Dirk locked the front door behind them and indicated the spiral staircase that led to up to the bedroom.

'Please, up there, make yourself comfortable. Would you like a drink?'

Hagen dropped his sports bag on the hall carpet alongside Dirk's. 'You got beer?'

'Coming right up.'

When Dirk entered the bedroom, Hagen was laid back on blue-and-white duvet, his head resting back on plumped-up pillows. One hand was stuffed down the front of his grey briefs, playing with the barely contained erection, whilst the other toyed with a pellet-like nipple standing out from his hairless chest. Dirk held out the beer towards him. Hagen's hand left his chest and took hold. He tipped the neck towards his mouth and sucked on the tip, looking up at Dirk with a new intensity in his pale-blue eyes.

'Taste good?' Dirk asked.

Hagen wiped his mouth with the back of his hand. 'Don't mean to sound ungrateful, Dirk. But I'd rather have my lips around your dick.'

Dirk sat down on the bed beside him and took the bottle from him between thumb and forefinger, placing it on the bedside cabinet. Dirk ran his palm over the flat of Hagen's belly and watched as his abdominals tensed reflexively, accentuating the egg-box musculature. Tracing the grooves with his finger, Dirk worked his way up to the two slabs of beefsteak that formed his mountainous pecs. They were rock solid and as smooth as glass. Dirk took hold of one nipple and tugged on it gently.

Hagen slipped an arm behind his head, flexing an impressive bicep. 'Are you just gonna play?' he teased. 'Or are we going to get naked and party?'

Dirk stood and crossed to the end of the bed, yanking the grey sweatshirt over his head. Then, bending over, he removed his white sports socks whilst he turned his head to see Hagen hook his thumbs under the high-cut waist of his briefs. Hagen spread his thighs and kept his eyes focused on Dirk as he hoisted his legs and peeled his underwear over his rock-hard arsecheeks. Low-slung balls came into view, and finally Hagen's cock and butthole were revealed in all their naked glory. He hiked his briefs over his calves then, flinging them aside, he knelt, palms on either thigh and tensed his impressive musculature. He held the pose.

'You like what you see?'

At that moment, the zipper on Dirk's jeans split wide open to reveal his prominent erection.

'Silly question.'

Dropping his jeans to the floor, Dirk kicked them aside, then clambered onto the bed to face Hagen directly. They paused a moment, sizing each other up. Dirk felt Hagen's hot breath on his cheek and, at the same time, Hagen threw his arms around Dirk. He smothered Dirk with a mighty hug. His grip was so strong, Dirk thought he'd squeeze the air out of his lungs. And then Hagen's mouth found his; grinding down against it, sucking the life force out of his body, demanding his complete surrender.

Hagen's stiff dick was poking into Dirk's thigh. Dirk's cock leapt up to slap his, whilst grabbing a handful of Hagen's solid pec and squeezing hard. Hagen whimpered; clutched Dirk's buttocks, thrusting his groin against Dirk's. They began to sweat. Moist, salty droplets running down each brow, flavouring their kisses. Dirk let his tongue roam over Hagen's face; his cheeks, his forehead. Hagen began to tremble.

'Suck me.'

Dirk pushed Hagen over onto his back and pounced on his breathtaking hunk of an uncut dick. Consuming it in one fell swoop, he filled his throat with Hagen's maleness. It tasted salty, raw, even a little fleshy. But Dirk savoured every morsel. He let his nose nuzzle into his blond pubic curls. Hagen gasped, grinding his balls against Dirk's chin. Slowly he began to fuck his throat. Slow, measured thrusts, deliberate in their intensity, stuffing Dirk's face, swelling his cavity till it was fit to burst. Reluctantly, Dirk felt forced to pull back. His fingers played along the length of Hagen's slick, rock-hard member, right up to the tip; gripping his heavy foreskin and pulling it forward to fully cover the bulbous, crimson helmet.

Holding it in place, Dirk forced his tongue under the tight fold of skin, poking and swirling his tongue beneath his silken coverlet. Hagen pressed his lips together, breathing out in short, sharp bursts. Dirk was in ecstasy. Oh, how he loved servicing cock. Better than a big, juicy steak, when it came to sating his appetite. Hagen's dick drew him like a magnet; drew his lips up to the hilt of the broad shaft with its irresistible attraction. His nose was tickled by pubic hair. He was glad to be the one to service this dick, grateful, even honoured. This prick needed a regular workout, but not for the purposes of size. That, Hagen already had in handfuls.

Hagen wrapped his powerful thighs around Dirk's ribcage and hooked his feet at the ankle, resting them over Dirk's broad back. Finally, he began to squeeze, lost in his own little world. Dirk let his tongue play over Hagen's hairless ballsac, and worked his way towards the other man's inner thighs, running the tip of his tongue over the prominent veins that had been pushed to the surface by the surfeit of muscle. Hagen spread his thighs wider to accommodate Dirk's explorations and finally unhooked his ankles, lifting them high and wide to present his hot, little hole for an intimate examination. Dirk prised Hagen's solid buttocks apart and buried his face in the crevice, licking and sucking and feasting on his manhole. Hagen's response was both vocal and physical, even as he started to yelp he was pressing the back of Dirk's head deeper into his crevice. Dirk held his breath and dove in, his head swimming, drowning in the depths of Hagen's deep end.

Dirk came up for air and Hagen flipped over onto his belly. Grinding his erection against the coverlet, Hagen's arse rose and fell.

'I believe you wanted me to fuck you?' Dirk asked dryly. Silly question.

Hagen looked over his shoulder, nonplussed. 'You want it in writing? Yeah, Big Daddy, I want you to fuck me.'

Dirk greased up Hagen's arsehole with lube. The tight ring-piece dilated at the touch of his fingertips; welcoming first one slick finger, then a second, then a third. Actively passive, Hagen pushed back to consume all that Dirk offered, and then some. Finally, Hagen was holding his own buttocks wide.

'Stick it in, Big Daddy. Just fucking stick it in!'

Sheathed in rubber now, Dirk's throbbing dick slid into Hagen with consummate ease. Disappearing slowly, right up to the nuts; stretching him wide. Dirk slid out equally slowly, then plunged back in up to the hilt.

As Dirk withdrew, Hagen let out a long moan; as Dirk thrust into him Hagen buried his face into the pillow and whined.

'Oh, yeah, Big Man. Fill me up. Fill me right up. All the way. All the . . .'

Dirk began to increase his rhythm. Forward and back, forward and back. Hagen struggled up onto his knees, his face still buried in the pillow, and began to rock backwards, matching Dirk's every thrust. Dirk let his hands glide over Hagen's meaty buttocks. Squeezing them, cupping them. Two solid hunks of muscle under a velvet coating. Warm to the touch, burning with desire. Dirk slammed into him, his balls slapping against him. Big balls swinging, heavy with come, swollen with passion.

Hagen spit on his hand, then reached back and began to jerk on his own tool. Pushing it back between his legs, Hagen stroked the exposed head against Dirk's hairy thigh and quivered. Dirk felt the slickness of Hagen's spit and then the stickiness of pre-come ooze from the tip and glide over his skin. Hagen's fingers juddered back and forth, jacking his length whilst Dirk lunged into him with no mercy.

Hagen's groans became louder, building inexorably as did his backward thrusts. His fingers diligently jacked his man-meat as sweat ran from Dirk's brow and splashed onto the other man's magnificent arse.

'I'm going to come, Big Daddy. Watch out, here she blows!'

Dirk felt the first blast of warm, pungent man-juice spray against his leg as Hagen began to grunt and squeal. A second blast hit his knee, then a third, and suddenly Dirk knew he himself was about to erupt. The unmistakable rumbling deep in his balls forced a path through his aching tubes, and finally exploded into the rubber teat as he thrust forward like a dog in heat. And again, and again, and . . .

Dirk slept on the wet patch; it seemed like a small sacrifice in the circumstances. Hagen snuggled up, his head on his chest, snoring gently. Sweet dreams. Dirk woke to find Hagen dressed, perched on the edge of his bed, lost in contemplation. Hagen swung around when Dirk reached out to touch his arm, and planted a sloppy kiss on Dirk's forehead.

'My instincts were good.'

Dirk raised his eyebrows, puzzled. 'Sorry?'

'You do know how to use that big thing.' Hagen reached down and gave Dirk's prick a final affectionate tug. He stood up. 'Well, I guess I'd better be going. Don't get up. I'll see myself out. Maybe, I'll see you at the gym. But don't worry, I'll be discreet.'

Dirk raised a quizzical eyebrow.

Hagen slipped on his jacket and picked up his sports bag. 'Oh, yeah. You had a phone call. Some guy called Jens . . . '

Dirk could barely disguise the look of panic that crossed his face. 'And you answered?'

'Give me some credit, Big Daddy! He left a message on the answering machine.'

'Oh.'

'Sounds like the guy loves you a lot.'

'Yeah. Yeah he does.'

Hagen walked to the doorway, then turned to look over his shoulder. 'He's a lucky guy. See you.' And with a final salute, Hagen disappeared out into the hall, down the stairs and out of the door.

Ten

Ahmet sat on the edge of the bed and lit a cigarette, throwing the packet and disposable lighter down on the bedside table with a clatter. The crisp, white bed sheets were thrown back. Jens lay naked at his side, shading his eyes with his forearm. Ahmet coughed. Jens looked at Ahmet's broad, tan, hairy back. It was incredibly hairy, like he was wearing a fur suit. One that started by circling his neck before coating his entire body all the way down to his feet.

Jens kept quiet to keep the peace. He hated it when Ahmet was in one of his moods. But he had learned to let him come around in his own time. It never helped to try and placate him.

For the past three months they had been embroiled in a relationship of sorts. A poor excuse for a relationship - Ahmet sneaking behind his wife's back and Jens behind Dirk's. And although Ahmet made some pretence to emotional engagement, Jens was not so easily fooled by his posturing. Ahmet always had to be on top of things, including Jens. He packed the wife and kids off to visit her relations in Frankfurt or in Hamburg, on as regular a basis as he reasonably could. And used this 'free time' to gorge his appetite for arse. Jens had played the willing recipient of his desire but for how much longer?

Once again, Jens had managed to piss him off, big style. Well, what had Ahmet expected him to say, anyway, he thought to himself. Was he supposed to be overjoyed to hear that Ahmet's wife was pregnant again? And couldn't he have chosen a more suitable time than just after they had finished their afternoon fuck-a-thon? Ahmet had barely allowed time for the come to dry on Jens' butt-fur.

Ahmet looked back over his shoulder and smirked. It made Jens' sick at heart. The guy looked fabulous even when he was acting like a complete shit. That curl of his lip exposing such perfect teeth. No one deserved to look so good without working at it. And the only thing

Ahmet seemed to work at consistently was being an arsehole. One day, Jens thought to himself, you, Ahmet, are going to be an ugly, old, fat, toothless slob whom nobody is going to want to touch with a barge pole. It came as cold comfort. Given that there was no justice in the world it would probably be another fifty years until that particular metamorphosis took place.

'You know your problem?' Ahmet asked pointedly. Attack clearly being his first line of defence.

Yes, you. You're my problem, thought Jens but all he said was: 'No, but I'm sure you'll be happy to tell me.'

'You see problems where there are none, and none where there are problems.'

'Would you like to give me an example?'

'No problem.' He sucked hard on his cigarette and exhaled a thick stream of smoke. 'You are too trusting. You think my little brother is so sweet, so nice?'

'Don't tell me, he's a mass murderer?!'

'Worse for you. He is in love with your boyfriend.'

'Oh, yeah. I forgot. And you are in love with me!'

Ahmet adopted a pained expression. 'It is simply my duty to warn you.'

It was more than Jens could take. He punched the bed. Then he stood suddenly and crossed into the living room. Kiddies' toys were piled high in one corner with a play pen alongside. He wrapped his arms across his body and shivered. He had seldom felt so naked and exposed.

'Come away from there! Come away from the window!' Ahmet's voice snapped from the doorway behind him. 'The neighbours!'

'Oh, yes. Mustn't upset the neighbours! Do please forgive me! And, anyway, what are you complaining about? I'm nowhere near the window. What? Your neighbours use binoculars?!'

Ahmet came up behind him, wrapped his arms around him. He

pressed his warm and furry body up against him, and laid his head against Jens' shoulder. 'I am a married man, my friend.'

'And don't I just know it. When do the wife and kids get back?'

'Sunday.'

'And then what?

Ahmet sighed theatrically.

'So, let's just call it quits.'

'You know I can't do that.'

'Let me go, Ahmet. You have your life and I . . . I have mine.'

'You belong to me.'

'No.'

'Yes! I let you kiss me. Does this not count!'

'I've got my own life.'

Ahmet sneered. Jens could hear the arrogance in his voice. 'Until my little brother proves me right. He will have your Dirk. But you?' Ahmet's tone softened. 'You will always have me.'

'And the wife, and the kids?'

'Why make it so difficult?!' Ahmet slapped Jens' sturdy behind and laughed. 'And while you think about it, I get something to eat. I'm hungry. You give me a big appetite.' He turned and entered the kitchen.

Having lined his belly with the contents of the fridge, Ahmet lit another cigarette and sat sideways on a kitchen chair, naked. One arm rested on the chair back, holding the cigarette. One heel rested on the bottom rung. Tan toes, with white nails, were splayed against the beige, tiled floor. His little paunch was stuffed with food. His eyes stared up at the ceiling, then flitted onto Dirk's face as he stood in the doorway.

Ahmet looked gorgeous, breathtaking even. Without a doubt he was one of the most handsome Bears that Jens had ever seen. And yet he regretted the fact that they had ever embarked on this fiasco of a relationship. Ahmet screwed with his head more than he ever did with his butt. Jens still could not get his head around how Ahmet could bat for both teams, and switch with such ease. In his hands, Ahmet was totally aroused and still he would avow his heterosexuality, wore it like a badge of pride.

'You want something to eat?' Ahmet took hold of his flaccid but still impressive cock with his right hand. He waggled it at Jens. Subtlety was not his forté. Still, it was a hard offer to refuse.

Somewhat reluctantly, Jens shook his head. 'I better be going, Ahmet. Ömer will be back from work soon. Or so you said.'

Ahmet stood, crossed the tiled floor and caught Jens roughly by the elbow as he turned towards the bedroom and his clothes. 'Maybe he will. Maybe not. Maybe he is even now fucking your boyfriend.'

Jens shook him off. 'I must go.'

Ahmet raised his hand, ran his fingers through his thick, coal-black hair. 'You will be back.'

'Don't count on it.'

Ahmet sat back at the kitchen table and spread the morning newspaper before him. 'You will be back.'

Eleven

At first, Jens thought it was the alarm ringing. But they hadn't set the alarm. Nevertheless, Dirk and Jens were being woken by a ringing sound, woken from a much needed sleep after a night on the town. The piercing sound of the telephone travelled from the living room, echoing down the hall and up the spiral staircase. Jens groaned. Dirk must have left the bedroom door open during the night. Five rings and then the answering machine kicked in. Then silence, as the pre-recorded message played unheard. Jens snuggled back down hopefully. Alas, Bodo's bass-baritone came booming out of the loudspeaker.

'I know you guys are at home. It's ten before twelve noon. High noon. Time you two were out of that pit of yours. What? Still no answer? Then I'm going to sing until you pick up the damn phone!' Bodo cleared his throat and began to warble. '"Do not forsake me, oh my Darling" . . . '

Dirk threw back the covers. 'I'll go get it.'

'Damn right you will!' Jens wrapped his pillow around his head, covering his ears from the dreadful caterwauling. 'And be quick about it.

Naked, Dirk sat cross-legged on the floor next to the phone. Picked up the cordless handset and extended the aerial. 'Will you shut the fuck up?! The last thing I need first thing in the morning is that racket!' He rubbed the sleep from his eyes with the heel of his hand.

'But Dirk, my friend, I thought you were a music lover?'

'Yeah, that's the problem.'

Bodo laughed.

Dirk yanked the receiver away from his ear, his head still thick from the night before. 'Do me a favour, Bodo. Keep your voice down a bit.'

'Feeling a little bit fragile, are we?'

'Didn't get to bed until four.'

Bodo clucked sympathetically. 'And then of course you still had to get up and come home?!'

'Yeah . . . ' Dirk cast around for a witty repast. Found one. 'Yeah, Volker didn't want me to leave but, like I told him, at least I'd kept the bed warm for you.'

'Think you're funny, don't you!'

'Don't think - know!'

'Don't suppose Volker would complain anyhow.'

'What? About your singing, or about my jokes?'

'About you keeping my side of the bed warm.'

'Now you're joking!'

'He's always had a soft spot for you, my friend.'

'Bodo, we both know Volker is terminally monogamous.'

'I think you could be the one to change all that . . . '

'Yeah, sure!' Dirk got to his feet and crossed to the window facing out onto the Hinterhof. Raising one arm, he rested the palm of his hand against the frame. 'You wouldn't have an ulterior motive for telling me this, now would you , Bodo?'

'Like?'

'I get to fuck Volker and you get to fuck Jens?!'

'You like the idea?'

'What you and Jens get up to is between you and him.' The answer seemed suitably vague and noncommittal 'But remember, Bodo. The guy does have some taste!'

'Fuck you!'

'Anyway -' Dirk changed the subject quickly to avoid further cross-examination '- where on earth did you get to the other night? Every time it gets to your round, you don't just disappear off to the bar - no, you just disappear. I was waiting for you for ages.'

'Got distracted.'

'How big was it?'

'Huge.'

'Tell me all about it!'

'I intend to . . . ' Suddenly his voice sounded muffled. Whispering? 'But not in front of Volker. You know what he's like. The less he knows _'

'- the better. Volker's there?'

Bodo mumbled, 'He's just come out of the shop and . . . ' His voice returned to normal. 'Yeah, we're in the area. Just around the corner in fact. Out for a ride -'

'So what's new?!'

'- on our bikes!! See you in about ten minutes, meathead.'

Twelve

How Jens ever got through his early morning class was anybody's guess. Maybe just on adrenaline alone. Everything had been okay, despite the fact that for the entire lesson, Jens' eyes had been hidden behind Ray-Bans. He had pleaded a migraine. Truth was, he had the mother of all hangovers. But somehow he had summoned up all of his depleted energy reserves and switched into performance mode as soon as the group were seated around the table. Running almost on empty, he had managed to stay awake throughout the hour and a half session.

Indeed, he had appeared to be his usual, charming self. His relationship with this particular group was now well established. It was a little like a mutual admiration society: they laughed a lot during their time together. Jens entertained them even as he taught them. And fortunately, they were more than happy to simply engage in conversation practice. Which was just as well on a day like today, since Jens was hardly in a fit state to discuss the precise meaning and usage of the third conditional.

Once the lesson was over, however, he quickly switched off. Wrecked. Now free until four p.m., he planned to head home and grab a couple of hours' sleep. Perhaps then he would feel human again. His stomach was playing up, too: groaning, churning, growling. Better get something to eat, that might help matters. A late breakfast and a long nap was in order.

He passed by Cafe Bleibruhig on his way to Savigny Platz S-Bahnoff and the train home. That would more than do. They made a great Omelette mit Schinken und Toast. Jens knew this for a fact, since he had had it countless times before. And the ambience of the place was laid back - to say the least - which, at this precise moment in time, was exactly what Jens needed. For the price of a cup of coffee you could sit and read a selection of newspapers and weekly magazines for hours on end. Perfect when you had time to kill between sessions. But today Jens wasn't in the mood to read; his mind was elsewhere. He took a table over by the window offering a comprehensive view of a bustling Kantstraße.

When the waitress took his order she gave him a wry smile. Maybe she was tipped off to his fragile condition by the sunglasses he still wore inside, or maybe it was the way his fingers pressed against his temple like it was the only thing keeping his head together.

Why had he done it? Why get so smashed the night before a morning class? A vain attempt to smother his troubled conscience. He hated this, hated sneaking around behind Dirk's back. Was Ahmet worth the hassle? The answer to that question was a big NO. And yet for some reason he was prepared to play this stupid game.

The waitress returned with a soup bowl sized cup of Milchcafé. He thanked her, attempting a smile.

What was it? What exactly was this hold Ahmet had over him? Jens didn't think he even liked Ahmet but, still, he was like a man obsessed. How many years had it taken Jens to feel comfortable with his sexuality? How many years before he could actually celebrate it? Ahmet didn't make Jens feel good about his sexuality. His own lack of acceptance dragged Jens down. And yet there was something darkly magical about the sex they had, something thrilling. In his secret heart, Jens took immense pleasure from the knowledge that Ahmet was a husband and father. Even as he admitted it to himself, Jens knew this feeling stemmed from some fucked-up part of his nature, but even so . . .

So much crap! Jens knew that this idea was just a pile of crap. The myth of the 'real man'. A myth that had been sold to him since the cradle. A potent myth, but a myth nonetheless. With his conscious mind, Jens knew that he all he was doing was buying into this lie - and yet Ahmet seemed to aggravate some deep, unreconciled wound in his psyche. Fuck! Fuck! Fuck!

'You think too much and you'll get a headache!'

A startled Jens looked up from twiddling his cup. Sabine sat down opposite him.

'Too late. I've already got one.'

'Need an aspirin?'

'Need a handful.'

'That bad?'

'And then some.'

Sabine reached into her bag. 'Only have two, I'm afraid.' She popped the tablets out of the foil covering and handed them over.

Jens swallowed them down with a gulp of coffee. 'So, what are you doing here at this time? Shouldn't you be staffing the front desk?'

'Kerstin is working a half-day today; I left her in charge. I've been in the office since seven. They can do without me for an hour.'

'That place would fall apart if it wasn't for you.'

Sabine reached over, squeezed his hand and smiled. Jens' order arrived. Sabine placed her order in turn. Jens tucked into his omelette with enthusiasm.

'You look hungry. When was the last time you ate? Last Thursday?'

'Let's call it comfort food.'

'You need some comfort. I have broad shoulders. Tell Auntie Sabine all about it.'

'Men. That's my problem.'

'I should be so lucky!' Sabine smiled, but the smile faded to concern when Jens didn't respond in kind. 'Is this about you and Dirk?'

'Yes . . . and no.' Jens peeled the gold foil from a small rectangle of butter and began to spread the butter on his toast methodically.

'Does that mean someone else is involved?'

'Naturally.'

Sabine turned her gaze towards the busy street outside. A bus pulled up. People got on. The bus drove away. 'I always envied you gay men.'

'Really? Why?'

'Oh, you know. The way you can have one partner, or two, or fifty-six if you were so inclined. But I guess there are always consequences.' She turned her gaze to focus once more upon him. 'Unavoidable consequences. Am I right?'

'It's funny. You think you've got it all sorted out in your mind.' He pointed to the half-eaten omelette with his knife, 'This is my primary relationship -' then pointed to the side salad '- and this is my bit of fun on the side.'

'Life is not so simple?'

'You just said one helluva mouthful, Sabine. One helluva mouthful.'

She toyed with her napkin. 'Maybe you should talk with Dirk?'

'Maybe.'

'Only maybe?'

'You're right.' He reached out and took hold of her hand. 'I should talk to him!'

With his classes cancelled for the rest of the day, Jens went home. He had told them that he was ill, although it was a lie. Still it seemed to be more than justified. He had stepped in at the last minute to help the company out of a hole often enough. Now it was time for the payback. He couldn't have worked at any rate. His mind was elsewhere. All of the things Ahmet had said were buzzing in his head. Not least, that Ömer had become a serious rival for Dirk's affections. But he was determined to sort things out once and for all. He would take the afternoon to prepare himself and then once Dirk walked through the door he would lay his cards on the table. Beg forgiveness. Talk things out.

He unlocked the door to the apartment, pushed against it and entered in, pleased that he would have the place to himself. Room to breathe and sort through some things. It was not to be.

The first thing he noticed when the door swept open was that it caught on something. That something was a trail of clothes on the hall carpet. A trail leading inextricably towards the spiral staircase up to the bedroom. Not one set of clothes, but two. Two checked work-shirts, two pairs of boots, two pairs of jeans, two pairs of sports socks, one athletic support hanging from the banister, one pair of French-cut briefs on the second step.

Jens followed the trail on tip-toe. Furious. Didn't they have an agreement? You don't shit on your own doorstep. You don't bring your tricks home to the marriage bed. But the closer he got to the bed-room, the louder the grunts and groans became. And as the volume increased, so did Jens' rage. For it was undeniable now: Dirk was hard at it and, unless he was much mistaken, Jens knew exactly who with.

Peering through the crack in the bedroom door, Jens' fears were confirmed. The curtains were closed, blotting out the sun, and two lit candles cast a warm glow over the naked flesh resting atop the king-size bed. Dirk was on his back, but a beautiful bubble-butt was strad-dling his face. His partner's head bobbed up and down, swallowing Dirk's impressive length. Consumed it with a gasping, slobbering enthusiasm. Dirk, in turn, sucked on his partner's balls, letting his fin-gers play with the cleft between buttocks spread wide and wanting.

With an urgency that surprised even Jens, Dirk manoeuvred his partner up to sit squarely on his face. Buttocks spread wide, embrac-ing Dirk's face. His mouth buried deep, snaffling and sucking on one juicy, tender arsehole. His partner groaned, threw back his head and .

. . There could be no doubting it was Ömer. Ömer in rapture. Riding Dirk's face. Parting his own cheeks ever wider, grinding his arsehole down. Groaning and grunting with rapture. 'That's it, baby. Eat me, baby. Eat my hole.'

Dirk pulled back and stuck out his tongue. He traced the puckered ring with the glistening tip. Then slammed his face back in with increasing vigour.

Ömer arched his back, rode the tidal wave of lust. He was battered by Dirk's tongue, swept away by the force of nature. And then the words tumbled out of Ömer's mouth, the words that bowled Jens over, knocked him for six. 'Eat me, baby. Lick my hole. Oh, I love you, baby. I love you, Dirk. I love you! I love you! I love you!'

And the realisation hit home. Jens had to clasp a hand across his mouth to stifle his shocked reaction. Love? Fucking hell! Just what was going on here?! Dirk's reaction shocked Jens even more, because he seemed simply to redouble his efforts. Encouraged? Pleased? In love with Ömer, too?!

Ahmet had been right. He had been telling him the truth. But Jens, like a fool, had not wanted to hear it - refused to believe it. And now here was the evidence slapping him in the face. Jens staggered back down the stairs. Unable to stifle the urge, he slammed the door behind him and made his exit down the stairs and out of the door without so much as a backward glance.

Thirteen

Ahmet aimed and fired, splashing saffron-yellow piss against the white ceramic urinal. Simultaneously, he released a sigh of relief, one palm pressed against the tiled wall to steady his gait, the other encircled his corpulent handful. When soft, it was still as big as most men hard; hard, it was twice the size of most men.

The door to the Gents' opened and closed behind him, first exposing then smothering the racket from the street. Casting an eye about him to ensure they were alone, the newcomer walked to Ahmet's side and stood silent and intent. Eyes front, Ahmet's gaze hardened to a frown, and the outpouring from his bladder halted abruptly. Menacingly, he jerked his head sharp right. But then, clearly pleased, his features melted into the warmest smile. And, after the pause, his free-flowing discharge resumed full force.

'André, what a surprise. Thirsty, are you?' Ahmet asked, winking and indicating down to his open fly.

'I'll have a glass . . . Maybe two?' André cupped his palm midstream, then brought dripping wet fingers to his lips and licked them. Careful not to let any droplets splash on to his smart, blue, pin-striped suit. It felt good to tease Ahmet, to watch the blood flow into his organ like air into a Zeppelin. 'But let's go somewhere more private. How about the first cubicle on the left? '

'After you.' With a jerk of his head, Ahmet indicated the doorway to the cubicle. Then looked down. 'Look what you have done to me! You have got me all hot. So hot.' André was clearly dying for it, a fact Ahmet had every intention of exploiting to my advantage. 'You have money? I have a need, my friend.' Ahmet shook loose the last few salty droplets from his crimson cockhead and turned his head to face his customer. André nodded. Folding his cock into his pants with some significant difficulty, Ahmet led the way.

*

By the time Jens entered the Klappe there was nothing to be seen. At first glance the place appeared to be empty, but it couldn't be. Jens had seen Ahmet enter and had waited for him to come out. No show. There was no other exit, save for the one through which he himself had just entered. Three cubicles stood to his left. One without a door, one with the door ajar and the last closed. Grey paint peeling, graffiti scraped on the panels. Then, unless he was much mistaken, Jens heard a grunt from behind the closed door. With a last quick check over his shoulder, he dropped to his knees and peered under the gap in the door. Two pairs of boots. As quietly as possible, he eased into the cubicle alongside. He looked around, saw the glory hole, threw the latch and seated himself. Peering through the spy hole, he caught sight of the action within.

The only thing that had run through Jens' mind since storming out of the apartment was the need to see Ahmet. And why? Fuck only knew! To fuck him? To be fucked by him? To get his own back on Dirk? But there had been no answer when he had phoned. So he jumped on the subway and made the journey with no assurance of success. Only hope.

What were the chances of seeing Ahmet on the street? What chance of seeing him enter the cottage just a hundred yards from his own apartment? Couldn't Ahmet wait five minutes?! Fat chance that the guy was after a piss. Public toilets served a host of public services. No wonder then, that the city council had all but eradicated them. All but this one. A welcome exception.

Jens pressed his ear up against the partition but could barely make out a sound. Maybe, if he strained really hard . . . ? Maybe if he placed his ear directly up against the hole? But no, that might have drawn their attention to him. Still, what was that? The muffled sounds of heavy breathing and clothing rustling, or simply his fertile imagination? Peering through the hole, he could not see very much at all. All he could see, at best, was blue denim and pin-striped enclosed crotches rubbing together. Hopefully it would get better than this. Jens figured that if he angled his head correctly, he might be able to see a bit more of what was going on. So, crouching down, he looked in and up and could catch glimpses of a moustachioed face with the unmistakable triangle of hair under his lower lip, which was definitely Ahmet, while the other guy looked like a goateed skinhead in a business suit.

There was some movement as the skinhead removed his suit jacket, hanging it neatly on the hook on the door behind him, no doubt. Jens peered in once more to see the skinhead, his bald head bowed in concentration, systematically unbuttoning Ahmet's denim shirt. He caught a glimpse of Ahmet's hairy chest. And, finally the shaved upper body of the skinhead with his big, fuck-off tattoo over one shoulder and upper arm and his two pierced tits - as his own shirt was discarded.

Then came the delicious sound of zippers being unzipped, trousers being pulled down and the sight of cocks being revealed. Ahmet's dick, rock hard and ready for action. The skinhead with a Prince Albert piercing. So Ahmet was faithful to his wife and Jens, was he? Oh, yeah. Sure he was! Cocks that now were being rubbed together? That was just accidental!

The skinhead dropped to his knees sucking hungrily on Ahmet's purple prince. Licking the balls, taking the ballsac into his mouth.

What the hell, thought Jens, as the blood began to pulse between his legs. Moments later, his cock was out, trousers round his knees, as he began to pull on his meat.

The skinhead was standing again, leaning up against the back wall of the cubicle. And Ahmet was rubbing his cock against the other man's arse crack. Then spitting on his fingers, greasing up and sticking first one finger, then two, three, four fingers into the skinhead's hungry hole. His customer, it seemed, couldn't get enough of it. He was pushing back, riding on Ahmet's fingers. Sucking them inside of himself. Pulling on his own cock.

Ahmet produced a condom from his shirt pocket and began to unroll it over his cock. He was fully erect, his cock fat and glistening with pre-come.

Jens was thirsty just looking at it.

Without further ado, Ahmet stuck his cock in - right in - in one fuck-off show of power. He was the boss man here. Skinhead pressed back, riding the cock furiously. And not just pulling, but yanking on his cock now.

Jens discarded all thoughts of jealousy. He was beyond that now. He was incredibly turned on. He stuck his fingers through the hole. He knocked on the wall. Ahmet was distracted from his labours, but did not seem in the least bit shocked. Not even when he saw the fingers poking through the hole and realised he was being observed. A third party, hot to trot. He was flattered.

The skinhead repositioned himself and stuck his shaved cock through the glory hole. Ahmet began to fuck him again, slamming him up against the wall of the cubicle. Jens licked the juddering cock-head, ran his tongue around the sculpted ridge, felt the cool metal of the skinhead's Prince Albert on his tongue. He took the cock into his mouth and sucked on it, sucked on it as if it were Ahmet's cock.

Cock and balls were now stuffed through the glory hole. The skinhead's body pressed up against the wall once more, his cock straining. Jens could feel the violence of Ahmet's thrusts as the skinhead's cock battered his own throat. Deeper and deeper. Harder and harder. The cock was pulsating in his mouth. Straining, bursting.

Jens stood, rubbed his own throbbing member against the skinhead's cock, lubricating it with his pre-come. He pulled gently on the Prince Albert, then dropped down on his knees to suck the skinhead's prick. He could actually hear the muffled moans from next door. Ahmet's testosterone laced grunts. Heavy breathing. The slap of flesh on flesh.

The skinhead was now emitting regular and very audible moans. If anyone came in here now, thought Jens, they were certain to be arrested. Saved by the come shot, the skinhead let loose and started to shoot. His come blasted the opposite wall of the cubicle, jet after jet of come. Jens blew too, spraying the scuzzy floor with his jism and, in doing so, heard Ahmet reach his peak next door. He had heard him come enough times to know that this orgasm was a prize winner.

Now Jens could hear the sound of toilet roll being torn from the holder as it echoed against the tiles. Everyone was cleaning up. Jens waited his turn, only stepping out when he thought the coast would be clear. His timing was almost perfect. Outside the cubicle, he only saw the back of Ahmet's head as he disappeared through the exit door. Jens washed his hands, alongside the skinhead businessman. He looked like a hunky bank manager or the like, with his suit and briefcase. Fixing his tie in the mirror, he gave Jens a broad smile, a wink and, with a 'ciao', he was out the door.

Jens let the cold tap run, cupped his hands beneath it, and splashed his face. Raising his head, he too now looked in the mirror. He watched the water droplets run down his face, hang from the end of his nose. 'Where to now?' He spoke to the empty space. 'Where to now?'

Fourteen

Bodo's feet had been buffed and scrubbed in the bath that morning. Volker knew that for a fact. He had done the soaping. Now at the end of another day's labour, he yanked off Bodo's workboots and peeled the first woolly sock from his size elevens. Bringing Bodo's foot to his face, Volker licked the salty under-sole. Squirming and wriggling like a child being tickled, Bodo fought the impulse to pull away and relaxed as Volker's lips gently encased each thick, square toe. Bodo's feet were immaculate. Big and strong and masculine. Volker would have crammed one up his arsehole if he could but have taken the fucker.

Yes, they had done or tried just about everything during the course of their two-year relationship. Still, Bodo managed to excite Volker as much as he ever had. Particularly his big, bearded, beautiful face and all the expressions that sex kicked into play. His lust was aggressive, vocalised in coarse terms of endearment that jostled with vulgar demands and all in a rasping drawl. Talk of marriage had not altered that. If anything, it enhanced it. They had talked about having a commitment ceremony sometime soon. Bodo had even got down on one knee. But beyond exchanging rings on their first anniversary, they had yet to get to grips with organising the event. Bodo had a habit of putting off until tomorrow what he could do today. But happen it would. The sooner the better, as far as Volker was concerned. He wanted to make a public declaration of his love for Bodo. Bodo, his big Honig Bär.

Bodo popped the button fly on his cut-off jeans and eased them down over his hairy knees, before hiking his T-shirt up above his tits. He then lay back on the sofa. Whilst one rough paw tugged and squeezed the neck of his scrotum, forcing two big red bollocks to swell fit to burst, the other was busy tweaking his own nipples. Volker looked longingly at his lover's eight fat inches of twitching power tool, as Bodo's cock strained and swayed, fully erect. At the same time he continued to suck and lick ferociously between Bodo's toes. Volker behaved like a complete glutton. He would have eaten Bodo if he could have.

'Volker! Volker, you bastard! You know what that does to me . . . I can't fuckin' hold back . . . can't fuckin' hold back! You horny little cunt, you fuckin', horny little bastard cunt!'

And without further stimulation, a translucent flash of jism flew from Bodo's quivering dong, straight up in the air. Bodo groaned and fired again and again. A regular pulse, as he clutched his ballsac. He pumped it out: painfully, ecstatically. Volker thought Bodo was going bring the neighbours running, he was howling so loud. But then the noise level subsided, as the last few globules trickled from Bodo's spent knobhead. Nevertheless, his body continued to tremble and shake for a good few minutes afterwards.

Having emptied himself now, Bodo rested back on the sofa. He closed his eyes, smacked his lips and grinned. Volker sat alongside him, snuggling into him.

Bodo threw a meaty arm around Volker's shoulder and drew him closer. 'Nobody makes me come like you do, Volker. No fucker. No way. You blow all my fuses.'

Of his ability to give Bodo the best orgasms he had ever experienced, Volker was supremely confident. For he was equally aware that Bodo's compliment came with the voice of extensive experience. Monogamy was never going to be part of any marriage arrangement between the two of them. Bodo loved sex. The more sex the better. A third-rate orgasm being preferable to none. And Berlin was so full of handsome and very available men . . .

For his part, Volker had never played the field. Perhaps he would have, if Bodo had not been the first in the queue. Bodo had come into his young life at a time when he had desperately needed the loving care of a big Papa Bear. As a small-town boy, he would probably have been eaten up by decadent Berlin and all the pleasures on offer had he not had Bodo's protective arm around him and a ready-made home to stay close to. But he was learning all the time, not least of all how to please a man. Once he had felt weak, but Bodo had made him feel incredibly powerful. Now Volker was leading from behind. Leading with his behind? Volker smiled. He could wrap Big Daddy Bodo around his little finger simply by wrapping his mouth around his toes.

Having climbed up the four flights of stairs, Jens paused to catch his breath before buzzing to enter. As the door swung open, the familiar smell of chlorine enveloped him like the arms of a sympathetic friend. He paid the entrance fee and was given, in return, a fluffy, cream towel and a key to his designated cabin.

A short while later, suitably stripped and attired, he made for the bar. There was an eerie silence about the place. Okay, so it was normal that on a mid-week evening like this, the sauna would be less full than on a weekend. But tonight it seemed more like a ghost town; there was almost no one was around. Just as well. Jens shrugged his shoulders. He was not in the mood for company. He would just get his beer and then lock himself away.

The bar was deserted. The barman, idly dusting glasses, raised a jaundiced eye as Jens entered, as if to say: 'What? You actually want me to serve you?' Will I ever get used to Berlin attitude, Jens asked himself. Back home, the customer was king - over here, the customer was all too often considered an unwanted and unnecessary distraction. Naja! He'd just let it go over his head. Climbing on to a bar stool , he ordered a Hefeweizen beer. But before it could be poured, someone sat on the seat alongside him. Jens turned his head and was met by the man's lecherous gaze. He next noted the broad smile, the square jaw, the moustache and close-cropped hair.

'Hi!' the stranger said, drinking him in. 'Sprechst du English?'

That question again: 'Do you speak English?' Jens had heard it so often. Another sex tourist? The stranger's accent was ripe with an unmistakable American twang.

'You from the U.S.?'

The stranger looked pleasantly surprised. 'And you?'

'German-American.'

'I've got a little bit of German in me too. But then I could take a whole lot more . . . ' He winked, and shuffled his arse against his seat. He couldn't have made his intentions any plainer if he had parted his buttocks and pointed to his hole.

Jens fixed a smile on his face.

'First time here?' the stranger asked.

'Yeah, just up from Köln until the weekend,' Jens lied.

'What's your line of business?'

'Construction.' Another lie.

'Oh! Blue collar . . . That's interesting!' The stranger licked his lips, clearly salivating. His chunky torso was carpeted with chestnut-brown hair, flecked with grey. A cute little pot of a beer belly rested on the tuck of his towel. He was clearly on for it but, unfortunately, Jens was not. Another time maybe, but not at that moment. The stranger let his eyes drink Jens in.

'And yourself?' Jens asked.

'What?' The other man answered as if distracted. He dragged his eyes away from Jens' hairy thighs.

'What do you do?'

'Lawyer, all the way from New York. Phil's the name . . . ' He held out his hand.

Jens took it. 'Chuck's mine.' One lie begetting another. Still he kept a straight face.

'Berlin's pretty hot, huh?'

'I wouldn't know, it's my first time.' Lying or acting? Same difference.

'Oh! A virgin . . . even more interesting!'

'Not quite. It's my first time here. You go to the baths in New York?'

'No, never!' the strength of Phil's response took Jens by surprise. 'There it's full of hairdressers and clones . . . ' The sneer in his voice was matched by the look on his face, 'Manicured men! I prefer a rough mix. I find you get that here in Germany or Amsterdam or just Europe, generally. White and blue collar. I like real men.' The smile returned to his face, that lecherous smile. 'Guys like you, you could say.'

Jens looked down and rubbed his palms together. He changed tack. Looking around, the place almost empty. 'Doesn't look like there's much action in here?'

'It's mid-week. I've just got to look harder! Keep an eye out - you never know who'll walk through the door!' The play of Phil's eyes left no doubt as to the implication. Jens was the only worthwhile guy who had entered in the last hour. 'I'd check out the damp sauna next to the showers. That can be pretty orgiastic if you can deal with the heat. Then you could do a round of the cabins. Someone as good looking as you should be able to take their pick.' He paused meaningfully. 'I've got me a cabin . . . ' He paused, meaningfully.

The implication was clear. Was it also clear that Jens did not pick up on the offer? Jens hoped so. He took a slug of his beer.

Phil coughed, changed the subject. 'So . . . Do you have a partner?'

Wrong question.

Phil ploughed on. 'Dumb question, I guess? Of course you do. A big hunk like you . . . '

Jens toyed with his beer mat. 'And you? Do you have a partner?'

Phil held up his wedding band. 'Been together five years.' He left a pause. 'So, what am I doing here, huh?' Phil chuckled. 'Gene - that's his name, my partner - Gene and I have an agreement, you know? He's back at the hotel right now. He picked up some guy in a bar earlier .' He ran the tip of his index finger around the rim of his beer glass. 'He said he might drop by later. You should meet him. I'm sure he'd love to meet you.'

Jens stood, just a little too abruptly. 'I think I'll check the place out.'

'Oh . . . okay!' Phil could barely disguise his disappointment. 'Might see you later then?'

'Yeah, maybe.' Jens picked up his glass and strolled towards the TV area and the cabins beyond. Another time, another place, Phil might have struck lucky. But not right now. And not after pushing all the wrong buttons. Yet another wide-open relationship! Jens had too much on his mind. He simply wanted time out, behind closed doors. A chance to hibernate and think things through. A chance to lick his wounds.

The sound of music filled the apartment. Swelling from the speakers and rising in waves. 'La Sonambula'. Cologne, July the 4th, 1957. Dirk smiled to himself. Jens always made jokes about his Callas obsession. He said the recordings - particularly the live ones - sounded as though they'd been recorded in a biscuit tin. Dirk didn't care. He liked the warm crackling tones, the immediacy of a live performance, the act of tightrope walking in front of an audience without the benefit of a safety net. Living life on the edge. A bit like his own life at the moment, he thought.

Earlier, much earlier, when he had heard the door slam, Dirk had been on his feet in a jiffy. He had run to the window and watched Jens walk away down the street. Too late to catch him up. Fuck! He and Ömer had hurriedly dressed and set out to find him. But they had had no luck so far. Now, after searching their usual haunts for the last couple of hours, there was nothing to do but wait and hope. Hope that Jens would ring. Ömer was still out there looking for Jens but Dirk, they had reasoned, would be better off sitting at home by the phone. The hours dragged past. And still no word.

All of this complicated relationship stuff. Dirk had always thought of Jens and his relationship as the safety net in his life. The one thing

that was at the basis of everything else, providing stability and allowing both of them to develop separately in the knowledge that they
had this firm foundation. Now, however, he found himself questioning whether this safety net was there at all. And when, precisely, had
it been removed? Okay, they had both drifted into the three-ways and
stuff, but that all seemed harmless enough, didn't it? And, okay, there
were those times when one guy would be more into Jens than Dirk, or
vice versa, which had - he had to admit - caused a few tears before bed-
time. But they had talked about it, hadn't they? Had sorted through
the issue of jealousy, hadn't they? Then Ömer came on to the scene
and suddenly things seemed to take on their own momentum. What
was the logical outcome of it all? If the safety net no longer existed,
would it be possible to remake one, but this time including Ömer? Or
was that something that Dirk alone wanted? Questions, questions,
and not a single answer in sight. Well, no easy answer. Relationships
were so fucking complicated.

As if on cue, Callas' voice came from the speaker. 'Ah! non credea
mirati'. It was the famous sleepwalking scene of the title. Her voice
mirrored how Dirk was feeling. Callas' character, Amina, has just
walked across a rickety bridge with a raging river beneath. Somehow,
she manages to get across, and the obvious danger of the situation
convinces her fiancé, Elvino, that she sleepwalks, and so is innocent
of the infidelity charge which had been brought against her. All's well
that ends well. If only real life were so simple, thought Dirk. Maybe
that was the appeal of this stuff - that even desperately complicated
situations somehow got resolved. Though thinking about it, there was
resolution and there was resolution. While Dirk might not have mind-
ed a bit of harmless sleepwalking, he didn't really fancy being walled
up in an Egyptian tomb like poor old Aida. Nah, there had to be an
easier way. Bodo had suggested that he and Jens should just sit down
and talk about what was going on. Which was, of course, the right
thing to do, but the time and place never seemed to present itself. And

what was that about? Both of them seemed to be avoiding the situation, running into a head-on collision. A crash. A bust-up, like today. If only they had talked it through . . .

It was around midnight when Jens finally emerged from his cabin. Surprisingly, the place was beginning to buzz. Maybe these guys hadn't struck lucky in the bars? Who knew. Having smoked a couple spliffs, Jens was too mellow to care. His anger had dissipated with each toke, as had his ability to think clearly or find a resolution.

Again he was hiding, lost in the pages of a German Illustrierte. Sitting on a couch near the TV area, flicking through a copy of Praline or other, similar, soft core sexposé magazines. Cheap entertainment for the masses. 'Housewife-Prostitutes Tell All!'; 'Sexual Aerobics: Light His Fire And Burn Those Calories!!'; 'Wife-Swappers Find True Love!!!' Jens, however, was a discerning reader - only interested in the naked photos of readers' husbands and the like, naturally. Naked heterosexual male flesh always gave Jens a certain perverse charge. Forbidden fruit? Heterosexual cocks proudly on display. 'One for the Ladies!!' Did all those dumb fuckers really believe they were being appraised and enjoyed by women? Who did they think bought the magazine?! Straight men could be so stupid. He drank deep from his fresh beer, wiped the froth from his moustache with his bottom lip and set the magazine he was perusing aside with all the others. The wet sauna was calling and he got to his feet.

An outer door led to an inner door before Jens hit the sanctum of the damp sauna. A double blast of menthol vapours and searing mist threatened to overwhelm him. The heat was blinding. As Jens' eyes grew accustomed to the dark and humid conditions, shapes began to materialise within the haze. Wooden benches framed the walls on either side. Two figures seated, two standing took the form of shadow puppets and, in profile, four voluptuous cocks jutted out proudly whilst being lovingly caressed. From some distance in front of Jens came the sound of dick being viciously thwacked, foreskin retracted and released, backwards and forwards. Jens' cock leapt reflexively and began to throb as the scalding heat matched the fire in Jens' belly.

As Jens made his way towards the far end of the sauna, he brushed past yet more anonymous, naked bodies; bodies that turned hopefully towards him, reached out to stroke his stiffening cock as he passed by. But he carried on regardless, determined to reach his destination. And, in finally doing so, he turned and sat on the sodden plank of the back bench.

Jens' hand fell to his lap and began to squeeze and pull, pumping and teasing his cock to a full-blown erection. The clouds of steam dissipated somewhat and, as Jens strained his eyes to see, a huge, stiff phallus emerged out of the darkness. With legs spread, the guy stood tall, slapping his stiffy with a vengeance. The moment Jens fixed his eyes on the guy's magnificent whanger, a shudder of lust swept through his entire body, threatening to make him pop his cork right there, right then. Abruptly, Jens let go of his own prick. He rested back, gazing in wonderment. Out of the clouds of steam stepped a second powerfully built figure. Back-lit by the dim light afforded by the double glass doors, muscular thighs led up to a nipped-in waist, topped by a broad chest and shoulders. Cock in hand, he walked to the wall beside Jens and stood sensuously wanking on a good eight inches.

Jens' heart beat rapidly inside his rib cage, pounding like a hammer, as every nerve in his body sprang to life. It was like a dream, like some fabulous wet dream. Such a debauched scene. Totally surreal and yet here he was in the midst of it all, trembling with lust; flicking his gaze from one hot length to the other and back again. He could see neither faces nor features. Just two mouth-watering members. What to do? Reach over and make a grab?

Any decision was to be delayed as the door opened not once, but three times, heralding new arrivals. Jens' partners in crime slowed down their exertions and grew still. Minutes passed. Moisture from the ceiling plopped on Jens' head like raindrops. The three newcomers prowled around but, finding no action, they exited again quickly. The three of them were left alone to get on with the business at hand.

The man standing beside Jens now sat himself alongside and, after a moment's hesitation, made his move. His big, horny fingers encircled Jens' cock and began to tug. Jens closed his eyes and surrendered to his senses; to touch and taste and smell and sound. It was enough to be so desired, to take comfort in this intimate contact with another male body. Jens reached across and took a firm hold of the cock on offer. The recipient of his attentions seemed only too grateful to hand over responsibility and let Jens take a turn. His thick, circumcised cock was dripping wet with sweat and condensation, a double handful that swelled to rock solid in response to Jens' touch. He was hard but his flesh felt like silk. He leaned forward and drew close to kiss Jens' cheek, then stuck his tongue in Jens' ear and licked the inside.

Whist massaging the length of the shaft with one hand, Jens cupped his palm around the guy's cockhead and rolled it over the bulbous head, around and around; the tip grew sticky with pre-come and Jens worked it with his thumb, spreading the goo in an even layer. The guy's mouth worked its way along the underside of Jens' chin, around and across his cheek, towards his mouth. Tender lips brushed against his. Jens sucked on his top lip, then the bottom. The guy parted his lips willingly. Jens slipped his tongue into the other man's welcoming mouth. Then the battle of tongues began in earnest.

How long were they like that? How long before Jens opened his eyes and saw for the first time that it was Ömer? Up close, where his eyebrows met, he was unmistakable; the phantom of the sauna revealed in all his glory. Shock. Jens was in shock. But he disguised it admirably, because he was so turned on. Maybe Ömer hadn't yet realised. And even as Jens was trying to get his head around this, the third guy was beside Jens on the bench, trying to force his head between their heaving bellies; trying to get his mouth around Ömer's cock. Jens was in an accommodating mood. He eased back, allowing the third guy access between them. Head and shoulders manoeuvred their way into the gap, folding across Jens' lap. The third guy fell onto Ömer's dick and began to suck hard.

Ömer groaned as his assailant's lips gripped and furiously worked his boner, the ravenous mouth encircling the bulbous head. Jens played with Ömer's nipples and sucked on his lips whilst squeezing droplets of lubricant from the other guy's cock. They were gone; both of them off their heads, but Jens' thoughts became more clearly focused. Ömer had let go of Jens' knob and in so doing Jens regained a measure of composure.

His mind was racing. Here he was poking his tongue into the same mouth that had so thoroughly convinced him that he was a cuckold. Then why was he clearly getting off on kissing Ömer? A form of sweet revenge? Instinct overriding all reason? Enough analysis! Jens was all fired up and was not about to halt the proceedings to cross-examine himself. But could he examine Ömer's body? With pleasure! Jens allowed his left hand to fall onto the curve of Ömer's shoulder and down along the fulsome bulge of his bicep. He imagined artwork under his fingers, a tribal tattoo freshly engraved in ink, as his hand slid over skin the texture of wet velvet. Jens' fingers traced the veins on Ömer's succulent, hairy forearm and beyond, to where his hand cradled the other guy's head as he bobbed and swallowed. Reaching up to his tits now, Jens' fingers' brushed against tensed up pecs, and nipples as sharp as tacks.

'Ughhh!' Ömer moaned. A guttural sound that was so full of testosterone it made Jens' toes curl. Jens tweaked and tugged again.

'Ughh! Ughhhh! . . .

The third man took his cue, intent on facilitating Ömer's climax. All it had taken was a little verbal encouragement to shift the suck-monster up a gear; working his mouth like a wild thing; moaning and snorting through lips pressed tight. He basted Ömer's roasting joint with a vengeance. For his part, Ömer seemed set to drive it home as he ate Jens' face with increasing rapture. Then Ömer buried his mouth into the nape of Jens' neck and ejected his bollock-load over the head of one very grateful recipient.

Having achieved his aim, the third man rested his head on Jens' thigh. Jens, in turn, laid a hand on the guy's head and, inadvertently massaged Ömer's come into his scalp. Finally, with a satisfied sigh, the guy got to his feet and strolled out the door without so much as a backward glance. Jens didn't bother to stifle his laughter. Ömer did it for him. He leaned forward, taking Jens' face in his huge palms and planted a big sloppy kiss square on Jens' lips. That shut Jens up. Resting forward against Jens' chest, Ömer let out an exhausted sigh of his own as Jens held him in his arms. Then he too got to his feet and, without a word, he was gone. Jens sat back, stunned. Hadn't Ömer recognised him? He must have recognised him! Or was this just his way of saying 'Fuck you!'? If so, it had worked. Jens' balls were on fire and here he was sitting on his ownsome. 'Thanks pal!' Jens said aloud, his words echoing off the walls into an otherwise empty void.

By the time he came out, neither Ömer nor the third man were anywhere to be seen. Jens showered and dried and headed for a drink. Ashamed. Confused. Frustrated. Angry. He needed a beer and he needed it badly. He reasoned that he had sweated out so much fluid that his body was threatening to turn into a prune.

Phil the lawyer was still propping up the bar opposite him as he parked his butt on a bar stool. 'Any luck?' he asked with no enthusiasm.

'Plenty', Jens replied.

Phil gave Jens a military salute and let his eyes fall onto the contents of his beer glass. Sitting on the stool wasn't easy; Jens' balls were aching to the point of distraction. He ordered another beer and, just as it was being delivered, saw from the corner of his eye that the seat next to him had been taken. That Phil, thought Jens, he just can't take a hint. Jens turned to say, 'Please, go away! I'm not interested!' but instead he found himself saying simply, 'Ömer . . . '

Ömer raised his index finger to Jens' lips and shut Jens up once more. Then he took Jens' hand and led him through a warren of corridors to 318.

'How did you know this was mine?'

'Just thought it. This where we met, remember?'

Jens turned the key in the lock. 'Hard to forget.'

Ömer locked the door behind them as Jens took a long swig out of his beer glass. It hit the spot, ice cold, and Jens was getting hotter by the minute.

'Lie down,' Ömer said, pointing to the bed. 'This time I do all the work.'

Jens didn't object. His cock was stiff as a poker and straining against the wrap around towel. It was cast aside in a jiffy and he lay back expectantly. Ömer dropped his towel to the floor, and Jens copped a full view of his now-flaccid penis and pendulous bollocks. Ömer had nothing, absolutely nothing to be ashamed of. He tossed Jens a condom, then tore the seal on a sachet of KY with his teeth and squeezed a glistening wad onto his index finger. Hoisting one foot up onto the bed, he bent over, parted his buttocks and proceeded to douse and then lubricate his own sphincter. Jens truly had a ringside seat.

'You're going to come inside my hairy hole, Jens. You're going to spray a condom full, if I have to ride you all night long.' And without another word, he climbed onto the bed and straddled the object of his desire between his thighs. Fixing Jens' pride and joy between his buttocks, Ömer slid backwards down the latex pole. His face was a picture, lips curled up in a big, blissful smile as he wriggled down from tip to base, simultaneously letting out a groan of pleasure and pain.

'Ohhhhhh . . . '

In the aftermath, as they lay in each other's arms, in each others sweat and ball juice, Ömer asked Jens that question again. 'You want a three-way friendship, or no?'

'Uh-huh . . . ' Jens grunted in reply.

Ömer wrestled Jens back, pinning him down with his full weight. 'All friends together. I do want this. And you?'

A smile spread across Jens' face, like the sun emerging from behind the clouds. 'Uh-huh . . . '

Now it was Jens' tongue that prevented Ömer from speaking any further . . .

When Dirk heard the key turn in the lock, he jumped to his feet and hurried out into the hall. Ömer entered the apartment alone. Dirk's shoulder's dropped in disappointment. And then Ömer smiled his glorious smile and beckoned for Jens to come in. Dirk heaved a sigh of relief and swept Jens up in a big Bear hug. They stayed that way for the longest time, each clinging to the other. Ömer stuffed his hands into the pockets of his leather jacket and stood aside. He looked on and smiled until the point when Jens reached out an arm and drew him into the scrum.

Finally, Ömer extricated himself. 'I think I better be going. You guys need time to yourselves.'

Jens kissed him. 'Thanks, Ömer.'

Dirk kissed him. 'Thanks for everything.'

'No problem. Take care of each other, you guys!' And with that, Ömer skipped off down the stairs. Hop, skip and a jump. Like a boy springing down a hill path and padding over rocks. Two beautiful feet. Toes that Jens had sucked, soles he had licked this very evening whilst Ömer trembled with pleasure. Now Ömer was bouncing down the steps now on those selfsame feet. And Dirk finally closed the door behind him, as his footsteps faded.

All was quiet now. Dirk took Jens by the hand and led him through to the lounge. They sat down side by side on the green suede sofa and, as Dirk put his arm around Jens' shoulders, Jens leaned into his lover, resting his head on his chest.

'God, but I'm sorry, Jens.'

'Me too.'

'I'm glad you came home.'

'Me too.'

'I've been so worried about you.' Dirk kissed Jens on his forehead. 'Do you forgive me?'

'Yes, I forgive you.'

'You're not angry anymore?'

'No. I've had plenty of time to think. I'm not even sure if I was angry. More shocked than angry. Jealous, maybe. But then I realised that I really don't have any right.'

'You have every right! I should have told you.'

Jens hesitated. 'Look, Dirk, I've got a confession of my own.'

Dirk was equally hesitant in his response. 'And what is that, sweetheart?'

'I've been . . . having an affair.' He corrected himself quickly. 'No. An affair is not the right word. I've been fucking someone and I didn't tell you.'

A pause. 'How long?'

'On and off for . . . three months or so.'

'Your own private fuck buddy.'

'Yes.'

'Do I know him?'

'I should think so. It's Ahmet, Ömer 's brother.'

'Really? That hunk? Good for you!'

Jens lifted his head from Dirk's chest and turned his face to look at him. Dirk was grinning like a Cheshire cat.

'Well, I hoped you wouldn't take the news too badly but I didn't expect such a positive response.' He lay his head down on Dirk's shoulder with a thunk.

Dirk gave him a squeeze. 'Fuck! You should have told me. I would have suggested a foursome.'

'You wouldn't if you knew him. He's crap in bed. Anyway, that's all over as of now.'

'Sure?'

'Positive. He's an arsehole.'

'Well, I'll be . . . '

'I'm glad you're taking it so well!'

Dirk chuckled. 'Actually, I've got a confession to make too, Honey Bear. I already knew you were carrying on with him.'

Jens sat bolt upright. 'You knew!'

'The guy has been sharing all the grizzly details with Ömer.'

'The arsehole!'

'Yep. He's been saying how you're a glutton for cock. How you bend over at any given opportunity. How you keep begging him to leave his wife and get it together with you on a full-time basis.'

'But you didn't believe him?!'

'Oh, the first two statements are true enough . . . '

Jens punched him playfully.

'But the last . . . Nah, you'd never leave me.'

'No, I wouldn't.'

'You know which side your bread is buttered on!'

Jens snuggled in close. 'Dirk?'

'Yes?'

'Earlier, when I saw you in bed with Ömer . . . '

'Yes, baby.'

Jens swallowed hard. 'I heard Ömer saying that he loved you.'

'He loves us both, Baby Bear.'

'I know that now.'

'So?'

'Let's go to bed.'

Again Dirk kissed Jens' forehead. 'Tired?'

'No. But I will be once you've given me a good fucking.'

Dirk stood. Looked down. Held out a hand to pull Jens to his feet. 'There you go again! Bending over at any opportunity!'

'I can't believe Ahmet said that, the arsehole! He's such a twisted little shit!!'

'Forget him.'

'Oh, believe me. He's forgotten already. He's history!'

Fifteen

Ömer's German was improving all the time, thanks to Jens and Dirk - and not just his sexual vocabulary, either. And he was also now attending Second Level German classes at the Volkshochschule every week to further improve his skills. It was like a community college offering a host of courses - not all of them language courses, by any stretch of the imagination - and it was also not anywhere near as fancy as Jens' language 'academy'. But it was cheap - it had that much going for it, at least. The classes were literally packed with Ausländer of every conceivable nationality. Some Turks, of course, and he had already made friends with a couple, Mehmet - the class clown, and a real chunky hunk called Kaan. But the best thing about the Volkshochschule was that it was cheap and easy to get to. And anyway, any class is only as good as its teacher. And Ömer liked his teacher a lot.

Frau Stubenrauch was her name. Not Eva, Sylvia or Brigitta Stubenrauch but simply and most definitely Frau Stubenrauch. She was not the most exciting teacher in the world, in fact Mehmet had been known to fall asleep in her class and snore through the second half of the lesson. But she had taken a shine to Ömer. She always made a point of correcting him carefully and complimenting him on the quality of his homework. Mehmet said it was only because she fancied Ömer. But that couldn't be true, could it? She was old enough to be his grandmother, wasn't she? The thought horrified him. But no, Mehmet finally admitted he was only winding him up, adding that it was Kaan who Ömer really had to worry about.

Dirk had had just about enough of Ahmet. The relentless telephone calls were driving him up the wall. Sometimes he would ring late at night after Dirk and Jens were both in bed. The answering machine would click on and the sound of the pre-recorded message would drift through to the bedroom. But the only message left after the tone would be the beep, beep, beep of an aborted call. Sometimes Ahmet would ring during the early evening when it was clear that Jens would be at work. When Dirk answered, Ahmet would apologise profusely, only to say that he would ring Jens there at his job. More often than not, though, when Dirk answered, Ahmet would simply hang up.

Just as well that Jens had admitted to his dalliance with Ahmet. Hell, Dirk couldn't blame him. The guy was fit! But he was also clearly mental. He understood why Jens wanted to give him the heave-ho. So why couldn't the guy accept 'no' for an answer?

It had to be Ahmet calling. Nobody else they knew would do such crazy things. Dirk started to refer to Ahmet as Glenn Close, she of Fatal Attraction fame. He half expected to come home one day and find a fluffy, furry, little bunny rabbit boiling in a pot on the stove.

Dirk picked up the phone for the third time in as many minutes. Again silence. It was the last straw. 'For fuck's sake, Ahmet! Get a fucking life!!' He was just about to wrench the hand set from his ear and switch the ringer off when he heard a voice, Ömer's voice, shouting, 'Wait! Dirk! It's me!'

'Ömer?'

'Sorry. I so sorry! Something is wrong with this phone!' Ömer sounded distraught. 'I try to ring you but you not hear me.'

Dirk attempted to lighten the load. 'You're coming in loud and clear now, Brother Bear.'

'Can I come see you?'

'When?'

'Now.'

'Now?'

'Yes, now. I sorry, Dirk. Ahmet, he threw me out of the apartment. Locked me out. Put my bags in the hall. I don't know what I must do.'

Dirk shot a concerned look at Jens who sat across from him on the second sofa, reading a book. Reading no longer, their eyes locked. 'What?' mouthed Jens, picking up on Dirk's vibe. Dirk shook his head.

'Dirk? Dirk?! My phone card runs out. Can I come? Please?'

'Where are you? We'll come and pick you up.'

'Prinzenstraße Bahnhof.'

'There's an Imbiss just outside. Wait there. Hold tight, brother. We'll be with you in twenty minutes.'

'Thank you, Dirk. Thank you so much.'

'No need to thank us.' Dirk hung up.

Jens was already on his feet. 'What on earth?'

Having picked up his car keys, Dirk was halfway out of the door. 'Grab your coat. I'll fill you in on the way.'

Ömer was waiting exactly where Dirk had suggested. Standing beside his suitcase and a rucksack, he looked every inch the lost little boy. Jens' heart went out to him. And his conscience was suitably troubled. How much had his own illicit relationship contributed to this present state of affairs, he wondered.

On the journey home, Ömer sat silently on the back seat. Both Jens and Dirk thought better than to interrogate him about the evening's events. He would doubtless explain all in his own good time.

It was only once they were safe inside the apartment, the door shut, Ömer 's baggage placed in the hall, that Ömer 's eyes welled up with tears. Dirk threw his arms around Ömer hugging him to his chest. Ömer reached out a hand and drew Jens in. Ömer was trembling, his whole body vibrating. He was also hyperventilating. Dirk and Jens cuddled him tight, to calm him down.

'Thank you. Oh, thank you. You guys. You are too good to me! I don't deserve it.'

'You're our friend, Ömer.' Dirk rubbed his back, kissed the top of his head. 'Of course you deserve it. It's our privilege to help you.'

'I do not know what I would have done.'

'It's our privilege,' Jens repeated reassuringly. 'You're okay now. You're safe. You're with friends who love you.'

Dirk looked at Jens and was reminded of exactly why he fell in love with him all those years ago. Because he was a good man, with a loving heart. They did not come any better.

'Thank you, my friends. Really. Thank you.' He yawned suddenly. 'I so tired.'

'I'm not surprised; you've been through the mill. Time for bed, I think,' said Dirk. 'We can talk all about it in the morning.'

In the bedroom, Dirk lit the bedside candles as Jens took off Ömer's padded check-shirt and slipped the T-shirt over his head. Dirk came up behind, stripped off Jens' shirt and vest. Ömer had another attack of nerves, freaking out completely. Jens held him tightly while Dirk extended his arms around them both, cuddling tight to calm him. Ömer 's body was hard and warm.

Jens pushed Ömer back on the bed. Dirk undid his shoelaces. Jens slipped off Ömer's shoes and socks. Dirk clambered onto the bed and embraced him tightly. As the two of them lay together, Jens also climbed onto the bed and made up the Cub sandwich. Reaching around, Jens undid Ömer's belt, pulled down the zip of his black jeans, cupped Ömer's bulge in his palm and drew him into life. Suddenly, Ömer was wide awake. Jens slipped his hand inside Ömer's black briefs, fumbled around in the warmth. Off came Ömer's pants and jeans together, yanked over his feet by Dirk. Ömer looked over his shoulder back at Jens and was met with a passionate kiss. At the same moment, Dirk took Ömer's soft, fleshy prick between his lips.

Ömer broke the kiss and looked lovingly into Jens' face. 'You kiss wonderfully.'

'So do you.'

'You're gorgeous.'

'So are you.'

'In Turkish, we would say: "Your eyes talk." There is love in your eyes.'

Jens smiled. 'In yours too, my sweet little Bear Cub.'

As Ömer grew stiff in Dirk's mouth, Jens slipped off the bed. Taking time out with a beer and a spliff, he watched Ömer and Dirk together. He had to admit, it was a beautiful picture. Two handsome Bears getting it on. It felt like an honour to simply be there and watch. Ömer knelt astride Dirk's face, his mouth level with Dirk's groin and he consumed Dirk's giant dick, sucking and gorging on it as if it was the last dick he would ever be allowed to swallow. Ömer's beautiful buttocks were pale - bathed in candlelight, caressed by candlelight. And Dirk's brutish fingers caressed them and pulled them gently apart to reveal the puckered rosebud between.

Ömer groaned slightly in anticipation. He looked over his shoulder directly to where Jens was sitting cross-legged on the floor. 'I love being rimmed.'

Jens smiled. 'You want me to rim you?'

'Are you fucking serious?' Ömer replied. 'I'd love you to rim me!'

On all fours, Ömer soon had a tongue buried deep in both ends. Dirk's in his mouth, Jens' up his arsehole. He was punching the mattress and waggling his arse, squirming with the pleasure of being so expertly serviced. Jens reached between Ömer's thighs and began to pull him off into his palm. His face buried deep in Ömer's crack.

Ömer placed his own hand over Jens'. 'Squeeze it hard! Harder! Squeeze it! Don't stop! Don't stop.'

First came the groan and then come was flying everywhere, spraying in every direction. Come splattering the bed cover. Ömer's heart was beating fit to burst, pounding against his chest, as he kissed Dirk hungrily. He came a massive wad. Jens' palm was covered, sticky, glistening with sperm.

'Stop it!' Again Ömer covered Jens' still-pumping hand with his own. 'Stop!' Too much feeling. And more than a handful of spunk.

It was now enough to let him sleep then, for Dirk and Jens to snuggle up beside him. They had done their duty. But it was no duty - it was, indeed, their privilege.

It was just a little less than a week since Ömer moved in and it had already become clear that the apartment was not big enough to house the three Bears comfortably together. With all the good will in the world, there simply was not enough room.

Ömer was out working the late-shift on the evening that Dirk poured Jens a glass of Sekt and sat him down at the kitchen table.

'He is looking for a flat of his own,' Dirk began.

'I know.'

'It just takes time.'

'I know.'

'And I was thinking . . . '

'Why does that not reassure me?'

'I was thinking . . . you're always saying this place is too small for us.'

'Yeah, so?'

'Wouldn't it be a good idea if we all pitched in together and got one big flat.'

Jens held his breath. Released it. 'Together?'

'Uh huh!' Dirk pressed quickly on. 'I mean, it makes sense. You've always wanted a study and you like Ömer a lot and he loves you and . . . '

Jens held up his hand. 'Whoa! Now it seems to me that it's hard enough for two people to live together in any kind of harmony without a third to contend with. A fourth if you count Ahmet.' Jens got up from the table and began to pace.

'What do you mean, Ahmet? Ahmet's a crazy man! He's not moving in with us. No way.'

'Thank God for small mercies. But it's all par for the course, isn't it?

No matter how hard you try, things get complicated.'

'So, what's the moral of this story? That a three-way relationship under one roof can't possibly work?'

Jens remained calm. 'That's not what I said. It probably can work, if all parties are of the same mind. And maybe it's a possibility I would seriously consider - sometime in the not-too-distant future. Unfortunately, I don't feel like I'm being given a choice here. We've been forced into a position where we had to take Ömer in and now I'm being put under pressure to make the arrangement permanent.'

'It's not just what I want, it's what Ömer wants too.'

'Talked about it already, have you? Thanks for including me in the process.'

'No! We haven't talked about it. But you know he'd be keen. He thinks the world of us.'

'And you think the world of him?'

'And so do you! I don't see the problem. Haven't we been through all this before? I love you!' Dirk rearranged his features into something resembling a pout. 'Don't you love me any more?'

'Oh no, Dirk. You can't pull that stunt anymore. Not the wounded, lost, little boy act. It doesn't cut the ice. This is too important. I don't need your bullshit theatrics.'

Dirk was not to be so easily dissuaded. 'Is that your way of telling me you don't love me anymore?'

Jens finally lost his cool. 'Of course I fucking love you, why else would I be here talking this through? If I didn't love you, I would have fucked off long ago.'

'I thought you'd be happy.'

'Why? You can't give me that speech about "sex is sex but love is something else entirely" again. Not in this instance. There's a third person involved here. And you keep moving the damn goalposts. I don't know where I stand anymore.'

Dirk came up behind him, placed his hands on Jens' shoulder.

'Come here . . . I'll show you.'

Jens shook him off. 'Always the same old routine. When will you ever learn? You can't just paper over the cracks. You can't solve this with a quick fuck!'

'I want you.'

'That's clear. But do you love me?'

'What kind of a question is that?'

'The same one you asked me.'

Dirk was exasperated. 'Look, will you stop pacing and sit down?'

Jens sat, albeit sideways, with his arms folded across his chest.

'Thank you. Now can we just calm things down?' Dirk consciously controlled his tone of voice. Adopted a calm, measured approach. 'Won't you just think about it? Think about us living together?'

Jens set his jaw. 'Yes, I'll think about it. But what if I eventually say no?'

'Then there's no problem. You are my first priority.'

Jens cast a sideways glance, expecting the worst. But there had been no irony in Dirk's voice, nor was there any in his expression. He had meant what he said.

'You are my first priority,'

And in that moment, Jens knew the decision he would ultimately make.

The hunt was now on in earnest. The Sunday edition of the Berliner Morgenpost came out late on Saturday evening and, having made a special trip to Zoologischer Garten train station in the city centre in order to pick up one of the first copies, the three guys now sat around the kitchen table scanning column upon column of apartments to rent. Dirk played secretary, with his big yellow highlighter in hand, circling any and all possibilities. They had already discussed which areas of the city they were interested in, how many rooms the new apartment would have to have and how much they were prepared to pay in rent. But outside of these parameters, there was still a lot left to debate. How important was a balcony, for instance? Or was the place angled to get the right amount of sun? After much heated debate, a list was drawn up and viewings arranged.

Sunday was taken up with a seemingly endless round of viewings. They had managed to narrow their choices down to half a dozen, but still it was tough going, looking at one place after another. Most notable was one dump with a pigeon's nest en suite, in place of a bathtub! No bathtub at all, just a series of pipes hanging from the wall. Given the extortionate rent, it was a wonder the rep kept his face straight. The three lads didn't. It was the best laugh they'd had all day.

'Let's hope we have better luck this time. This is number five on our list, and the others haven't exactly been ideal,' Dirk muttered as they drove down the street, checking for house numbers. The numbering system was crazy to Jens. On one side you could have number two, and on the other three hundred and two. Dirk had explained it to him, but he still couldn't get the hang of it - especially since it seemed to change from street to street. He was getting a headache from all the eye strain.

'Look, there!' said Ömer, pleased with himself.

'Number ten.' Jens pointed a finger. 'And there's a parking space directly in front. Maybe it's an omen.'

After parking the car, they clambered out and stared up at the building. It was impressive. A traditional Berliner Altbau. Ornate balconies and all of the original fascia.

'Let's hope it's as beautiful inside as it is outside,' Dirk said as he buzzed in to the main entrance.

'It's at the back,' Jens reminded them as they passed through a stone archway and across a sunlit courtyard to the Hinterhof.

Up four flights of stairs, the door to the apartment stood ajar. Inside appeared to be empty. 'Anyone at home?' Dirk called as they entered the cavernous hallway. The rep appeared through a doorway to the right. A look of recognition passed between the four of them. They smiled. This guy was family.

It was an open viewing and they'd expected the place to be crowded. 'Are we the first?' Jens asked.

'The one and only,' the rep replied.

'Really?' Ömer was incredulous.

'Afraid so. And I was just about to go . . . '

Jens looked at his watch. 'Sorry we're late - we had difficulty finding the place.'

'No problem. I have time. But make sure to close the front door, won't you?'

Dirk grinned. 'Should I lock it?'

'It'll lock automatically. But I don't expect anyone else. And if they do come . . . '

'Tough.' Dirk smiled, finishing his sentence.

'Exactly.' The rep laughed. He held out his hand. 'My name is Bastian.'

Bastian was a big built man, a hunk with a grip like iron. Six feet of solid masculinity. Closer to fifty than forty, fit and tanned. His thinning hair was cropped fashionably short. A salt-and-pepper beard. A big ol' Daddy Bear, all dressed up in jacket, shirt and tie. Dirk could only wonder what treasures lay buried beneath his formal attire.

'Follow me,' said Bastian, leading the way into the large reception room.

They entered into a large sunlit room, spacious and newly decorated. The walls were white, the floorboards stripped and polished, the ceiling still covered with the stucco work that older apartment buildings in Berlin still boasted. Double-glazed French windows led out onto a large terrace with a view out over the rooftops of the city. It was breathtaking. Dirk strode forward and opened the balcony door, and all three of them walked out onto the terrace.

'Wow! We could eat out here in the summer months,' Jens

enthused as he looked at the glorious view beyond the tree-lined canal.

Bastian smiled. 'What can I tell you about this place? Well, it is a hundred and forty square metres, comprising four rooms, two bathrooms and two kitchens.'

Jens ran a hand over his goatee. 'The advertisement said that it had originally been two apartments.'

'That's right.'

'That's good. We won't have to fight over the bathroom first thing in the morning.'

'And, if we decide we don't like each other, then we each can stick to our own end of the apartment,' Dirk added.

Bastian continued: 'The apartment, as you can see, has been completely refurbished. The four rooms are all roughly the same size.'

'And the rent?'

'One thousand seven hundred Deutschmarks, pro Monat.'

Dirk, frowned slightly, and pinched the end of his nose with thumb and forefinger. 'It's a bit expensive.' Dirk knew that that was a lie, but it didn't hurt to chance his arm. 'Don't think we could go above one thousand five hundred.'

'I could speak with the owner if you are interested. Put in a good word for you.'

'Let's see the rest of the place.' Jens nudged them in the direction of the hall.

They toured the apartment not once, not twice, but three times. Ömer was giddy from rushing from room to room. Jens and he could barely contain their enthusiasm, but Dirk played it cool. At last, they returned to the terrace and Bastian left them alone to 'think it over'.

'I've fallen in love with this place! I could really imagine me, us, living here,' Ömer whispered enthusiastically.

'Dirk, this is exactly what we were looking for!'

'I know it is. Almost too good to be true. Now, if we can just get them to lower the rent.'

'Don't blow it!' Jens was adamant. 'I know what you're like. You love bargaining. Just don't blow this deal.'

'Trust me,' Dirk replied. 'If we have to pay one thousand seven then we pay one thousand seven, but if we don't . . . '

Bastian reappeared in the doorway. 'You need more time?'

'No,' Jens said firmly, and shot a warning glance at Dirk 'We really, really like the apartment. But there are some details we're not sure about.'

Ömer was hopping excitedly from one foot to the other. 'Yeah, we really like the place . . . '

'But?'

'The price. You said that you could maybe cut us a deal?' Dirk reminded him.

'I could.'

'And will you?'

'I'll talk to the owner. Tell him that lots of people came to see the flat. That everyone thought that it was too expensive. That you offered the most and are his best bet. Maybe you won't get it for one thousand five. But maybe one thousand six. I can be very persuasive.'

Dirk grinned. 'I don't doubt it.'

Jens placed a hand on Dirk's shoulder. 'That's real friendly of you, Bastian.'

Ömer 's face broke into a broad smile. 'How can we ever thank you?'

'Put your heads together. I am sure that you guys can think of something appropriate, eh?'

Without further prompting, Dirk crossed the floor and placed his hands on Bastian's shoulders. 'Are we thinking along the same lines?'

Bastian grinned and blushed. 'I suspect so.'

Dirk swept Bastian up in a big, grizzly Bear hug. Bearded cheeks brushed up against one another. Their mouths searched for and then found each other, Dirk's moist tongue darting between Bastian's lips.

Not to be left out, Jens and Ömer quickly joined the pair and formed a scrum. Ömer slipped Bastian's jacket off, over his broad shoulders and powerful arms. Jens undid the tie wrapped around Bastian's thick, bull neck. Dirk popped the buttons on Bastian's shirt. The older man's barrel chest swelled and a forest of silver chest hair revealed itself. Belt buckle undone, fly unzipped, Bastian's trousers fell swiftly around his ankles. Jens squatted down to untie Bastian's shoe laces. Then Bastian stepped out of both trousers and shoes in one deft move, his lips never once releasing Dirk's tongue from their grip. Ömer peeled off Bastian's socks and threw them aside with all the other items of clothing. Now all that was left to be removed were his snug-fitting briefs.

Still kneeling at Bastian's feet, Jens reached out a hand and gently cupped the bulge in the front of Bastian's pants. A moan escaped Bastian's lips but somehow he managed to hold fast to Dirk's tongue. Jens felt the semi-erect member swell against his palm. He wrapped his fingers around it, squeezed it, felt it swell even more. Releasing his hold, he let his fingers trace the stiff, tubular cock that threatened to burst free from its constraints at any moment. Unable to resist what was clearly going begging, Jens lowered his mouth and consumed Bastian's cockhead through the stretched cotton.

The cotton grew transparent and moist with saliva. The purple circumcised cockhead flushed beneath the fabric. Then Ömer could no longer resist, either. Positioning himself behind Bastian, he hooked his fingers under the waistband and eased the pants down over firm, hairy buttocks. Up front, Jens helped with his own hands. Bastian's stiff prick and fulsome bollocks burst free from their cotton enclosure. With his briefs slipped down to his hairy ankles, Bastian now stepped out and kicked them aside. He stood there, naked and proud. Jens launched himself upon the stiff prong that throbbed in his face whilst

Ömer buried his own face in the salty crack of Bastian's arsecheeks.

All the time, Dirk's mouth fed on Bastian's. His hands roamed across the hairy chest, tweaking the erect nipples, and then slid around the supple flesh of Bastian's waist. He could feel Bastian's heat in the passion of his kisses. Could feel Bastian's mouth slam up against his own. Yawning wide, Bastian chewed on Dirk's lips and tongue, wanting more.

Finally, Bastian dropped to his knees. His mouth opened wide, begging to be filled. ... Ömer, Jens and Dirk stood before him, more than willing to fill his aching need. First, he took Ömer and Jens' cocks in his fist, squeezing them hard, watching them swell, his tongue hanging out provocatively before Dirk interrupted his minute examination and forced his own prick deep into Bastian's throat. Now Bastian began feasting on all three stiff, supple cocks in turn. His mouth consumed first one, then the next, then the third, spoilt for choice. Bastian indulged himself in a surfeit of cock. His mouth was drooling, dripping with saliva, hungry for man-meat. He wanted to gobble up all three cocks as if his life might depend upon it.

Bastian felt Dirk finger his arsehole. Slick fingers, lubricated with saliva. He knew what was coming, and he wanted it. Oh, god, how he wanted it. That feeling of fullness. That feeling of a rock-solid pole up his arse. Filling him up. Dirk put him out of his misery, mounting him quickly. The condom proved no barrier to intimacy. Bastian was on all fours, happy to be at the receiving end.

'Fuck me. Fuck me,' Bastian growled. 'Oh, yeah, fuck me, you big Bear-stud.'

Dirk fucked him good. Pumped his hips backwards and forwards, slamming into Bastian. Pulling out. Slamming all the way back in again. Bastian received him willingly, beads of sweat breaking out on his brow as he thrust backwards to meet each lunge.

Dirk pulled out again but this time Jens was greased up, rubbered up and ready to take over. Bastian looked back over his shoulder and, as Jens lined up his cock, he pushed back taking the full length in one hungry movement. Jens needed no further encouragement. He started to thrust, building up a tempo. Building up a tempo until he was fucking like a rabbit, bucking his hips to beat the band. In and out. His latex erection pulsing out, drawing Bastian's ring-piece with it.

And finally, Jens withdrew and Ömer immediately took his place. He buried his cock up to the hilt in the selfsame hole. He filled it to capacity, hammering home his advantage with his magnificent weapon. Bastian was dripping with sweat, relishing the pounding he was getting. Moans and groans and gasps escaped his mouth as he slammed back, impaling himself time and again on Ömer 's big, fat dong.

Dirk matched Ömer stroke for stroke, thwacking his cock for all it was worth. His eyes transfixed on the junction of cock and arsehole, and he licked his lips. He felt the familiar rumble in his ballsac and knew he could not hold back much longer, knew that any second now, he was going to empty his jizz over Bastian's chunky butt. Could not help himself. Here it was, working its way up his tubes, man-juice forcing its way to the surface. Had to be released, simply had to . . .

'Oh, oh, oh . . . ' Just as predicted, Dirk shot his wad over Bastian's firm, hairy buttocks. He watched as his milk-white juices splashed over Bastian's arse, and ran over the curves and dripped into the crack as Ömer rode Bastian towards his own end. Jens came next. His come sprayed high and wide, on and on. Finally, Ömer pulled free. Tore off the condom and blasted Bastian's arsecheeks with a torrent of jism so copious it threatened to drown each glorious buttock with its volume.

Bastian came in his own palm. He raised his cupped hand to his face and drank deep. Once his palm had been licked clean, he stuffed his dripping fingers into his mouth and lapped up all that what was left. He ate every glob of his spunk, every morsel, every last trace. Smacking his lips, he wiped his mouth with the back of his hand. All gone.

With nothing else close to hand, Jens used his T-shirt to mop up the come on Bastian's saturated arse. 'No problem,' Jens said as he screwed it up and flung it aside, 'Dirk will buy me a new one, won't you, Dirk?'

'Fortunately, you still have your shirt, don't you? So that one can go in the wash, can't it?' Dirk placed his tongue in his cheek. 'Unless you want to keep it as a housewarming present?'

The four of them collapsed down into a heap on the floor. The polished, wooden floorboards were warmed by the sun. Four tired Bears. They snuggled up against each other; loving kisses were exchanged. They cuddled into stillness.

Finally, Dirk broke the silence. He asked, 'So, what's he like then, this owner?'

'A lot like me.'

'Then maybe we should thank him personally?'

'You just did! Meet your new landlord.'

'Does that mean that we have a deal on the apartment, then?'

'I would guess so. I'm pretty satisfied.'

They grinned; rubbed Bastian's chest, and his furry ass.

'So do you want to shake on it then?'

'I think you guys just did!'

Sixteen

The best thing about moving apartments was the glorious sight of so many beefy, hairy bodies stripped to the waist. As well as sweaty torsos and bulging biceps, humping the furniture, countless packing cases and electrical goods up four flights of stairs. Squeezing past each other on the stairway; some guys going up as still others came down. No one complained. Not even Sabine, although she had refused to go topless herself. She was wearing the T-shirt Dirk and Jens had given her as a special thank you as the only female present. Emblazoned on the front was the slogan, 'Honorary Bear for a Day.' She was thrilled with it, and pulled her weight accordingly.

The sun shone down, flooding the apartment with light. All of the windows were thrown open, allowing a gentle breeze to waft through the cluttered rooms. It had taken the best part of six hours to empty one flat, transport the stuff in relay, and fill the new one. It was after five o'clock when Volker placed the last packing case in the hall and shouted, 'That's the lot!' He found his comment greeted with a spontaneous burst of applause from all concerned.

Out on the terrace, Jens handed out the beer. A huge pot of chilli was simmering on the stove. Freshly baked bread and bowls of salad stood ready and waiting on the kitchen table; the crates of beer were lined up. It was a way of saying thank you.

Sadly, Bodo couldn't be there to help. Still, the assembly toasted his health and wished him luck. He would need it. He was working security at some Beer Festival out in Brandenburg. Brandenburg lay just outside the city boundaries and was home to a significant portion of the Rechts Radicale. Fascist skinheads were expected to turn out in force and run riot. Bodo's towering presence would doubtless be significant motivation to persuade them to behave. Last year, they had torn the place apart. This year, they would have Bodo and his team to contend with.

Out of Bodo's giant shadow, Volker had come into his own. He was louder, brasher and more confident than expected. And unless Jens was seriously mistaken, he was flirting - flirting with Dirk. Or rather, flirting back, subtly but unmistakably. Jens had to smile. Who would have guessed? Certainly the point was not lost on Sabine. She cornered Jens in the kitchen.

'You know him,' she whispered conspiratorially, 'that little muscle packet?'

'Who? Volker?' Jens replied, stirring the pot.

'Yes, him.' She leaned in close. 'He's a bit keen on Dirk, isn't he?'

Jens laughed. 'You could say that.' He brought the wooden spoon to his lips and sampled the chilli. Perfect. 'Strange really. I mean he's normally as quiet as a mouse. When Bodo's around, he wouldn't say boo to a goose.'

'You have to watch out for that type -' Sabine touched the end of her nose knowingly '- A Dark Horse!'

Jens chuckled. 'Sabine!'

She reached for a carrot stick and began to crunch. 'And you're cool about ?'

'About flirting? Sure! I have no problem with flirting. It can be just for fun, you know? It doesn't have to lead anywhere.'

'Oh, it makes me sick!' she said, annoyed.

'What flirting?'

'No, not flirting!' She grabbed another carrot stick from the bowl. 'I mean, why are gay men so gorgeous? They're all so gorgeous. It's just not fair!'

'What are you on about?'

'I'm on about that lot, out there.' She waved her hand in the general direction of the terrace. 'If I met any one of them in a bar, I'd snap them up!'

'Shade! Shade! Shade!' Jens replied - 'Sorry! Sorry! Sorry!', in the manner of a popular TV advertisement. 'I'm afraid they all prefer someone with a little more body hair!'

'I know, that's why I'm sick!'

'Well, if it's any consolation, Sabine, not all gay men are handsome. That is a definite. Gay men are just men at the end of the day. The good, the bad and the ugly, I'm afraid. Don't get so upset. You know, the grass is always greener, and all that? I saw this big Turkish muscle hunk the other day tending the grass verges over by Ernst Reuter Platz. Obviously straight. Well, I imagine so. I tell you, what I wouldn't have given to have been Pamela Anderson for an hour! '

She poured another glass of wine. 'Believe me, Jens. It is no consolation.'

'What are you going to say next, that it's "such a waste"? And then I'm supposed to say, "Believe me, Sabine. It's not wasted?!"'

'It's enough to make me want to be a gay man.'

'Then I take that as the highest compliment.'

Seventeen

Spring was in the air. The time of year when, traditionally, a young mans fancy turns to . . . Bodo was hardly 'young'; he was forty if he was a day but, nonetheless, Bodo was feeling horny. So, nothing new there. The working day over he had decided to take some much-needed rest 'n' recreation. And, rather than heading straight home to his Baby Bear, he decided to stop off at the woods.

For a city as densely populated as Berlin there were, perhaps surprisingly, sizeable chunks of woodland and a number of parks - the 'green lungs' of Berlin. And Bodo knew every square inch off by heart. Places where many of the city's inhabitants headed on the weekend to swim, walk, or, in the case of men like Bodo, to fuck and suck. Indeed, in the particular spot Bodo was headed towards, the leather men of the city liked to get together after the bars shut to have massive outdoor orgies. But it was still too early for that. At this time it would be commuters like Bodo - just a bunch of horny guys wanting to get their rocks off before heading home to the wife and kids, or lovers, or alone.

As he steered his Yamaha Virago into the car park, Bodo noticed that it was nicely full. This was good since it meant that there would be enough guys cruising the pathways to make it more than certain that he would meet someone to satisfy his urges. It also gave him a chance to show off his low-slung metal monster. The Virago was not just any old motorbike. Its burgundy chrome shone in the evening sunlight. Climbing off the padded leather seat, he adjusted his straining cock. Then he locked up, and headed down the well-trodden path into the forest.

At first, Bodo moved slowly through the dense foliage, allowing time for his eyes to adjust to the dark shadows cast by the trees. He walked deliberately, knowing exactly where he was going, but still keeping his attention focused on the figures he could see around him

- other men out looking to fuck or get fucked.

After about fifteen minutes of walking, Bodo came to the horse trail, and from this point on he was heading into the darkest and most secluded part of the forest. It was here that things really started to heat up and, sure enough, Bodo had no sooner re-entered the shade of the trees than he saw a couple of guys hard at it. The taller of the two guys was leaning with his back against the trunk of a tree, his big cock disappearing down the hungry throat of another man who knelt respectfully on his knees. The big guy had his shirt open, with his two hands pinching and tweaking his nipples. Bodo stopped to have a look. This was one of the things that he really enjoyed about coming out here - he could live out his voyeuristic fantasies - just like live porno happening before your eyes. The big guy was aware now of Bodo's presence and, while looking Bodo up and down, he pinched his tits even harder, pulling the nipples between forefinger and thumb. This spurred the cocksucker to even greater demonstrations of worship.

Bodo, however, didn't move. He was enjoying the sight of these two men getting it on - enjoying the looks of pleasure that washed over their faces - and he just wanted to look. This was their scene, and he was just an onlooker. The fact that he could join in at any moment was a real turn-on, making his cock swell even harder inside his custom-made, black leather jeans.

The man on his knees slurped hungrily on the cock, letting it slip in and out of his mouth, his hands busy playing with the other guy's ballsac - taking it in both hands, pulling it down and away from the body, dividing it in two. Then he moved his mouth to take first one shaved ball and then the other, cramming them both into his mouth while at the same time pulling his own swollen cock out of his jeans. Out and proud, he began to wank it. The big guy's hands were hard at work, too - one hand rubbing over his own chest, while the other grabbed his cock and started to jerk it with a feverish motion.

Bodo was completely lost in this private performance - moving his eyes from one man to the other - watching their reactions. Enjoying the fact that they wanted to have him watch.

The big guy's fist moved faster and faster and then with a whoop he let fly. Ropes of creamy come shot from his cock spraying the adjacent foliage. Bodo smiled to himself, and with one last grab of his crotch - and a smile and a wink - he was off. The Vorspeise was over, now it was time to snare the main course.

Early yet. A dirt track. The earth solid underfoot. He ducked under a low branch. An evening breeze blew gently, rustling the leaves on the trees.

At the point where two tracks crossed he saw the Turk. Out there in the open, sunlit. Bodo emerged from the shadows, his eyes fixed directly on the Turk. The two men passed each other slowly by and then, turning simultaneously, they stood their ground.

The Turk was definitely handsome: short and stocky, with a thick moustache and short, combed-back hair. His clothes were unremarkable - just blue jeans, black shirt and bomber jacket. Both men eyed each other appreciatively. Still neither one made a move. A stand off? Finally, the Turk turned sideways and walked deliberately into the bushes. Bodo followed his cue.

A trail led into the thicket. The Turk walked purposefully ahead, leading the way to a small clearing, one he was obviously familiar with. Bodo followed closely behind. Once satisfied that they were hidden from the eyes of the casual passer-by, the Turk stood still, turned around and waited. Bodo drew close, stood directly before the Turk and reached out a hand. His fingers brushed against denim - and more: the feel of big, ripe balls and a thickening length of pipe. Bodo traced the contours with his fingertips while the Turk stood stock still, his face impassive, but his eyes darting this way and that. On the lookout? Not knowing where to look? Bodo smiled. He felt in control. He was going to take his time; to enjoy the effect his ministrations were having. The Turk's fruitful basket was now filled to capacity. A couple of kiwi and one big, plump banana. Fumbling for the zip, Bodo gripped the metal tongue and began to ease it down over the swollen mound. The teeth parted company. A mountain of white cotton burst free from the yawning gap and Bodo's fingers felt the warm bulge brush against his knuckles. He reached for his own zipper.

Bodo was hard, hard as rock. Now with his cock free of his fly and out in the open, he felt the kiss of the evening breeze on his glistening cockhead as he fully retracted his foreskin. The Turk pulled down the waistband of his own briefs and hooked it under his slack, shaven ballsac. His circumcised dick was now fully exposed. What's more, it was up and throbbing. Once again, Bodo let his fingers trace the length, now exposed, and the Turk whimpered and moaned. Bodo leaned down to kiss the Turk's mouth, but found himself presented with the guy's cheek. He chuckled quietly to himself. The old, old story. You can fuck me but you can't kiss me. It's too intimate. Well, his loss.

There was to be no similar resistance when Bodo dropped to his knees and began sucking cock. Clearly, the Turk loved being serviced. Maybe he couldn't get lip service at home. He thrust deep into Bodo's throat, holding firmly to the back of his head, and fucked Bodo's face. He jabbed his cock into the depths with slow, pulsing thrusts, then he closed his eyes and threw back his head. Then opened his eyes again.

Bodo broke free, looked up. The Turk suddenly seemed a little agitated. Bodo looked around. Out of nowhere, shadow figures had emerged from the bushes and encircled them. Watching. A couple had their cocks in hand, stroking them lovingly. But the strangers kept their distance. They were content to settle down and enjoy the performance. Bodo was not one to disappoint them.

Bodo set to work on the Turk's bollocks, and soon all else was forgotten. He took one ball in his mouth, rolled it around on his tongue. The Turk rubbed his cock against Bodo's bulging cheek, rubbed it against his full beard, and jerked on it. Muttering something barely audible as he did so, and not in German, that was for sure. He had worked himself up into a lather and now he was mumbling away, words bubbling out of his throat in a constant stream, his eyes closed tight shut once more.

Sensing the inevitable, Bodo got to his feet. Standing tall, he leaned in once again to the Turk's face. Their foreheads rested together and Bodo allowed his tongue to lap a sheen of sweat from the Turk's cheek. No resistance. The Turk was quaking now. He was minutes, if not seconds, from orgasm. Moaning low, grunting, his entire body was focused on this one objective. Bodo listened for the inevitable rise in intensity. He jerked languidly on his own cock, letting the Turk work his own in turn. Jerking faster, increasingly urgent. Losing his reserve, the Turk pressed his face up against Bodo's. Faster. Jerking faster. And then the yelp as the Turk let fly into Bodo's open palm. Each spasm ejecting still more, coating Bodo's hand with a thick, sticky puddle.

At last, the orgasm was over. Both men reached into their pockets, produced tissues and cleaned up. Bodo could not help noticing the Turk's wedding ring. He smiled. Wonder what excuse he gave the wife this time, he thought to himself. The Turk smiled back, unaware, and, pointing at Bodo's dick, he simulated a hand-job. Bodo shook his head; he wasn't ready to come yet and so he stuffed his swollen dick back inside the confines of his fly. The Turk smiled apologetically, rubbed Bodo's shoulder and headed back to the path.

Bodo looked at his watch. Seven p.m. He would allow himself another half-hour. Working late, that would be his excuse as always. Working up a sweat would have been closer to the truth. A couple of minutes and Bodo caught sight of a hunky figure up ahead and he quickened his pace. As he drew closer he could see the man's features more clearly. Short hair, bearded, maybe thirty years of age. That sounded fine to Bodo, so he continued to walk quickly in pursuit of his quarry. The guy looked around, and seeing Bodo's rapid approach, he stood to one side, leaning against the trunk of a tree. Bodo slowed down, and walked slowly past. Allowing his eyes to meet those of the stranger full on - to try to ascertain whether the interest was mutual - and then he was past him. Bodo gave the man a lingering look and walked on. After another thirty metres, Bodo stopped and waited. The stranger approached, but as he reached the point where Bodo was standing, he looked down and quickened his pace. Hmm, thought Bodo, evidently not interested.

Still, it was all a game, and sometimes the rules were anything but clear. This was one of the things that fascinated Bodo about cruising. So he waited a little, and then he followed. But this time the stranger wasn't walking slowly, and he was moving deeper and deeper into the wood, without so much as a backward glance at Bodo. It was clear that this guy wasn't interested at all.

His hard luck, thought Bodo as he stepped off the path and into the bushes. Sometimes, the chase could be just as exciting as the capture, and Bodo did not really take any of it very seriously. Unzipping his fly, he pulled out his semi-hard cock and sighed with relief as he emptied his bladder. A heavy stream of golden piss splashed onto the ground. Finally empty, he zipped up again. That was better!

Bodo stepped back onto the path and continued to walk, but slowed his pace as he rounded a corner and noticed a familiar face. It was one of the two guys he had been watching earlier - right at the beginning of his cruising: the cocksucker. Their paths criss-crossing for a second time. This time Bodo could see him more clearly and, on this occasion, without a cock or ballsac rammed in his mouth. He smiled as Bodo passed him, giving a friendly nod of his head. He was handsome, thought Bodo - maybe 5'6" tall, with short, cropped hair under a baseball cap and a goatee. Plus, the guy was a superlative cocksucker. Bodo had already seen him in action, seen how the guy didn't just suck cock, he blew it away. Bodo turned to look back and the man was still watching him, so Bodo gave a little nod of his head to indicate for the man to follow him.

Up ahead was a small copse where the bushes grew thickly, protecting them from prying eyes or intruders. Bodo slipped inside and waited. Within moments, the stranger was beside him. Bodo leaned down and kissed the man tenderly on the lips. The man responded, opening his mouth to allow Bodo's tongue to slip inside. He tasted minty. Spearmint, thought Bodo, as he stuck his tongue even deeper. The guy began to suck on it. At the same time, he reached up to play with Bodo's nipples, first brushing them gently with the palms of his hands, getting them hard, and then gripping them between thumb and forefinger beneath the cloth of Bodo's shirt. A moan escaped from Bodo's lips.

Opening the buttons of Bodo's shirt, the man slipped his hands inside and ran them over Bodo's hairy chest. This time it was the stranger's turn to moan. Obviously Bodo had what this guy wanted. Hair and more hair. The guy ran his fingers through Bodo's rug of a chest and actually quivered as he did so. The misty-eyed look on his face was close to ecstasy.

Bodo opened the guy's shirt and sucked on one of his nipples, biting it gently between teeth and tongue. The guy reached forward, fumbling with Bodo's fly. Desperate, it seemed to get Bodo's cock in his fist. Mission accomplished, he knelt down and licked the head of Bodo's cock, running his tongue around the crown, savouring the taste of sweaty meat and the smell of leather. He gripped the cockhead between his fingers and pressed it gently to open up the piss-slit and then he stuck the tip of his tongue inside, caught the last, lingering vestige of piss.

'Big dick,' the guy said. 'Big salty dick. I'd love you to piss in my mouth, Big Daddy.'

Bodo shook his head. 'Don't have any left to give, Baby Bear. I just took a leak. Taste this instead.' Roughly, Bodo rubbed his meat back and forth across the other guy's face and beard, then buried the guy's head in his crotch. The earthy smell of Bodo's ball-musk seemed only to excite the other man's passion still further.

Holding Bodo's cock in his iron grip, he took it into his mouth, centimetre by centimetre. Real slow. When it was all in, and his face was up against Bodo's bush, he reached around to grip Bodo's leather-clad arse - indicating that he wanted his face fucked good and hard. Bodo was more than ready to oblige. Slipping out and in, he built up a rhythm.

Bodo looked down at his cock slipping in and out of the stranger's mouth and smiled. 'Oh, yeah, little Bear Cub. Suck on me. Suck on Papa Bear. I could ride your sweet face for hours, and watch you take care of this big, fat dick of mine for hours, too. You'd like that too, wouldn't you?'

The man's eyes turned to look up at Bodo. His mouth was wide open and the head of Bodo's cock was resting on his tongue. He nodded without losing hold and his face broke into a big Teddy Bear smile.

Bodo leaned over a little and allowed a dribble of saliva to drip from his mouth and land, with perfect aim, on the back of his cock-head. The whole time the man's kept his eyes focused on him, watching the spit thread from Bodo's mouth and drop onto the cockhead. Then Bodo slowly slipped his cock back into the man's mouth. The stranger sucked furiously.

Again, Bodo pulled his cock out, but this time until only the tip of his cock was inside. This time he dribbled more spit onto his cock-head, but allowed it to run from his cock into the guy's open mouth. The guy pulled on Bodo's balls, stretching them down. Then, opening his jaws wide, he took the cock back into his mouth. Bodo was total-ly turned on and close to coming. But he was not about to let it hap-pen, not just yet. He tried to ease his cock out of the cocksucker's mouth, but found the stranger was more than a little reluctant to let it go. There was a soft, yearning look in his eyes. It almost made Bodo capitulate. But no, he yanked his dick free. And not a minute too soon.

All change. Bodo helped the guy to his feet and leaned forward to kiss him. The guy quickly proved to be as enthusiastic a kisser as cocksucker. They took it in turns to nuzzle and nibble their way through each other's beard. The young guy chewed on Bodo's chin and used his versatile tongue to lick and lap the sweat from Bodo's face. Bodo struggled to open the other man's trousers. That job done, he dropped to his knees. The guy's cock was straining against his jockstrap. As Bodo pulled down the thick, elastic waistband, the guy's cock sprang free. Bodo could see the shiny glint of the man's Prince Albert ring. A thick one too. He leaned closer and took the stiff dick into his mouth in a single, swift movement. Bodo wasn't used to sucking pierced dicks, and always thought that the way they rattled against his teeth was somehow amusing. But it never stopped him from enjoying them. This was a good cock, too, a shaved cock and balls with a nice cropped bush of pubic hair. He licked both balls, teased them, tickled them with his tongue, then slathered his way up and down the shaft until hot beads of saliva were dripping down onto the smooth surface of the guy's tender bollocks.

Having worked up an appetite, Bodo was now hungry for some serious arse action. He turned the guy around, indicating for him to bend over, and quickly got stuck into his arsehole. Licking and sticking his tongue into the sweaty crevice. The guy was moaning with satisfaction, yanking his own buttocks apart, as Bodo's tongue fucked his fur-framed hole.

Bodo reached through the guy's legs and took hold of the other man's shaft, pulling it backwards and down so that he could suck on it. He flipped his tongue from pierced cockhead to hairy hole and back again, driving the poor man wild. He stretched the other man's buttocks wide and spat directly onto the guy's pulsing sphincter. No doubt about it, this hole had seen some action in the past. And was about to see some more. Much more.

The guy began to plead with Bodo, to whine, to beg, 'Fuck me! Oh, fuck me, you big, horny stud of a Papa Bear! Fuck me now!'

Bodo stood up and got the guy into position, up against a tree. Leather jeans around his ankles now, and condom in place, he rubbed his cockhead up and down the guy's saliva-drenched crack. The guy moaned his assent, and Bodo slipped his rock-solid cock into the guy's hole; slipped it in until it was buried up to the hilt. The guy never flinched, only sighed. Then pushed backwards to match Bodo stroke for stroke as he began to thrust his hips.

'Papa Bear is going to come up your arse, baby. You want that? Huh? You want that?'

'Oh, yeah. Oh, fuck, yeah, Papa Bear!'

Bodo grabbed the guy's hips and plunged forwards. Eyes closed, he could smell the pine, the earth, the scent of sex in the outdoors. He loved it. Sex in the open air. He loved it. Fucking a stranger. Fucking a guy who he did not have to chat up, or buy drinks for, or make small-talk with. Just someone who shared his urge. Someone who would take his cock and consider it a privilege.

He could hear the slap of flesh on flesh as his pelvis slammed against the guy's sturdy butt-cheeks. His big balls were ascending, tightening, primed and ready to blow. He felt the delicious ache deep in his nuts, the ache heralding the inevitable. Then, all too soon, he was coming, shooting his load inside the dark recesses of the other guy's ravenous hole. His entire body was shot through as if by electricity, the sex-charge of orgasm coursing through his veins. His mind was a blank; stars exploded before his eyes. And then, unable to help himself, he threw back his head and started to laugh out loud. Laughed with pleasure. Laughed with joy. Laughed with every spurt. Laughed when he heard the guy before him groan and spray the tree trunk with a joyous load of his own.

He was still chuckling to himself ten minutes later as he climbed back onto his bike and turned the key in the ignition. Nowhere else but Berlin, he thought to himself. No place else. Sex could be so uncomplicated. Why did people find it necessary to make it so complicated? Fuck 'em, thought Bodo, as he revved up the engine and laughed again. Fuck 'em!

Eighteen

It had been a long, long day of cleaning, shopping and preparing. Jens was exhausted and he still had to get his head shaved, shower and get dressed. How the fuck did he ever let Dirk talk him into this party? Of course, it had been all Dirk's idea. A big party to celebrate 'our' new apartment. Invite lots of our friends, prepare a big buffet and get in lots of wine, beer and stuff. So how come Jens had ended up doing most of the work? Because Dirk was no mug - but Jens was!

'And what's the criteria for giving out invites? We both know we could never invite everyone. They would never fit in this place, big as it is,' said Jens.

Dirk wore an angelic expression. He raised his eyes heavenward and said nothing.

Jens stuck his tongue firmly in his cheek. 'No. Don't tell me. Let me guess. We all draw up a list of guys we fancy who might be on for an orgy? '

'Not such a bad idea, Jens,' he replied. 'Wish I'd thought of it!' And that was that.

Of course all of that had been some weeks back, and they had not really discussed the matter since. However, when the guest list was eventually drawn up it did indeed include only the huskiest of Bears and with it the promise of a night of unbridled passion. A promise that had hung in the air from the moment the invitations were dispatched. And now here it was, with guests due to begin arriving in a few hours' time. So, where the fuck was Dirk anyway? And Ömer! They had only 'popped out to the shops' and that was literally hours ago.

As if on cue, Jens heard the key turning in the lock and the sound of stifled laughter as Dirk and Ömer entered the apartment.

'Where the fuck have you two been?! I've been working my bollocks off whilst you two - well, what? Got lost, did you?'

Dirk just chuckled, turned to Ömer. 'Ahhh! I think he missed us.'

'Missed you? I'll murder the pair of you.'

Ömer looked sheepish, but Dirk carried on regardless. "Oh Jens, you're just getting all worked up over nothing. We just went out to the supermarket to get the beer and the wine and all the other bits and pieces. Just like we said we would.'

'And where exactly was this supermarket located? In fucking Dresden?!'

Dirk adopted his most soothing tone. 'Jens, Jens, Jens . . . ' Repeating his name like one gentle stroke upon another. Each stroke was intended to smooth down Jens' ruffled fur. 'You know how the queues are on a Saturday afternoon. All those Berliners rushing around like madmen and madwomen trying to clear the place out.'

Jens threw up his hands in a gesture of submission. 'At least you're here now.'

'We are.' Ömer batted his luxurious eyelashes in the most disarming way. Coy, apologetic and flirtatious, all at the same time.

Jens had to laugh. Then, 'Did you manage to get everything on the list?'

'Sure. Ömer's going to set the bar up in the kitchen. I'll just strip off this sweaty T-shirt and then get stuck into doing your hair.'

Jens' bath was run. Steam rose from the foam-covered surface. Bare-arsed, Jens bent his head over the sink as the electric hair trimmer clicked into life and vibrated in Dirk's firm grip. One slip and they would all be electrocuted! And yet there was something reassuring about the familiar buzz of the appliance, psyching them both up into party mode. A necessary prelim: a shared routine and a shared intimacy. As Dirk guided the blades in loving strokes over the contours of Jens' head and neck, the bowl became powdered with bristles that looked like iron filings drawn to a magnet.

'Stop moving your head so much. Keep still!' Dirk commanded, adjusting Jens' head with both hands.

'Sorry.'

'Do you want to end up looking like the last of the Mohicans? Or do you want to look your best?'

'I want to look my best.'

'Good. Then hold still!'

Jens grinned. It was the same procedure every time.

At last, Dirk switched off the appliance. 'All done.'

Jens raised his head and looked in the mirror on the bathroom cabinet directly in front of him. He ran a hand over his freshly shaven head. 'Oh, yeah. That looks much better. Thanks.'

Dirk brushed the last few hairs from Jens' neck and shoulders. Looking at their reflection in the mirror, Jens was captured by the sheer domesticity of it all. Fuck it! He had to admit, they made a very handsome couple.

'You want me to do you now?' Jens asked, looking around for the trimmer.

'Nah, later. I want to set up the bedroom.'

'Got something special in mind?'

'Naturally.'

Getting the bedroom ready was like an act of love. Laying down a cover over the bed; scattering cushions over the fur rugs; placing small bowls with condoms and lubricant strategically around the room. A selection of the best Bear porno videos was chosen, organised into a playlist and arranged by the television. Dirk was sure that they would keep Ömer happy, at least. The first one, already slipped into the machine, was running as a sort of foreplay. The first of numerous incense sticks were lit and lots of coloured candles flickered, casting a warm, seductive glow over the proceedings. The sound was turned down on the video and the music cranked up on the mini hi-fi. Dirk was proud of his handiwork. Now it was down to the chemistry of the guest list to work its necessary magic.

Jens and Ömer came in to admire Dirk's set up. 'Looks pretty professional to me,' said Jens. 'You know, you're completely wasted in your job, Dirk. You should have stuck to working in that brothel.'

Ömer looked from Jens to Dirk, a shocked expression on his face, before both Jens and Dirk burst out laughing. 'It's just a joke, Ömer. Honestly!'

Jens trimmed Dirk's hair and beard before the big guy followed Ömer into the shower. Fortunately, Ömer was already out and towelling himself down, otherwise it would have been highly unlikely that they would have been ready on time. But ready they were. Once everything was in order they sat around on the sofas, sharing a cool beer together, chilling out for five minutes before the pandemonium was due to begin.

At about nine o'clock the buzzer sounded. Well, this was it - the first guest was about to arrive. Guess who? No surprise. With a loud roar, Bodo burst through the door. Volker followed in his wake, clutching a six-pack of beer to his leather-vested chest.

Dirk was first to wrap his arms around Bodo and clap him on the back. 'Should have known you'd be first one through the door.'

'I'm the first? Damn! So none of the hunky men you promised me are here yet?

'The first three are.'

'Who are they, then?' Bodo asked, with that unmistakable twinkle in his eye.

'Me, Jens and Ömer, of course!'

'So . . . the best is yet to come?'

'Fuck you!' Dirk punched him playfully on the shoulder.

'Shouldn't that be the other way around?'

'Eh?'

'Thought it was more usual for you to say "Fuck me"!'

'Up yours!'

'In your dreams!' Bodo turned to hug Ömer, sweeping him up in his arms and smothering him. He lifted Ömer's feet off the floor in the process. 'Ah, but now this little one? Maybe if I stood him on a chair?'

Jens stood with his arm around Volker's shoulder, watching the evening's entertainment begin. Finally, he leaned into his ear. 'Come into the kitchen. Let me get you a drink.' He raised his eyebrows. 'These guys will be at it for hours.'

In the kitchen, Volker's gaze was instantly drawn to the sight of the mountain of food laid out over every available surface. There was enough to feed a small army of hungry men. Setting the six-pack down alongside a myriad other bottles, he remarked, 'You've been very busy. That's a helluva lot of food for one party.'

'Just remember. We're catering for Bear appetites. I only hope it's enough!'

'Did you do all this?'

'Most of it. The food, anyway.'

'I'm impressed. It looks delicious.'

'So, help yourself. Can I get you a drink for starters? What do you want?'

Dirk suddenly appeared in the doorway with Bodo towering over his shoulder and Ömer at his elbow. "I'm sure Bodo will have his usual pink gin, and as for Volker? What about a large lemonade shandy? Mmm, can't you just feel that cooling liquid pouring over your hot, eager tongues? Whaddya say, big boys?'

Bodo clipped the back of Dirk's head. 'Whaddabout, "Fuck you!"'

'Sorry,' Dirk replied. 'That's my line.'

With everyone clutching a beer, they settled down on the sofas once again. Bodo made small talk with Jens and waiting for the promised parade of hunks to arrive. Dirk was entertaining the rest of the assembled group, as was his forté. Ömer, meanwhile, just basked in the light of the admiring glances.

While trying to concentrate on what Bodo was rambling on about, Jens could feel himself teetering on the edge of anxiety. Parties, for him, were always fraught with anxiety. Would there be enough to eat, or enough to drink? Would enough people show up? Would everyone enjoy it? His natural instinct at parties was to hide in the kitchen, but tonight he had to play host. Beer helped. Helped him to be more of a social lion, a role that seemed to come effortlessly to Dirk - with or without alcohol. Stealing a glance at his watch, Jens realised that it was still early yet. The party wouldn't get into full swing before ten. Eleven?

Bodo had noticed that Jens' attention was elsewhere, and had seen the quick look at the watch. Shuffling in his seat, he turned to Jens. 'So, do we get a tour of the apartment?'

Jens was relieved. Anything to break the tension. 'Follow me. Volker?'

'Later. I'll have a look later, if that's okay?'

'Sure . . . '

First stop was Jens' playroom, as it was known. Equipped with a desk, computer, CD and bed, it functioned as a study, really, but when he needed his own space he could always lock himself away. It was his private space. As they entered, Jens reached for the light switch, but Bodo held him fast. Wrapping his arms around Jens, he hugged him to his chest. 'What's up? You seem really stressed out.'

'That obvious, huh?'

'If it's the party that's got you worrying, you shouldn't bother. There's nothing at all to worry about. Everything is going to be fine. Believe me.'

'Glad you think -' But Jens was not able to finish the sentence. Bodo shut him up by crushing his lips down upon Jens'. His powerful tongue thrust between his lips and wriggling deep within the warm and wet recesses. If Jens was at all surprised, he did not show it. It was as if he had simply been waiting for the inevitable to happen, and he responded in kind by gripping Bodo's powerful back and pressing up against him. His fingers clawed at the soft flannel material of the checked workshirt encasing Bodo's hulking shoulders.

Bodo took hold of Jens' right hand and drew it down, placing it firmly on his crotch. His rock-hard erection was demanding some attention. 'You're stressed. But I'm all excited.'

Jens pulled away slightly and then, giving Bodo's cock a firm squeeze, he moved away. He reached down and adjusted his own fly. 'The night is young. Better save something for later, Big Man.'

'Spoil sport!'

'What about Volker?'

'Leave him to me. Now, lead on.'

'You guys were gone a long time,' said Volker, seemingly oblivious to what had just taken place. 'It's a great apartment, isn't it?'

Bodo reached down to ruffle Volker's close-cropped hair. 'Oh, we were just admiring the view over Berlin from the balcony out back. It's really spectacular. Come with me, Volker, and I'll show you.'

The buzzer sounded as Bodo led Volker by the hand in the direction of the bedroom balcony. Bastian, their landlord, and his partner Bernd were at the door. Framed in the doorway, these two men in their late forties made a handsome picture. Bernd was big and brawny, with cropped silver hair and sculpted goatee to match. He looked more than a little like some film star. Dirk, being lousy at that sort of thing, could not put a precise name to the face. George somebody-or-other, with sexy, Latin eyes that were playful and flirtatious. Both Daddy Bears were carrying bottles of Sekt - just something small for the party.

'We've also brought you a special something for your housewarming.' Upon saying this, Bernd took out a small package from inside his jacket. Unwrapping it, Dirk saw that it was a video. His quizzical expression was answered by Bastian.

'It's one of our own home videos. Thought you guys might appreciate it. We use it as our . . . how would you say it . . . ?'

'Our calling card,' continued Bernd, looking Dirk straight in the eye. 'We've made a couple of private videos. But this one is definitely the best.'

'Well, this is one video I look forward to seeing,' said Dirk, somewhat dumbfounded at their brazen overture but aroused nonetheless. 'In fact, maybe we could show it this evening. We sort of have a video show organised in the bedroom. Videos "plus", if you get my meaning.'

'Oh, I do. I certainly do,' replied Bernd. 'Bastian told me all about you guys. He said that you were real party animals. Friendly. Accommodating. And a whole lot of fun.'

'That we are. That we are. And the fun begins right here.' Dirk gestured to the kitchen. 'So what can I get you guys to drink, then?'

'Beer,' said Bastian.

Bernd frowned, momentarily. 'Afraid I'm driving. It'll have to be a large lemonade shandy, I'm afraid.'

'But will that get you into the party mood?' Dirk asked pointedly.

Bastian chuckled. 'Oh, it doesn't take much to get Bernd in the mood, does it now?'

The buzzer sounded again. This time it was Ömer's turn to dance in the hallway as his friends Hassan, Seyhmus and Kaan arrived. Three muscular packages of Turkish delight. There were kisses all around, and everyone delighted in the shared affection. At last, Ömer had an opportunity to play host. Stepping to the forefront, he introduced his friends around to an appreciative audience.

After that, the front door bell never seemed to stop ringing. The flat quickly filled to capacity. And with it, an increase in sexual heat in direct proportion to each new arrival.

Twelve o'clock and Dirk took a look into the bedroom to see how things were progressing. Comfortably full, if not yet cram-packed. Ömer was up against the far wall, feasting on the face of some Turkish guy, both of them with their stiff, circumcised cocks out and proud. And over in the corner, some other guy - Seyhmus, was it? - sucking Bastian's thick dick. Dirk wondered whether he should join in, then thought better of it. Plenty of time yet. He took a deep breath and left to look after the rest of his guests.

In the lounge, the Marianne Rosenberg 'Hit-Mix' CD kept the party in full swing with its series of gay camp classics. Some guys were dancing to the music. Still others, clustered together, were straining to have their conversations heard above the bass boom. Dirk caught sight of Jens across a crowded room. Their eyes held fast, sharing a satisfied smile. Everything was going great guns. Time was flying by, all too quickly.

It was already three o'clock in the morning, and the party had begun to wind down. Many of the guests had already taken their leave, albeit reluctantly. Even Volker, whom Dirk had accompanied downstairs to organise transport for him. Still, it was far from over yet.

'I saw Volker leave earlier. Dirk was going to get him a taxi,' said Jens rearranging what little food was left. 'However did you manage that, Bodo?'

'Oh, that was easy. I just reminded him that he's got to go visit his sister tomorrow morning. And that since I've got nothing in particular on, that I can afford to stay out a bit later.'

Jens grinned at his reasoning. Bodo and Volker's relationship was a funny one. Bodo, the gregarious fuckmonster, and Volker, the one who preferred the quiet life. Still it took all sorts. But they worked well together, and they both seemed to be happy, which in the end, Jens figured, was the main thing.

'Hey, what's up, little guy?' said Bodo, noticing the momentary pensive expression on Jens' face. 'I hope you're not going to start fading on me, just when I was getting into the swing of things.' With that, he crossed the kitchen and took Jens in his arms without another word. He kissed him passionately; took his hand and led him up the hallway. They entered the orgy room, which, despite the late hour, was busy with the last remaining guests.

Bodo turned Jens around so that they were facing each other. He leant down to kiss him tenderly on the lips, then ran his hands over Jens' powerful chest. he opened up Jens' shirt and reached inside to tweak the stiffening nipples. Hard as bullets. Jens responded by sticking his tongue deep into Bodo's hungry mouth. The shirt now fully unbuttoned, Bodo yanked the tail free from Jens' shorts. He rubbed his hands over Jens' hairy chest; ran them down to the belly button, feeling the taut muscle beneath the fur. Bodo reached his hands up to Jens' shoulders and slipped the shirt off, at the same time running his fingers down the other man's back as he hugged him closer. Now reaching down, he probed into the back of Jens' leather shorts. No underwear.

Bodo's kisses moved to Jens' cheeks, his neck, his shoulders and his tits. Then Bodo was on his knees, pressing his nose up against Jens' crotch before unbuttoning the shorts. Reaching into the fly, he prised the hard cock free. Jens gave a helping hand by undoing his belt and allowing his shorts to slip down to his knees. Bodo lathered his cock with his tongue, nibbling and chewing. As they were positioned up against the wall, it gave Jens an opportunity to look around the room. In the dim light he could make out Ömer and Bernd on the bed, sixtynining. In the corner, Bastian was on his knees sucking on two cocks - those of Seyhmus and Hassan. Bare-bollock naked, their arms were around each others shoulders, mouths clamped together. Hassan was flexing his stomach muscles and his pierced tits. A tattoo on his left pec pumped hard. Seyhmus was clean shaven. His pubic hair was cropped back, revealing a bald cock and balls. Mouth-watering meatballs.

Jens was enjoying this debauched scene. He was tantalised by Bodo's talented lips and tongue, for Bodo was a born cocksucker. A cock-hungry fiend, really. He took Jens' dick in his mouth right to the hilt, then slid back to reveal the entire length of Jens' big, shimmering cock, before swallowing the whole pork sword back down again. Jens was also enjoying the feel of the new ring ball-weight that Dirk had given him as a present for his birthday. Bodo's tongue now played with the weight, going all around the ring. And below, he licked and caressed Jens' balls in a tongue bath. Bodo pulled off his own shirt, and Jens reached down to play with Bodo's nipples, careful not to break the connection between cock and mouth. Bodo began to growl. Jens pinched harder. The growl turned into a howl, bouncing off the walls.

Bodo reached into his pocket, fumbling about, and produced a small bottle of Jungle Juice. He held it up to Jens, who grasped it, twisted the white plastic cap free and held it under his nostril. He pressed his index finger up against one nostril and inhaled deeply, repeating the process on the other side. Suddenly, his face was burning ad his head was swimming. He was instantly drunk as amyl nitrate fumes filled his head; coursed through his blood stream. His focus was solely on the divine moment. His prick was buried in Bodo's ravenous mouth. Everything else forgotten. Only the junction of cock and mouth had importance. Dirk was long forgotten. As was his disappearance with Volker. Long forgotten.

In a darkened shop doorway, not two hundred metres from the entrance to the apartment building, Volker was on his knees. Dirk's cock was pounding the back of his throat.

They had been walking to the nearby taxi rank with the best of intentions. Hadn't they? The empty suburban streets were devoid of life. Street lamps were casting their sombre glow. But then, Dirk's little finger had brushed up against Volker's. Their hands had gripped each other. It was but a short step into the deep recesses of the supermarket entrance.

Volker had Dirk's jeans around his ankles within seconds. His desperate need for Dirk's thick, long cock was finally going to be sated, for Volker was like a man possessed. Without any preliminaries he zoned straight onto his target: cock. Dirk's cock, to be precise. It was as if he had been waiting for this moment for the longest time and, having finally been presented with opportunity, he was going to make the very most of it.

Gripping the base of Dirk's shaft with his fist, Volker's head bobbed up and down on the flushed and straining arrowhead. Fuck, thought Dirk, this guy really sucks dick like a professional. Volker seemed determined to force Dirk's cock to release its creamy load. Wordlessly, he worked his mouth, as if he was begging for Dirk's dick to release its contents.

Dirk towered above him, his cock buried deep in Volker's throat, and he fucked the other man's wet cavernous throat. Looking down upon him, Jens couldn't help but smile. Bodo had taught him well, though he was clearly a natural talent. His technique was very impressive. Straining his neck, Volker moved his mouth forward and back over the length of Jens' cock as Dirk whispered words of encouragement. 'Beautiful baby. Sweet little Bear Cub.'

Suddenly Volker yanked his head back. 'Oh, no.'

Dirk gasped, looked down. 'What is it, Little Bear?'

'Not here, Dirk.'

'Eh?'

'Not now. Not like this.'

Dirk gasped again, perplexed. 'What?' What?!'

'I want you, baby. But not like this.'

'Then how?'

'In bed. I want to take you to my bed.'

'But Bodo?'

'Bodo travels all the time. Yes?'

'Yes.'

'You can come over. We can do this properly.'

'Ah, no, Volker. I want you now!' He attempted to persuade Volker to accept his cock in his mouth once more. Placing his hand on the back of his head, he pressed him forward.

But Volker was adamant and he pressed his lips together. As a form of consolation, he kissed Dirk's cock, then kissed his balls. 'No, Papa Bear. You deserve better.' Volker eased himself up onto his. 'Soon, Dirk. I'll give you all my love. I promise. I'll be worth the wait. Soon.'

Bodo aimed long, luxurious licks down the length of Jens' cock, from base to tip. He ran his tongue around the ring of the cockhead. Then up onto Jens' belly. Bodo rose slowly on his haunches, now facing Jens, and gave him deep, soul-kisses. Then Bodo grappled with the belt on his faded Levi's and let them drop. Beneath the blue, he was wearing a jockstrap. His cockhead was attempting to struggle free from the side of elasticised pouch. He stood, standing proud, his hands braced against the wall on either side of Jens' head, his legs spread wide. His asscheeks were pulsing as his pelvis met Jens' all-consuming stare.

Looking over his shoulder, he cocked his arse at Dirk, who now stood watching from the doorway. 'Come on, Dirk. Give it to me. I want you to fuck me. Hard. Fuck me real hard.'

Dirk was only too willing to comply. He stripped deliberately, discarding his shirt, his jeans, his underwear and socks in a heap on the floor. He stroked his impressive erection, then walked across to the bedside table, plucked a condom from the bowl and unrolled it slowly down the full length of his prick. He was taking his time, making Bodo wait. His big dick, engorged with life-blood, was held up to the light and he lubed himself up. It was hardly worth the effort, as Bodo was already lubed up. But that was not the point. Dirk was showing off, putting on a performance. A performance that was having exactly the desired effect, because Bodo was clearly drooling.

'Enough!' Bodo growled. 'Enough, you prick-teasing bastard. Get over here and fuck me now!' He parted his buttocks. His arse was more than ready and willing.

Dirk grinned and crossed the room. He positioned himself behind Bodo, placed his dick between his buttcrack, then teased Bodo's anus with his cockhead.

'Stop playing, Dirk. Just stick it in. Please! Just stick it in!'

Dirk pressed gently forward. His cock slipped in with an ease that he rarely experienced.

'Yeah, all the way. Get your cock in all the way.' Bodo leaned forward, his mouth consuming Jens', and Jens clung to Bodo's big, hairy, trembling body.

'Fuck, Bodo! It feels so good to be up your arse,' Dirk said, holding still.

Bodo broke free on Jens' hungry mouth and twisted his neck to look over his shoulder as best he could. 'Fuck me!'

Dirk began to pump his hips. 'Like this?'

'Don't stop, big guy.'

Jens reached his arms around Bodo and gripped Dirk's arsecheeks, easing their forward motion, guiding each thrust of the hips. As the momentum increased, Bodo attempted to steady his gait, spreading his legs wider, planting his size elevens squarely on the floor. He bent at the knees, shuffling his hands higher up the wall, above Jens' head, in an effort to support himself. Jens found himself presented with Bodo's armpit bushes and caught a whiff of the musky man-scent that emanated from them. His fur was moist and smelled of an evening's worth of fresh, manly sweat. Unable to resist, Jens' buried his mouth right on in there. He sucked and nuzzled, first on one armpit, then the other. He savoured that special and wholly erotic masculine tang that he knew could only be found in the armpits of a big, horny Bear. Dirk, meanwhile, gripped and clung to the hair on Bodo's back with one hand, whilst the other reached around the front to hunt for the stiff, pink nipples almost lost amidst the forest of Bodo's chest hair.

The back of Dirk's legs began to ache with the strain of his deep butt-thrusts and so, after looking around, he motioned to the bed. Bernd was already there, taking up one half and getting seriously fucked by Ömer. Jens slipped free of Bodo's grip and joined the other pair. Kneeling over Bernd, he lowered his mouth onto Bernd's juddering dick. And then all hell broke loose.

Dirk manoeuvred Bodo to the bed, never breaking their intimate connection, and forced him down, face first, onto the heaving mattress alongside the squirming mass of bodies. Bodo pushed himself up, positioning himself on all fours with his arse in the air, allowing Dirk easy access. Dirk, in turn, took full advantage. Mounting Bodo from behind, he stuffed his dick deep within his willing hole. Bastian crossed the room and knelt on the bed, positioning himself so that Bodo could feed on his stiff Daddy Bear cock. Filled at both ends, crammed full, Bodo's mouth and his arse ached with the fullness of cock. He was stretched to the limit.

Over in the corner, Seyhmus and Hassan remained hard at it. They were now playing with each other's cock as they watched the developments on the bed, transfixed. Dirk gave a nod of his head to indicate for them to come over and join in. They didn't need a second invitation.

The bed groaned under their collective weight, but somehow it managed to hold firm. The heap of bodies melding into a solid mass of flesh and hair and muscle and sweat and sex. Bernd now lay on his back, Ömer was squatting over his face getting professionally rimmed. Jens was fucking Bodo, his dick slipping in and out in a steady rhythm. Dirk, meanwhile, was stroking his cock as he looked on. Bastian was lying on his back, both legs in the air getting roundly

fucked by Seyhmus, while at the same time sucking furiousl
Hassan's fat, circumcised cock. Dirk continued to stroke his own cock;
he spat on his palm and lovingly stroked his pride and joy. Some
housewarming, thought Dirk to himself, it's fucking red hot. His eyes
flicked between the TV screen and the debauched scene. The video
running on the television had nothing on this. The video couldn't
communicate the sweat, the feel of one manly body on another. The
physical heat. The smell. The headiness of the atmosphere. The scent
of sex in the air. A salt-and-meat smell of fresh sweat and dick-musk
and pre-come.

Ömer started to moan as Bernd's tongue plunged deeper, ever deeper into his arsehole. His buttocks were being prised apart, as if Bernd
wanted to stick his head inside. And then, suddenly, Ömer came,
albeit unwillingly. He had wanted to hold off longer, but had been
physically unable to do so. He yelped with the pleasure/pain of
orgasm. A rope of come lassoed high and wide, splattering Bastian as
he leaned forward, looking on, covering his shoulder and his furry,
matted chest.

Hassan lay back on the Bear-fur rug, his legs were slung over Dirk's
shoulders as Dirk ploughed into his trough. Bodo was still being
fucked by Jens. Bastian was on his knees licking Seyhmus' balls and
the base of his cock as Seyhmus jerked it over Bernd's head. Ömer, at
the head of the bed, was looking on. He was toying lazily with his
spent cock. On and on. How long? Time seemed to lose all meaning.

Dirk pulled out of Hassan. He positioned himself so that his and
Hassan's legs were interlocked, scissors-like, their balls touching base
and their cocks side by side. Jens did the honours, sheathing them
both in fresh rubbers. And as Dirk's fist clamped both dicks together,
forming one giant rubberised rod, Bodo squatted astride and above
them. Holding his arsecheeks wide, he lowered himself slowly down,
grinding his hips to facilitate entry, forcing a way in, then impaling
himself on both stiff pricks in a single swoop. Getting fucked by two

cocks simultaneously. Fucking hell, thought Dirk as Bodo bounced up and down, Fucking, fucking hell. It was a tight fit, for sure. Dirk felt his dick rub up against Hassan's, felt the grip of Bodo's ring-piece squeezing then together into one single monster cock.

The expression of ecstasy on Bodo's face deserved to be captured on camera. Jens took the photo. Seyhmus was sucking on Bodo's right tit, Bastian on the other. Bernd with his cock resting on Bodo's head. Ömer was grinning in the background. 'Cheese.'

As the flash faded, Bodo erupted like a volcano. His white-hot lava sprayed everywhere. And everywhere it touched, it caused a chain reaction. Bastian and Seyhmus splattered the prostrate Hassan and Dirk with steaming rivulets of ball-juice. Bernd shot his load over Bodo's head and onto the fur rug. Hassan and Dirk emptied their ripe plums into the blistering rubbers. And Jens, at long last, camera discarded, gripped his cock tightly in his fist. His come pulsed out in a high arc, as he opened his eyes wide to drink in the scene.

They cleaned themselves up, exhausted. The mass of bodies drifted off like ghosts in the night to their respective quarters. Seyhmus and Hassan to Ömer 's bed. Bastian, Bernd and Bodo - the three Big Bs - would share Jens'. Dirk and Jens, however, could stretch out or cuddle up in the relative luxury on Dirk's king-size mattress. And cuddle up they did, wordlessly and comfortably. Dawn's early light began to peep through a crack in the curtain. All was silent.

The quiet before the proverbial storm.

The next thing Bodo could remember was being shaken roughly by the shoulders.

'Leave me! I want to sleep!' he mumbled through an increasing, if reluctant, state of consciousness.

Dirk was doing the shaking. Jens stood close by.

'He's in no fit state to go home to Volker,' Dirk said. 'He's a wreck.'

'Who are you calling a wreck?' Bodo mumbled.

'Bodo?' said Jens. 'It's two o'clock in the afternoon. C'mon now, big guy.'

'Two o'clock? It's early yet! It's Sunday, I can sleep as long as I like.'

'Not here, you can't. Volker's been on the phone. He's worried. He wanted to know where you were. C'mon now, you big lug.' Dirk threw back the sheets and together they both dragged Bodo reluctantly to his feet. But it was hardly worth the effort. As soon as they released him, Bodo fell back onto the bed, bounced a couple of times and then was still.

All Jens and Dirk could do was laugh. Not least because Bodo had woken with a stiffy. Laying flat against his hairy belly, it was straining up towards his chin.

'Sounds like the party's still going on,' Bodo muttered, smacking his lips.

'Only in your dreams!' Jens replied.

'You've been out cold for hours. Of course it's over! Everyone else went home ages ago,' Dirk added.

Jens chuckled. 'Welcome to the real world.'

Bodo opened his eyes with some difficulty. They were sleep-encrusted, and sensitive to light. 'What are you two looking at?' Bodo asked, grumpily.

Jens grinned. 'A Bear with a sore head, unless we're much mistaken?'

Dirk leaned forward and clasped Bodo's throbbing cock in his fist. 'Or a Bear with a sore dick, if this big thing is anything to go by!'

Nineteen

Dirk was running through the dark empty streets. The ringing sound was still some way off in the distance. He'd have to increase his pace. Where was the sound coming from? What the fuck was going on? Just up ahead was a big intersection. Cars, buses and lorries were rumbling past, and there was no sign of any traffic lights. How come there was never a policeman on duty when you needed one? And still the ringing noise, off in the distance. He'd just have to get across the street somehow. But suddenly there were huge parachutes falling from the sky, falling all around him. Dirk dodged this way and that, but it was no use. A big silken parachute landed right on top of him. He was trapped. He'd never get to the source of that ringing sound now. Never manage to find out who was ringing. Ringing? Telephone? With a start, Dirk woke up. The sheets were wrapped around his head and the phone was ringing loudly. 'Fuck! Fuck it!' he growled as he scrambled out of bed and made a mad dash to the living room. 'Hello! Hello!' he called brusquely into the receiver. Who the fuck was ringing him at this hour of the morning anyway?

'Hi, Dirk? This is Volker. Did I wake you? I'm sorry.'

'No. No. Yes, this is Dirk. And you did wake me. But don't worry about it. I'm up now and in a couple of minutes I'll even be awake.'

'I'm sorry, Dirk. I just wanted to catch you on your own . . . I know that today is your day off, and I was wondering if you wanted to meet up. Maybe go for a bike ride in the Tiergarten?'

Although it was indeed Dirk's free day, he had had other plans for it. Like lying on the sofa and reading. Or maybe going to Teufelsee for a swim. Or maybe going to the gym for the morning. Or whatever. The main thing was that it was his day and he had planned to spend it by himself. Just taking time out to do his own thing. And yet here was Volker ringing him, obviously needy. Dirk, being who he was, couldn't let a friend down in his hour of need. Plus, Volker had the cutest arse in all of West Berlin. Almost!

'Sure, Volker, that'd be great. But I do have a number of things to get organised first, so could we make it later in the day? Say about fourteen hundred hours, or so?'

From the longer than expected pause, this was not quite what Volker had in mind. But what the fuck? It was Dirk's day, and he was determined to make sure that he got to spend some time alone.

'Yeah. Sure, Dirk. But listen, if you've got something else planned, then that's okay. We could always leave it for another time . . . '

'No, Volker. Honestly. It's fine. Plus, looking out the window now, it looks like it's going to be a hot one. So it'll be fun to get out on the mountain bike and ride around the Tiergarten.'

Having arranged to meet up at the zoo at 1400, Dirk put the phone down and returned to bed. He hadn't seen Volker for ages. Not since the night of the party. Oh, he had expected to, but days, weeks, had passed without a word. And now this, out of the blue. Well, there was no point worrying about it - he'd find out what it was all about later in the day.

The gym wasn't at all full when Dirk arrived. Just a couple of the regulars pumping iron, and Muscle Mary working the front desk. This was just how Dirk liked it. Not having to wait to use any of the equipment. No crowds of teenagers trying to impress each other. No, that was not Dirk's style at all. This was much more the way he preferred it: just Dirk and his body, his mind focused on the task in hand.

A couple of hours later, he was soaping up in the shower. His muscles ached slightly with that refreshing feeling of them having been tested to their limits. It was a comforting sensation. It made Dirk feel alive. Not just living within his body, but actually making his body work for him. Bending and shaping it to his will. Mind over matter.

Back at home, he prepared lunch. Steak and salad. And plenty of both. Food for the mind and for the body. Then it was time to chill out, read a little and get some letters written. Dirk really valued these days at home alone. No Jens. No Ömer. No one to disturb him. Not that he didn't enjoy living with them both, he surely did. But there were times when it was nice to be by himself, to do what he wanted to do, rather than to have to reach a consensus the whole time. For now, he needed to recharge his batteries. He somehow suspected that he would need every drop of juice he could store up.

At ten to two in the afternoon, Dirk cycled up to Zoologischer Garten railway station. No sign of Volker. Still, it was early yet. He hadn't given much thought to this meeting since the phone call that morning. Now with only minutes to go, he wondered what it was all about. He had never been that close to Volker - deliberately so.

Bodo, of course, was the reason. Bodo had been his friend long before Volker had come along. Dirk still remembered the morning when Bodo had called round to tell them the news. His eyes had lit up as he told the tale of the 'cute little Bear' he'd met the night before, who was only visiting Berlin for the week, but planning to move here in the near future. And how they had not got any further than kissing and hugging since Volker - for it was, indeed, him - wasn't interested in one-night stands. Bodo's face had been rapturous, but behind his back, Jens had raised an eyebrows at this revelation. Both men knew that it wasn't quite Bodo's style, fuckmonster that he was. Still, it had been funny to see him so entranced by this Volker.

Anyway, Volker had moved to Berlin. He and Bodo soon set up house together, and they were happy ever after. Well, almost. Bodo's testosterone got the better of him after a couple of months of couple-dom. One night Dirk and Jens had been in F-FABrik. After having been to a party, they had called in for one last beer. Dirk had been standing talking to Jens, when he noticed Jens look over his shoulder.

'Don't look now, but Bodo has just come up out of the fuck-pit downstairs. And by the looks of him, he's been well and truly fucked.'

And that was that. From that point on, Bodo had led a double life. The homebody that hung out with Volker and the fuckmonster that would call into F-FABrik for a quickie of an evening, or else take advantage of those times when work took him out of town . . .

Suddenly the reveries were interrupted. 'Hi, Dirk. You were early.'

Dirk looked up as Volker leaned over to kiss him hello. 'Oh. Hi, Volker. Sorry, I've been elsewhere. Daydreaming.'

'Well, whoever he was, I'm sure you were having a good time together.'

As Volker was saying this, Dirk looked at what he was wearing. It wasn't the typical Volker gear. In fact, this was like a whole new Volker. He was wearing a hoop-necked, green camouflage vest that showed off his abundant body hair and muscular shoulders. The masses of hair on his shoulders, arms and back matched the fur on his face. Combat shorts, green army socks and boots completed the outfit. And around his neck, he wore a chain with dog-tags, his eyes hidden behind a pair of dark sunglasses.

'Wow, Volker, when did you get into all of this stuff? I never thought that you were interested in the whole fetish scene.'

'Well, I wasn't. You know I always thought fetish meant rubber and stuff like that. And then last Christmas, Bodo bought me this vest. He said that it would show off my hairy shoulders and back. You know how he is about this whole body hair thing . . . '

'Woof! I do indeed, Volker. I do indeed'

'Anyway, I figured that I would need to get shorts to go with it. And so Bodo came along with me, and before I knew it I had got the whole outfit. So what do you think of it, anyway?'

'As I said before, Volker. Woof! And double woof!! What more can I say?'

Volker smiled enigmatically and, nodding, he steered his bicycle in the direction of the park and set off at a clip. Dirk followed. Their path led up along the side of the Zoo, ripe with smell of the elephant house, then up towards the Lion Bridge that formed the central point of the gay cruising area and onwards to the so-called Tuntenwiese, which was the main gay sunbathing area. Setting their bikes down, they spread out their towels, stripped off and stretched out, baking in the sun. Volker lay on his front, his beautiful backside on display for all to see. It was yet another side of Volker that Dirk had never seen before, and a side he very much liked. His attention was drawn especially to the small tattoo of a grizzly bear etched on Volker's left butt-cheek. Dirk found his eyes on it, time and again. His interest did not go unnoticed.

'You like my tattoo, or do you just think I've got a nice arse?' Volker was being flirty.

Dirk resisted playing the game for the moment and slipped on his Ray Bans, hiding his hungry eyes from view. 'Is it new?' he asked casually.

'The tattoo? Fairly new. Had it done a couple of months ago. Bodo picked this design, by the way.'

'Sorry?'

'The design. The tattoo on my arse. He said it was perfect.'

'The tattoo or your arse?'

'Both.' Volker smiled.

'Well, he certainly wasn't wrong there.'

'I'm glad you think so.'

'Oh, yes!' Dirk sighed, unable to disguise the desire in his voice. 'You have one hell of a well-trained piece of arse. You should bring it out more often.'

'Good of you to notice.'

'And as for that juicy-looking cock?'

Volker hesitated momentarily. 'It's all yours, if you want it.'

'Oh, I want it, sure enough.' Dirk licked his parched lips. 'But, Volker . . . ?'

'But what?'

'This could get really messy.'

'Then we'll just have to be extra careful, won't we?' Volker turned his face away from the sun. 'He's away, you know. Bodo. He's away for the next few days.

'He's got a gig down in Leipzig, hasn't he?'

'That's right, security for a rock festival. '

'How long is he away exactly?'

'He left yesterday afternoon. And he won't be back until Friday evening. Another two days' time.'

'So . . . '

'Well, it means that I've got the place all to myself and I can do as I please.' This time there was no mistaking what Volker was getting at.

Dirk sat up and crossed his legs. 'Are you sure you should be doing this, Volker?'

'What? Seducing you, you mean?' Volker grinned.

Dirk frowned and turned his face away. 'I mean, isn't this all a little out of character? You've never played around. Never wanted to, as far as I knew.'

'Maybe I'm just growing up.'

'Is that how you see it?'

'Look, I was twenty-one when Bodo and I got together. He's the only guy I've ever been to bed with. I thought it would always be that way. But he took me places, showed me things . . . It's given me an appetite. I want you to feed that appetite.'

Dirk covered his exposed groin with his hand in a vain attempt to cover his arousal. 'You want to go now?'

Volker stretched and relaxed. He smiled to himself. 'Oh, we've plenty of time yet. Let's just enjoy the sun for an hour.'

Once inside Volker's door, it was like a whirlwind had been let loose in the apartment. The two of them tore at each other's clothes in a mad frenzy to get naked, the faster the better. The last hour they had spent in the Tiergarten side by naked side. The wait had made Dirk crazy, like an extended foreplay getting each other ready for this. This passionate consummation. This frenetic kissing and sucking. Dirk thrust his tongue deep into Volker's mouth. Volker sucked it in, feeding on it.

Now both were naked. Volker dropped to his knees and buried his face in Dirk's crotch, sniffing the sweat, the manliness. Using just the tip of his tongue, he licked along Dirk's inner thighs and then the base of his ballsac. Dirk shivered. Then slowly, Volker moved his tongue from side to side and worked his way along the seam of the ballsac until he reached the base of Dirk's stiff cock. He licked the base of the shaft, bathing it with his soft, pink tongue. Then just as he reached the head, he moved back again to the sac. Again he licked Dirk's balls, taking them into his mouth, wetting them with his saliva. He sucked on them as if they were two ripe, juicy plums. Releasing them somewhat reluctantly, he worked his way back up the cock shaft. Dirk's body was shuddering as Volker ran his hands over the other man's belly. Dirk reached down to play with Volker's tits, but Volker lifted his hands away, putting them at Dirk's side. The message was clear. Leave me to do this, I'm a giver.

Again Volker was about to take Dirk's cockhead between his lips, but suddenly he moved back to ball-sucking. Dirk was going crazy. His cock was quivering and vibrating with lust. The head of the cock was slick with pre-come. Volker massaged it with his forefinger and thumb, spreading it all over the cockhead, making it glisten in the late evening sunshine that was filtering into the hallway.

'Oh fuck, Volker. This is too much.'

Then Volker licked Dirk's balls again, taking the shaft between his lips and loving it with his tongue. He was again at the cockhead. This time he hesitated maybe a couple of milli-seconds before licking the entire cockhead and then burying it in his mouth. Without stopping, he swallowed and swallowed until the entire length was deep in his throat. Volker held still, and reached around to grip Dirk's firm buttocks. Pulling them towards him, he established a fuck-face rhythm. Once Dirk was pushing, Volker ran his hands over Dirk's belly hair, and up until he was flicking Dirk's tits. He took the nipples between thumb and forefinger, tugging and twisting them with a vengeance.

Dirk reached down and took hold of Volker's head in his hands, steadying it for the long, slow thrusts as he buried his dick deep in Volker's mouth. Then Dirk pulled Volker to his feet and spun him around. His hands reached round and he began to play with Volker's tits. He kissed and nibbled Volker's back, his shoulders, his neck, his ears. Volker leaned backwards, turning his head to kiss Dirk on the lips. He extended a tongue tasting of Dirk's sweaty cock. Dirk kissed him deeply, hungrily, tasting his own dick and his own pre-come.

At the same time, Dirk rubbed his cock between Volker's cheeks, between that glorious tattooed arse. He pulled back and spat on his hand, massaging his saliva on his cockhead before sticking it back between Volker's arsecheeks for a second time. He rubbed it slowly back and forth, establishing a rhythm. Volker began to pant, his hot breath on Dirk's cheek. Dirk reached down and wanked on Volker's cock. He felt its length grow harder in his hand. Good and hard. Huge.

Volker squeezed his thighs together. Tighter. Dirk's cock was fucking him between his asscheeks. Dry fucking, it was called. Well, there was nothing dry about this fuck. Dirk's cock was slippery with sweat, pre-come and spit. Slipping in and out of Volker's hairy crevice, Dirk could feel the head of his cock hitting against the base of Volker's ballsac. He could feel the tension mounting in his balls. The exquisite sensation of his cock being sandwiched in Volker's hot, sweaty arsecrack, sandwiched between Volker's buttocks and ballsac.

His cock was now straining, getting ready to burst. His hands were busy: one pinching a nipple hard, the other jerking Volker's cock furiously. Volker was thrusting his arse backwards, milking Dirk dry. Dirk's thick moustache tickled and caressed the back of Volker's neck as he folded over him, his cock primed and ready to shoot.

'You fucking hot, little Bear Cub,' Dirk whispered, grazing his beard against Volker's cheek. 'I'm going to nail you to the wall with my fucking spunk.'

The friction of cock between hairy butt-cheeks was just too much. Dirk groaned manfully and strung his come over Volker's hairy thighs. Come oozed and slathered its way between Volker's legs. He rubbed them together, spreading the sticky deposit over his inner thighs. Dirk collapsed against his furry back of him, his bollocks well and truly spent.

'Whew!' said Volker, crushed by Dirk's weight, struggling to stay upright. 'That was some fucking scene. Wherever did you learn to fuck like that?'

'Oh, you know us Catholic boys. We have to be careful!' Dirk replied, as he nuzzled his beard against Volker's ear.

In retrospect, Dirk wasn't sure what the whole thing had been about. Sure, the sex had been great. Spectacular ,even. But now it was over. The come shot was in the can, and it was back to reality. What the fuck would Bodo think if he knew that Dirk was fucking his boyfriend behind his back? Sure, Bodo was fucking all and sundry. And Jens, Dirk and Ömer had all had him in the recent past. But somehow Bodo, for all of his 'What's sauce for the goose . . . ' moralising, was glad to have Volker as a homebody. It provided him with a stable base. And that was something that Bodo wanted - nay, needed - above everything else. If Volker was now going to go out and fuck around like Bodo, then there would surely be trouble. Dirk knew it was crazy. He knew that Bodo knew it was crazy. But that didn't really stop the emotions welling up. And the jealousy. Dirk figured that this was at the bottom of it all: Bodo could fuck around all he wanted, because he knew that he was never going to leave Volker. He knew exactly what

Volker meant to him; knew the importance of this relationship. But if Volker started fucking around, he might meet someone he preferred to Bodo. And Bodo couldn't deal with that: the possibility that he might lose Volker.

Was Dirk just catastrophising or had he really opened up a can of worms this time? Just as Jens had often predicted, his cock was going to lead him into trouble. No doubt about it!

Twenty

The day had started off well. Jens took his time over a late breakfast. Brunch, really. A leisurely hour, tucking into Brötchen and croissants fresh from the corner bakery. Honey, jam, cheese, salami and ham toppings and freshly brewed coffee followed cereal and fruit juice. It was the first Saturday in May, and the sun was blistering down. The temperature was up to 28 degrees, transforming Berlin as it always did from dull and grey to European Haupstadt. Ömer was out at work; Dirk was off riding his bicycle. And the guy opposite his kitchen window was lying naked on his terrace, soaking up the sun. What a glorious view.

Seemingly oblivious to Jens' prying eyes, his neighbour had slipped off his scant, black bathing trunks and spread his legs to bathe his groin in the delicious rays of sunshine. Lounging back on a steel chair, an orange towel cushioning his back and legs, he stretched out his legs and feet, resting them on a second chair. The thin metal bars of his balcony frontage reflected the sun, yet obscured nothing.

A brown body, slathered with sun oil, glistening like a baby seal. No tan line. None, at least, that Jens could see. The neighbour threw his head back and ran oiled up fingers through his hair. Crossing his legs at the ankle, he flexed his feet and picked up his mobile phone. He dialled and re-dialled, talking to his friends on his indispensable Handy. While he chatted, he played with his flaccid, fleshy penis and scrotum: flicking them, rearranging them this way
and that.

An hour passed. Jens luxuriated in this bird's eye view. There was something proudly illicit about it, odd even. His neighbour was undeniably straight. Jens had watched the parade of girlfriends trot though his apartment with unremitting regularity. There were no curtains in his neighbour's apartment to obscure the view from Jens' kitchen window. The only blind in the bathroom, and this also obscured nothing. When the light glowed of an evening, the raffia blind became transparent. He had seen the guy on the lavatory, jerking off many a time. If only he knew. It thrilled Jens' voyeuristic nature to consider the possibility that his neighbour did know and could not care less.

Like now. The neighbour stretched out his legs and rearranged himself on the two metal chairs, absentmindedly toying with his cock as he held the mobile phone to his ear. Finally, call over, he pressed the OFF button and reached for his micro-briefs, slipping them over his feet before he stood and turned so that his semi-erect cock and balls met Jens head on. He eased his togs up over sturdy, muscular calves. He seemed in no rush and, it was clear from where Jens was sitting, that he had nothing to be ashamed of. With his togs at half-mast, he held the pose and smoothed his chest lazily. Then his goods were eased once more under their Lycra cover. The neighbour turned, exited through his balcony door to the darkness of the flat beyond, leaving Jens flushed and flustered, his appetite yet to be sated.

It was time to take a cold shower, and then maybe head off to the gym. Today was a day off and he had time, maybe, to do some arm work. Curls, dumbbell raises, on and on until exhaustion. Pumped up, he would maybe slip on a muscle vest and go for a walk in the park. Bask in the light of the sun and admiring glances. The pay-off for his hard work. Lustful glances. He could do whatever he pleased. The day was all his.

If only.

Now afternoon sunlight streamed through the kitchen window warming Jens' back as he sat at the dinning table toying with his coffee cup. Still he felt a shiver run through him. Because Jens was no longer alone. Ahmet sat opposite.

In this moment, Ahmet looked to Jens like he did the first time he had laid eyes on him - frightening. His square, shaven head; his bull neck and hard features. He looked like the epitome of every bully-boy

Jens had ever known. There was his cruel mouth. When he smiled, as he did now, it looked more than ever like a sneer. The guy was always holding something back, always playing games. He wore the arrogant smirk of someone who possesses some hidden advantage, and he wore it effortlessly.

Ahmet was rambling on about nothing in particular. He had a raspy voice, like he gargled with glass. It was also deep, throaty and thick. He spoke slowly and methodically. Still, his grasp of German was impressive. Also, he frequently checked Jens' understanding, peppering his conversation with the obligatory: 'Weiß du?' - 'You know?' But at this precise point in time, Jens didn't understand anything. He had switched off and wasn't listening. Instead, he focused on his coffee cup, watching the dregs swirl round and round. The whole time he was asking himself some questions: Do I really still find him attractive? Undoubtedly. But do I like him? No, I don't like him. I really don't like him. So why am I feeling aroused?

Had Jens known it was Ahmet ringing at the front door, the questions would never have needed to be asked - he would never have buzzed him into the building in the first place. He was more trouble than he was worth. But when the buzzer sounded, Jens was talking on the phone. Dirk had rung to say that a problem had cropped up at work, that he would be home later than expected that evening. Then Dirk had mentioned that Bodo had rung, was back in town and wondered if the two of them would like to meet for a few beers later. Jens was thus preoccupied and didn't bother to screen the caller via the intercom. More fool him. Now here he and Ahmet were.

It was not the first time Ahmet had called by the apartment, but it was the first time he had been inside. In the recent past, Jens had often spied him from the lounge window, standing down at the Imbiss across the road, eating a take away Kebap or drinking beer from a can, and all the time intently staring up at the apartment, without ever once crossing the street or the threshold. It had given Jens the creeps on a number of occasions. Ahmet gave him the creeps right now.

Jens had offered Ahmet a coffee. He asked for and got a beer. A little early in the day to be drinking, Jens thought, but anything for an easy life. He would stick to coffee. He was sure to need a clear head.

Some brothers were like chalk and cheese. Ömer and Ahmet? Like sweet and sour. All that was sweet and loveable about Ömer seemed to have curdled and gone sour in Ahmet. That is, if the sweetness was ever there in the first place. Unfortunately, it wasn't so obvious to the untrained eye. Ahmet still looked good enough to eat. Like chocolate when you're on a diet. And, in this case, bitter chocolate. Always tempting, but ultimately offering only empty calories. Yet the most frustrating aspect of it all was that whilst Jens was fully aware that the packaging was more attractive than the contents this muscle packet still made him salivate.

What could he put it down to? Animal magnetism? Certainly there was something of the beast about Ahmet. Those thick, forearms covered in fur; the mat of hair smothering his chest . . . Oh-oh! Jens needed a distraction. He stood and crossed to the sink, turned on the mixer tap and rinsed his cup methodically, all the time hoping that the bulge in his jeans was not too obvious in profile.

'Any chance of another beer?' Ahmet said, crunching his now-empty can in one swift move.

Jens took the can from his unwelcome guest and put it in the blue bin, the bin for recycling. He was generally keen to improve the environment. Pity he couldn't affect his immediate environment so quickly and easily. 'Are you really sure you want one? Like I said, Ömer won't be back for hours yet. And I really do have a lot to do.'

Ahmet lit a filterless cigarette and gazed off out of the window. It seemed there was to be no discussion. He plucked a fleck of tobacco from the tip of his moist tongue and then exhaled a stream of smoke down his flared nostrils.

Jens took a can from the fridge and held it out at arm's length, exhaling a sigh of resignation down his own flared nostrils - though flared for an entirely different reason.

Ahmet took the beer and continued to stare off into the middle distance as he opened the can mechanically, brought it to his lips and took a long pull. His face broke into a smile. 'So, what are we going to do until Ömer comes back?'

Out in the beer garden, the air was noticeably fresher. It was mid-afternoon; the sun shone down and, as always in such weather, the beer garden was packed. Fortunately, a cool breeze blew through the bank of trees. Dirk lay two beers down on the table. Rearranging his trouser snake, he seated himself on the bench beside Volker. He brought the glass to his lips and drank deep. Froth from the head of the pint clung to his bushy moustache. He retrieved it with tongue and bottom lip. 'I've been thinking about you,' he said hoarsely to Volker, from the corner of his mouth. He was trying to look casual to the group who had formed a drinking circle around the next table. 'Hoped I didn't hurt you that last time . . . that I wasn't too big, too rough?'

'Couldn't sit down for twenty-four hours, that's all!' Volker joked.

Dirk laughed. 'At least I didn't split you in half!'

The sun and sky were clearly visible through the leafy branches above their heads. For a moment, it seemed that all grew still.

'Did you tell Jens?'

'No. Did you tell Bodo?'

'No. But somehow I don't think he would have a problem with it if he knew.'

'Jens neither . . . But it's nice to have some secrets!' Dirk took a swig of his beer and pressed on. 'I'm going to have your hole, little Bear Cub, have no doubt about it.' Dirk's voice was low and guttural. 'I'm going to chew you up and spit you out time after time.'

Thankfully, the group nearby was oblivious to Volker's ears burning and cock pulsating with blood rush. 'Let's go somewhere private and get bollock-naked,' Volker urged. 'I want to service you, Dirk. I want to take your big, beautiful dick. All of it. Every thick, long inch. Up to the fucking hilt. I'm aching for you to fill my hole, Dirk. I want you to ride me good and hard.'

Dirk's eyes fixed on his beer, his throat still dry. 'And I want that too, son. Fuck, yes. I want it bad! Pity Bodo's at home.'

Under the table, Volker dropped a hand to rest on Dirk's inner thigh and cupped his solid bulge. 'How about booking a room in a hotel for a couple of hours?' It would be more comfortable than the woods.'

Dirk chuckled lasciviously. His hand covered Volker's and pressed it down. 'Got it all worked out, haven't you, my little Bear?! So what are we waiting for? Drink up!' Not so much a request, as a firm command.

Jens was rattling his chains to no effect. He should have known better the moment Ahmet had produced the handcuffs from his coat pocket, he thought. One last fuck for old times sake? How could he have been so dumb! It was not as if he had wanted sex with Ahmet, rather anything to get rid of him. Now here he was, gagged and strapped to the bed. That was the last time he would ever offer anyone a sympathy fuck!

Ahmet had Ömer backed into a corner. He had lain in wait for his return and Ömer hardly knew what hit him when he had walked through the door. Jens had never seen such rage as Ahmet now exhibited. His face was blood-red and the thick, blue vein in his neck throbbed fit to burst.

Ahmet towered menacingly over Ömer, screaming directly into his face. 'You bring shame upon our parents, shame upon the family, shame upon our heritage. Only shame! You deserve only punishment. Do you hear me?! I will punish you. You want to be a girl? Okay, I treat you like a girl.' And with that, Ahmet reached to unbuckle his belt.

Ömer braced himself for the worst and then everything became a blur.

Ahmet was swung around and slammed back into the wall. Bodo held him there by the throat. 'Now then, what do we have here?'

Ömer, his throat dry with fear, could only mutter, 'Bodo?'

Bodo looked over at Jens and then to Ömer. He smiled. 'Someone left the door ajar. A little unfortunate for your friend here, wouldn't you say?'

Ahmet tried to wriggle free from Bodo's iron grip. It was a complete waste of effort. Bodo turned back to face him. 'Stop wriggling, you little piece of shit!' His tone was so menacing, Ahmet was forced to comply. 'Now, I don't know exactly what your game is, my friend, but I did hear enough to know you're up to no good.' Bodo raised his index finger and used it to punch the message home on Ahmet's ribcage. 'Now - don't - you - ever - ever - threaten - my - friends - again! Do you hear me?'

Ahmet choked on his reply. Bodo yanked him forward and then slammed him back into the wall a second time. Ömer thought he could hear his brother's bones rattle.

'I said, do you hear me?!'

Ahmet nodded his response but Bodo didn't loosen his grip.

'Good. Because if you ever so much as lay a finger on one of my friends again, I shall personally see to it that you die a horrible death. Got that?'

Another nod.

'And remember, you don't just have to worry about me. Because I've got my family to back me up. And if you think I'm big then let me put you straight, my friend. I'm the baby!' And with that, Bodo grabbed Ahmet by the collar, jerked him around and marched him to the front door. Finally, with the aid of a well-placed boot, Ahmet was over the threshold. 'Now get out of my sight, you sad, self-hating, little closet-case. Don't ever let me see your ugly face again.' Ahmet scurried off down the staircase as fast as his workboots could carry him. Bodo shouted a final reminder. 'Do you hear me? Keep away, or else!' And he slammed the door shut behind Ahmet for good measure.

Bodo marched back into the room, slapping the dust from his hands.

'Thank you,' was all Ömer was able to say, tears filling his eyes.

Bodo wrapped him up a big Bear hug. 'Nichts zu danken.'

Ömer buried his face against Bodo's chest. There was a muffled cry from Jens. It took Bodo a few seconds to remember that there was someone else in the room. He turned an eye to Jens, who was straining against the binds that tied him to the bed.

'You wait your turn,' Bodo said dryly. 'I'm enjoying myself here.'

Twenty-one

It had been ages since they had been back to the sauna. Everything
and nothing had changed. It had been freshly decorated, recarpeted,
retiled but effectively it was no more than a new gloss coat on the
same old grind. The clientele had changed; there were lots of new
faces. But all the same types: pretty boys, hairy Bears, skinheads and
leather types with the regulation leather lace tied around their necks
in contrast to the fluffy towels around their waists.

For the most part, the staff remained as the only permanent fix-
tures. The long and the short and the tall. The bald, the tattooed and
the pierced. The friendly ones remained friendly. The prissy ones
remained prissy. But it was all very much business as usual. Jens and
Dirk had never felt as though they were treated like regulars - which
suited them fine. Not to say that the sauna ever went without its share
of regulars. The ones you would see each and every time you dropped
by, no matter what time of the day or night, nor no matter what day
of the week. Yet even these residencies went in phases. A week, a
month, six months, a year. Eventually to disappear, only to be
replaced by another contingent. Doubtless, the staff had seen it all -
and all too often. No wonder they gave off such an air of studied bore-
dom.

But to Jens and Dirk it felt like a breath of fresh air, for absence had
made the heart grow fonder, no doubt about it. They settled into their
usual double cabin, number 318, undressed and headed for the bar.
They had barely ordered the first beer when, much to their surprise, a
familiar voice hissed in their ears. 'What the fuck are you two doing
here?'

Bodo was at their shoulders. And even more surprisingly, Volker
was with him.

'We could ask you the same thing!' Bodo replied.

'I wouldn't have come, only Volker here has decided it's time he took a walk on the wild side.'

'Is that true, Volker?' Dirk asked, amazed.

Volker blushed, as was his habit. 'I guess so.'

'Where's Ömer? I thought you only came as a threesome these days?'

'You mean you haven't heard?' Jens asked.

'Heard what?' Bodo replied.

'He's found himself a boyfriend.'

'Never?! This is bit sudden, isn't it?'

Jens shrugged. 'No, not really. It's been coming for a while. Seems he's decided he needs a Bear of his own. Which is fair enough.'

'Yep,' Dirk nodded. 'You met the guy. He was at our housewarming party. Kaan? He left early, couldn't stand the heat!'

'Is he moving out, then?' Volker finally piped up.

Jens answered. 'Maybe. Maybe not. We don't think Kaan exactly approves of our living arrangements.'

'Well, I want to hear all about it.' Bodo paused. 'But we've only just arrived and I promised to show Volker around,' Bodo added, apologetically.

'I imagine we'll still be here when you get back,' Dirk replied.

Bodo grinned. 'See you soon, then. '

'Don't get lost. Oh, yeah, I forgot. Not much chance of that, is there? Ha!' Dirk said.

'Ha! Ha! Ha!' Bodo replied, showing him the middle-finger. 'Sit on that and swivel!'

'Only if you're lucky,' Jens called after them.

Dirk turned to Jens, as soon as they were out of earshot. 'So, what do you think?'

'About what?'

'Us having them two? Don't you think we owe it to Volker to break him in gently?'

'And if I said no?'

'That's your privilege. You know that, don't you, sweetheart?'

'Not that line again!'

Dirk frowned.

Jens suddenly felt an overwhelming tenderness towards him. 'Thank you.' He said in all sincerity.

'For what?'

'For considering my feelings. For really considering them. We've come a long way.'

'Have we?'

'Yes, I think we have. Don't look so guilty! I'm proud of us.'

'Don't!' Dirk sounded choked. 'You'll have me in tears.'

'But I mean it, baby.'

Dirk swallowed hard. 'Okay . . . ' He grinned. 'So . . . does that mean you're on for it?!'

Jens punched him playfully. 'If you are.'

Dirk perked up on his stool. 'Damn right!'

'Volker will think all his birthdays have come at once.'

'That's what I'm hoping!'

Ömer woke from a deep, untroubled sleep. And as the day drifted into focus, one question came to the forefront of his mind: 'When was the damage undone?'

The bed was deliciously warm and comfortable, cosseting his body. He allowed himself the opportunity to luxuriate in all the sensual feelings it produced. Muscle melting against cool cotton sheets. Another Sunday afternoon, and no work today. He could stay in bed all day if he chose too. Would he choose to? He smiled and turned on his side. There was no rush to decide.

As he was only half-awake, other questions danced into consciousness. When did he reach this place of quiet and serenity? He had made his own way, fought tooth and nail through a wilderness of years towards self-acceptance. The path had seemed endless, every second step blighted by man-made obstacles. So many detours, so many unhappy endings. Finally, to be forced to cut all ties with his family, though fortunately not his culture. No, there were plenty more where he came from. And he knew happiness now. A measure of happiness he had never known before. The realisation hit him, not like a ton of bricks but like a . . . well, a feather pillow. He was a happy man.

At long, long last he was no longer alone. He had friends. And he had his arm wrapped around his lover's waist, the flat of his hand pressing against his hairy belly. And another thought crossed his mind, and brought with it a chuckle to his throat: 'Maybe life is not a bitch and then you die, like Jens says.' And with that thought in mind, Ömer snuggled even more closely into his lover's furry back.

Kaan slept on - worn out from the night's exertions, no doubt. Ömer smiled to himself; he could still feel the tender echo of Kaan's thick, long length inside him. Kaan fucked like a stud bull. And Ömer, having always found it greater to receive than to give, was the perfect match. Somewhere deep in Kaan's psyche, sex equalled love, inasmuch as it assured him he was loved. Ömer was happy to reassure him of his love as often as physically possible. The love they made was never less than wonderful. Affectionate sex, liberally sprinkled with kisses and cuddles. The kind of sex he had always longed for. And he felt that despite all of the recreational couplings he had indulged in, despite his loving relationship with Dirk and Jens, that what he and Kaan had together was different, unique. A special closeness. And he found he didn't even want sex with anybody else - that was the crazy thing!

Ömer closed his eyelids and buried his face against Kaan's hairy back; felt his own beard-stubble brush against his lover's black fur. He held still and listened to Kaan snoring gently. Sometimes, Ömer would wake in the night to find Kaan making no sound at all and then the fear would grip him. What if Kaan were to die? It was the closest Ömer ever came to panic. Then he would reach out a hand and touch . . . warmth. The warmth of Kaan's body was a given. Then Ömer would snuggle up against his back, just like this; would wrap himself around Kaan's solid, stocky body, toes touching toes, just as he was doing now. Then sleep would come quickly.

Kaan woke to find Ömer snuggling up against his broad back and snoring gently. The fit was perfect. Kaan lived for moments such as these. He would have to tell Ömer how much he loved him. He didn't say it often enough, though he felt it nonetheless. He was still struggling with verbal demonstrations of affection, but he knew Ömer needed to hear it. And goodness knows, he deserved to.

Kaan turned, shifting Ömer over onto his other side. The snoring stopped. Silence reigned, save for the gentle beating of hearts. Kaan wrapped his arm around his lover's waist. Perfect peace. Ömer shuffled back, his buttocks nestling into Kaan's groin. Then the inevitable - Kaan's sleeping beauty began to wake. Within seconds it was fully roused, forcing its way into the crack of Ömer's arse.

'Ömer?'

'Uh-huh?'

'You awake?'

'I am now.'

Kaan's fingers brushed Ömer's erect nipples and his body almost crackled with electricity. A bolt of pure pleasure warmed his entire body.

'You want to make love?'

'Uh-huh?'

'I love you.'

Ömer turned over. 'I love you too.'

Once they had returned from the tour, it did not take much to get Volker and Bodo back to Jens and Dirk's cabin. No more than an invitation, in fact. Once inside, all four discarded their towels and clambered onto the double mattress. The bed was barely big enough to contain all four hulking Bears. And the heat generated by the close proximity of naked, furry flesh made the atmosphere electric.

Dirk knelt beside Bodo and laid a hand on his hairy chest. 'Guess we two better get this off to a start,' he said. He looked to Volker and Jens, then back down at Bodo with such lust in his eyes that it startled even Jens.

A pause, then suddenly both big men came together in one resounding clash of lips, tongues and fur. Sucking on each other's mouth as if for a last breath.

Volker's face was a picture. It was as if the poor baby had not had a clue. As if he did not know that Bodo and Dirk were well experienced in satisfying one another's desire. Jens felt like he could almost see the penny drop behind Volker's eyes: 'So that is why Bodo and Dirk are so close.' Now watching the passion with which the two big Daddy Bears gripped each other's flesh, it was as if he could fully comprehend the depth of shared emotion.

Jens shuffled backwards, out of their way. His eyes were transfixed by their expert performance. Groping and grinding, a pulsating mass of hairy flesh and naked muscle now grappled in a heap before Jens and Volker's very eyes. Bodo and Dirk were lost in loving one another, oblivious to Volker and Jens. Wrestled onto his back now, Bodo hoisted Dirk's legs in the air and buried his face deep in the crack of his best pal's furry arse, slobbering and sucking.

Dirk was yanking on his power tool for all he was worth. 'Yes, you fucker, eat my fucking hole. Show me you love me. Fucking do it!'

Bodo kept mumbling, 'Dirk, I fucking love you, Brother Bear. I fucking love you,' he repeated, as he continued to gorge his appetite.

'Eat my fuckin' shithole!' Dirk demanded. 'Show me you love me. Prove it!'

'I love you,' gulped Bodo. 'I'm proving it'

Bodo worked his nose like a bloodhound sniffing out a fox hole, frantically snuffling the entrance. Dirk reclined like a lion being groomed, a big cat being serviced by its mate.

Jens couldn't hold back from the action any longer and in seconds he was on his knees, His quivering tongue stuck firmly in Dirk's navel. Drawing a trail of saliva to Dirk's erect nipples, Jens tweaked one with thumb and forefinger, the other held between gritted teeth. Jens looked over to Volker. He appeared to be shaking with excitement. Jens could almost see his heart batter against his white T-shirt.

'Come on over, Volker,' Jens gasped, indicating Dirk's mighty cock.

Volker hesitated, but only for a moment. Crawling on his knees, he dropped onto all fours for a closer inspection. His eyes grew wide, spellbound. 'That is one big cock,' he mumbled.

Hesitantly, Volker lowered his face for an intimate examination. The smell of it. The taste of it. Tentatively, the glistening tip of his tongue poked out to probe the wrinkled rim of foreskin. He grew in confidence as his Dirk's big dick strained and twitched at the stimulus. A greater expanse of tongue flicked over hairy bollocks, then lapped the underside of Dirk's shaft from base to tip. Emboldened, Volker's mouth swooped to consume Dirk's prick clear up to the nuts.

Dirk was plainly ecstatic at this turn of events. He yanked Jens up to position himself in line with his mouth and consumed Jens' knob, feeding on it, his rabid lips pumping double time. Bodo knelt tall between Dirk's open thighs, his cock held aloft over Volker's bobbing head. Jens' thumb and forefinger continued to nip Dirk's nipple, whilst he reached his other hand over to grip Bodo's rock-solid shaft and began to pull. Bodo moaned in gratitude and his balls responded by rising high in his low-slung pouch.

Volker was begging Dirk to come, drooling from the corners of his mouth. 'Come on, Dirk, give it to me . . . give me your spunk . . . all your spunk, Dirk...' His fist encircled the neck of Dirk's ballsac, forcing the swollen orbs to strain against taut skin. Dirk let go of Jens' cock. He looked down at Volker's gobbling mouth and began grunting, 'Dirk is going to give you his full load, Baby Bear. Dirk is going to give it to you!' Volker's mouth enveloped both bollocks, his cheeks straining to accommodate. He sucked hard, and then sucked harder. And with a groan that threatened to bring the ceiling down on everyone, Dirk's entire body went rigid. Quick as a flash, Volker increased the suction on Dirk's bollocks, doubling the intensity. Pointing towards his toes, Dirk fired a stream of thick, white jism. Volker was now perfectly positioned to watch as wad upon prolific wad splattered onto Dirk's belly. Dirk pressed back into the mattress, squirming as Volker teased the last vestige of sperm from his heavy bollocks.

In the instant, Bodo began to moan fit to burst, as Jens' hand continued to hammer down on his rod.

'I'm going to come . . . ' was all he needed to say as Volker leapt upon Bodo's bollocks, consuming both in one fell swoop, sucking on the knobsac like a vacuum pump. Bodo began grinding his hips as Volker pumped his cheeks, hastening Bodo's explosive climax. And boy, did he come some. He sprayed Dirk's prostrate body with a glossy coat.

As Bodo's eruption subsided, and his breathing returned to normal, a stillness rested over the proceedings. Jens took a moment to reach under the bed and produce a kitchen roll. He tore off a handful and passed it to Bodo.

Bodo took it gratefully. 'You really think of everything!'

Jens smiled. 'I try.'

As Bodo wiped their respective juices from Dirk's belly, Jens resumed jacking his erection. Volker's eyes were fixed intently on it, as he lovingly stroked his own. Spitting on his palm, Volker coated his shaft with his saliva, holding it at the base between thumb and forefinger, showing it off, before stroking it again. Jens smiled to himself. Volker was practically drooling. His lips were parted slightly and he kept wetting them with the tip of his tongue, his eyes never shifting from Jens' pulsing man-meat. They angled their bodies to face each other, as Dirk and Bodo shuffled aside to make room. Now, this was something they both wanted to see.

Bodo could not resist offering a helping hand. He reached out and slipped his fingers between Volker's sweaty arsecrack. He let his middle finger tease the trembling sphincter, felt Volker press down upon it, allowing access. He whimpered ever so slightly as Bodo's finger entered in.

'I think my baby wants you, Jens. I think he wants you up his hole.' Bodo smiled. 'You do, don't you, Bear Cub?'

Volker gripped and squeezed his balls, jacked on his cock and continued to press down further on Bodo's wriggling finger. 'Ummmnn!' Again he licked his lips.

'You want to fuck my baby's arse, Jens. My baby wants you to fuck him good and hard.'

Volker moaned.

'You hear that? He wants it bad, Jens. What do you say?'

'Yeah,' Jens growled. 'I want to fuck his arse.'

'So what's stopping you?'

Dirk leaned over and rolled a condom over Jens' throbbing organ, dressing him to impress. Bodo and Dirk then climbed off the bed, leaving their partners to it. They sat themselves side by side on the floor, and the two friends each wrapped an arm around each other's shoulders as they relaxed back to enjoy the show.

Volker rolled over like a puppy who wanted his belly tickled and raised his knees to his chest, his buttocks parting automatically, presenting his anus in a gesture of total submission.

Jens shuffled across the mattress, positioning himself for maximum penetration. He quickly poured lubricant on his fingers, put the bottle aside, and began to slather Volker's ring-piece. outside and in. Volker was in rapture, aching to be filled to the brim. And Jens was only too willing to put him out of his misery.

Cock against ring now. Jens' fat, rubbered-up phallus was pressed hard against Volker's tight, hairy, aromatic ring. He eased gently forward, inching his way towards the heart of Volker. He took his time, savouring the moment.

'Ohhhhhh!' Volker moaned. 'Ohhhhhh! Oh, yeah! Oh, yeah, Brother Bear! Oh, yeah!'

And finally, Jens hit base. He held still for a moment. And then, almost imperceptibly at first, he began to rotate his hips. Volker's reaction was instantaneous. He wrapped his hairy calves around Jens' sturdy waist and, crossing his feet at the ankle, gripped him tight, holding Jens in place.

And Jens' mouth fell upon him, smothering Volker's lips with passionate, slobbering kisses, getting as good as it gave. A film of perspiration coated both their bodies; made their skin glow in the dim amber light, as their bodies wrestled with each other. Jens pumped his hips and Volker pleaded for more. Man-sweat was running down the walls.

Jens clambered up onto his knees, severing their connection. But within moments he spread Volker's legs wide apart and, holding them at the ankle, he slammed his way back in, impaling Volker fully. Jens slapped his hips against Volker's rump as he began to thrust in and out once more. He looked mesmerised as he looked down at the exposed point of their intimate contact - puffy anus and slick, stiff dick.

Volker was a picture as he lay back: big and beefy and hung like a horse. His cock, plump and veined, was an impressive length topped by a prize strawberry helmet. Youth and experience were blending together now, reunited - and the fruit of two big balls grew once again from the trunk of a tree.

Jens' humping became more determined, because Volker's hole was urging him on. 'Yes, baby, love your big, ol' Brother Bear. Jens loves you. Jens loves his little Baby Brother Bear. He's going to prove it, too. He's going to give you his cream, all the cream in his Big Brother bollocks . . . ' Volker's erection was straining full force and he began to slam his fist down over his fat organ, tossing it beyond his belly button, tightening and releasing his arse muscles as he sucked Jens ever deeper. Volker was pleading again, pleading for Jens' dose, soliciting with dirty talk of his own, and with words of love. But not for long. Jens' balls were only too happy to oblige.

'That's a good boy. Jens is nearly there. He's going to shoot you full to the brim. He's going to love you with every inch of his big, hard dick. Going to love you, Little Bear . . . Going to love you . . . LOVE YOU!!!!'

With a tight grip on Volker's peach of an arse, Jens lunged to the very core and cried out in agony, in ecstasy as the first wave of a spectacular orgasm hit. He planted the fullness of his rich, ripe seed inside Volker's warm, nurturing depths. Volker clenched his arsecheeks rapidly. Tightening and relaxing, tightening and relaxing, draining the goodness out Jens' dick, draining it into the rubber, capturing it all in the straining rubber.

In the split second that Jens shot his last, Volker threw his head back and ejaculated. An elongated streak of spunk flew through the air and hit the wall behind his head with a thud, the second and third hit his face, the fourth, his neck. Globs of his own semen dripped from his moustache and beard. He stuck out his tongue and retrieved every drop he could manage.

Jens remained inside Volker for a little while longer. Unwilling to break the connection, he wanted to reassure Volker of his deep and abiding affection. Finally, he grew soft and prised himself free. Discarding the condom, he collapsed down beside Volker, rolled him on his side and cuddled him from behind. His hand resting on Volker's hairy belly, his nose nuzzling up against his furry back in one final tender gesture. There were, finally, two heaving chests and one pair of satisfied smiles.

Bodo and Dirk were far from relaxed, because both were up and hard. Tugging on each other's raw meat, their deep soul-kissing forged a deep soul connection. Bodo's hips thrust in rabbitlike stabs to meet Dirk's pounding fist, speeding up the inevitable. There were more resounding smacks as their mouths thrashed together, before Bodo's mouth opened in a silent scream. Then the juddering groan began. Desperately whacking Bodo's chopper, whilst thrusting his tongue into his yawning mouth, Dirk delivered the final thwack. And Bodo did the business; squirting his own burden in an arc, spurt upon reflexive spurt, matting his furry chest. Drenching it, as Dirk came too, directing his wad towards Bodo's belly, delivering a double dose. A double come-shot.

The essence of four big men, the love of comrades, mingled with the sweat and the heat. The stench of sex, the heady stench of man-sex, permeated the atmosphere, lulling then to sleep. Four Bears now lay side by side on the one bed, cuddled up close. Sleep came easy.

Dirk and Volker stood side by side in the showers. They had left Bodo and Dirk back in the cabin, snuggled up in each others arms, snoring away blissfully. Dirk pumped a handful of liquid soap from the dispenser into his palm, lathered his hands and spread them over Volker's muscular back. He soaped him up, and he soaped him down.

Volker looked back over his shoulder and smiled. 'It worked like a treat. Just like you said.'

'Perfect timing!' Dirk replied. 'And just the right amount of imagination.'

Volker stretched and yawned. 'That Jens of yours. He is one serious fuckmonster!'

'Impressed, were you?' Dirk let his soaped-up fingers slip between Volker's buttcrack, and touch his tender anus.

Volker trembled. Then he gasped, 'What do you think?'

'I think that you are a terrific little actor.'

'But I wasn't acting with Jens back there . . . '

'I'm not talking about that part of the performance. I'm talking about the rest of it. People would believe that butter wouldn't melt in that hot, little mouth of yours.'

'I have a great teacher. The best.'

Dirk's hands returned to Volker's back, swirling the soap around, swirling the fur around. 'I do love Jens, you know.'

'And I love Bodo.'

'And I love you too, little Bear Cub.'

'Likewise, Daddy Bear.'

'And I think it would be wise if they never learned we'd set them up.'

Volker grinned. 'Naturally.'

Dirk sighed. 'I think this could be the start of a beautiful four-way relationship.'

Volker reached a hand behind him and stroked Dirk's thickening cock. 'Oh, I do hope so, Daddy Bear. I do hope so.'